RANDOM HOUSE

LARGE
PRINT

This Time Tomorrow

ALSO BY EMMA STRAUB
AVAILABLE FROM
RANDOM HOUSE LARGE PRINT

All Adults Here

THIS TIME | TOMORROW

Emma Straub

RANDOM HOUSE LARGE PRINT

Copyright © 2022 by Emma Straub

All rights reserved.
Published in the United States of America by Random House Large Print in association with Riverhead Books, an imprint of Penguin Random House LLC.

Cover design: Grace Han

The Library of Congress has established a Cataloging-in-Publication record for this title.

ISBN: 978-0-593-60768-8

www.penguinrandomhouse.com/large-print-format-books

FIRST LARGE PRINT EDITION

Printed in the United States of America

1st Printing

This Large Print edition published in accord with the standards of the N.A.V.H.

For Putney Tyson Ridge

Only when a story was finished, all fates resolved and the whole matter sealed off at both ends so it resembled, at least in this one respect, every other finished story in the world, could she feel immune, and ready to punch holes in the margins, bind the chapters with pieces of string, paint or draw the cover, and take the finished work to show to her mother, or her father, when he was home.

Ian McEwan, **Atonement**

• • •

This time tomorrow
Where will we be?

The Kinks

• • •

Until the future!

Leonard Stern,
Time Brothers

PART ONE

1

TIME DID NOT EXIST IN THE HOSPITAL.
Like a Las Vegas casino, there were no clocks anywhere, and the harsh fluorescent lighting remained
equally bright during the entire stretch of visiting
hours. Alice had asked, once, if they turned off the
lights at night, but the nurse didn't seem to hear,
or maybe she thought it was a joke, but in either
case, she didn't respond, and so Alice didn't know
the answer. Her father, Leonard Stern, was still in
his bed in the center of the room, attached to more
lines and cords and bags and machines than Alice
could count, and had hardly spoken for a week, and
so he wasn't going to tell her, either, even if he did
open his eyes again. Could he sense the difference?
Alice thought about lying in the grass in Central
Park in the summertime as a teenager, letting her

closed eyelids feel the warmth of the sun, when she and her friends would stretch their bodies out on rumpled blankets, waiting for JFK Jr. to accidentally hit them with a Frisbee. These lights didn't feel like the sun. They were too bright, and too cold.

Alice could visit on Saturdays and Sundays, and in the afternoon on Tuesdays and Thursdays, when her workday ended early enough that she could hop on the train and get to the hospital before visiting hours had ended. From her apartment in Brooklyn, the subway ride was an hour door-to-door, the 2/3 from Borough Hall to 96th Street, and then the local all the way to 168th Street, but from work, it was half an hour on the C train, a straight shot from 86th and Central Park West.

Over the summer, Alice had been able to visit nearly every day, but since school had started, a few days a week was the best she could do. It felt like it had been decades since her father was still himself, when he looked more or less the way he had for Alice's whole life, smiling and wry, his beard still more brown than gray, but in reality, it had only been a month. He'd been on a different floor of the hospital then, in a room that felt more like an underdecorated hotel room than an operating theater, with a photograph of Mars that he'd torn out of the **New York Times** taped to the wall, alongside a photo of his ancient and powerful cat, Ursula. She wondered whether someone had taken those things and put them with the rest of his belongings—his wallet, his telephone, whatever actual clothing he'd been wearing when he checked in, the stack of paperback books he'd brought with him—or whether they'd been thrown away in one of the giant flip-top waste bins that lined the sterile hallways.

When someone asked how her father was doing— Emily, who she shared a desk with in the admissions office; or Sam, her best friend from high school, who had three children, a husband, a house in Montclair, and a closet full of high heels to wear to her job at a terrifying law firm; or her boyfriend, Matt—Alice wished for an easy answer. The longer it went on, the more the question turned into an empty phrase, the way one might say **How are you?** to an acquaintance passing on the sidewalk and keep walking. There were no tumors to excise, no germs to fight. It was just that many neighborhoods of Leonard's body were falling apart in a great, unified chorus: his heart, his kidneys, his liver. Alice understood now, as she never truly had before, how the body was a Rube Goldberg machine, and every time one domino or lever got knocked sideways, the whole thing would stop. When the doctors poked their heads into the ICU, it was just the word **failure,** over and over again. They were all waiting for her father to die. It could be days or weeks or months, no one was quite able to say. One of the worst parts of the whole thing, Alice understood, was that doctors were almost always guessing. They were smart people, and the guesses were informed by tests and trials and years of experience, but they were guessing nonetheless.

Alice saw it now: all her life, she'd thought of death as the single moment, the heart stopping, the final breath, but now she knew that it could be much more like giving birth, with nine months of preparation. Her father was heavily pregnant with death, and there was little to do but wait—his doctors and nurses, her mother in California, his friends and neighbors, and most of all, the two of them. It could only end one way, and it would only happen once. No matter how many times a person was on a bumpy airplane, or in a car accident, or stepped out of traffic just in time, no matter how many times they fell and did not break their neck. This was how it went for most people—actual dying, over a period of time. The only surprise left would be when it happened, the actual day, and then all the days that followed, when he did not push away the boulder or stick his hand out of the ground. Alice knew all of this, and sometimes she felt okay with it, it being the way of the world, and sometimes she was so sad that she couldn't keep her eyes open. He was only seventy-three years old. In a week, Alice would turn forty. She would feel immeasurably older when he was gone.

Alice knew some of the nurses on the fifth floor and some of the nurses on the seventh floor—Esmeralda, whose father was also named Leonard;

Iffie, who thought it was funny when Leonard pointed out that the hospital lunch often had apples three ways: apple juice, applesauce, and an apple itself; George, who lifted him most easily. When she recognized one of the people who had cared for her father in an earlier phase, it felt like remembering someone from a past life. The three men who worked the front desk were the most consistent caregivers, insomuch as they were friendly and remembered the names of people like Alice who visited over and over again, because they understood what it meant. They were led by London, a middle-aged Black man with a gap between his front teeth and an elephant's memory. He remembered her name, her father's name, what her father did, everything. His job was deceptively easy—it wasn't just smiling at the people with bunches of balloons who came to visit new babies. No, visitors like Alice would show up and show up and show up until there was no reason to come back, just a long list of numbers to call and things to do and arrangements to make.

Alice pulled her phone out of her bag to check the time. Visiting hours were nearly over.

"Dad," she said.

Her father didn't move, but his eyelids flickered. She got up and put her hand on his. It was thin and bruised—he was on blood thinners, to keep him from having a stroke, and it meant that every time the nurses and doctors poked him with another needle, a small purple blossom appeared. His eyes stayed closed. Every so often a lid would open, and Alice would watch him search around the room, not focusing on anything, not seeing her. At least she didn't think so. When she could get her mother on the phone, Serena would tell her that hearing was the last sense to go, and so Alice always talked to him, but she wasn't sure where her words were going, if anywhere. At least she could hear them. Serena also said that Leonard needed to release himself from his ego, and that until he did so, he would be forever chained to his earthly body, and that crystals would help. Alice couldn't listen to everything her mother told her.

"I'll be back on Tuesday. I love you." She touched his arm. Alice was used to it now, the affection. She had never told her father she loved him before he went into the hospital. Maybe once, in high school, when she was miserable and they were fighting about her staying out past her curfew, but then it had been shouted back and forth, an epithet hurled through her bedroom door. But now she said it every time she visited, and looked at him when she said it. One of the machines behind him beeped in response. The nurse on duty nodded at Alice on her way out, her dreadlocks tucked into a white cap with pictures of Snoopy on it. "Okay," Alice said. It felt like hanging up on him, or changing the channel.

2

ALICE ALWAYS TEXTED HER MOTHER after leaving the hospital. **Dad ok. No different, which seems positive?** Serena sent back a red heart emoji and then a rainbow emoji, indicating that she had read the words and had nothing to add, no follow-up questions. It didn't seem fair, abdicating all responsibility just because you were no longer married, though of course that was exactly what divorce meant. And they'd been divorced for far longer than they were married—more than three times as long, Alice thought, doing the math. Alice had been six when her mother had woken up, told them that she'd had a self-actualized visit from her future consciousness, or from Gaia herself, Serena couldn't be sure, but she **was** sure that she needed to move to the desert to join a healing community run by a man named Demetrious. The judge had told them how rare it was for fathers to have sole custody, but even he couldn't argue. Serena was fond, when she was in touch, but Alice never wished that her parents had stayed together. If Leonard had remarried, there would be some other person there holding his hand and asking the nurses questions, but he hadn't, and so it was just Alice. Polygamy would be excellent in cases like this, or a passel of siblings, but Leonard had only ever had the one wife and the one daughter, and so Alice was it. She went down the stairs into the train station, and when the 1 train arrived, Alice didn't even pretend to take out a book and read before she fell asleep with her forehead resting against the scratched, dirty window.

3

ALICE AND MATT HADN'T MOVED IN together, because having two apartments always seemed like a great trick, a truly revolutionary way to be in a committed relationship, if you could afford it. She'd lived alone since she was in college, and truly sharing space with another adult every single day—kitchen, toilet, and all—was a level of commitment Alice did not aspire to. She'd read a Modern Love column once about a couple who kept two apartments in the same building, and that seemed like the dream. Alice had lived in the same studio since she was twenty-five and finally out of college, having limped through art school as slowly as she could. It was the garden-level apartment in a brownstone on Cheever Place, a tiny street in Cobble Hill where one could always hear the roar of the Brooklyn-Queens Expressway, which lulled Alice to sleep at night like the ocean. Because she'd been there so long, Alice paid less for rent than the twenty-five-year-olds she knew who lived in Bushwick.

Matt, improbably, lived in Manhattan, on the Upper West Side, which was the neighborhood Alice had grown up in, and where she worked. The first time she and Matt went out to dinner and he told her where he lived, Alice had thought he was joking. The idea that someone her age— five years younger, actually—could afford to live in Manhattan was absurd, even though Alice had long understood that where someone could afford to live often had little to do with their own pay-check, especially if it was in Manhattan. He lived in one of the gleaming new apartment buildings near Columbus Circle that had a doorman and a package room with a special cold section for peo-ple's FreshDirect deliveries. He was on the eigh-teenth floor and could see all the way to New Jersey. When Alice looked out her window, she could see a fire hydrant and the lower half of people's bodies as they walked by.

Even though Alice had a key to Matt's apartment, she always stopped at the desk before going to the elevator, the way visitors were supposed to. It wasn't unlike going to the hospital and giving her name. Today, one of the doormen, an older man with a shaved head who always winked at her, just pointed toward the elevator as she approached, and Alice nodded. A free pass.

Around the glossy marble corner, a woman and two small children were waiting for the elevator. Alice recognized the woman immediately but zipped her mouth shut and tried to be invisible. The children—both towheaded boys, maybe four and eight, ran in circles around their mother's legs, trying to whack each other with tennis rackets. When the elevator finally arrived, the kids darted in, and their mother trudged behind them, her thin ankles sockless in her loafers. She looked up when she turned to face the doors, and that's when she saw Alice, who sidled in right next to the buttons, tucking herself into the corner of the small cube.

"Oh, hi!" the mother said. The woman was pretty and blond, with an earnest tan, the kind that accumulated gradually on tennis courts and golf courses. Alice had met this woman—Katherine, maybe?— when she'd brought the older child to the admissions office at the Belvedere School.

"Hi," Alice said. "How are you? Hi, guys." The children had abandoned their racket swords and were now kicking each other in the shins. A game.

The woman—Katherine Miller, Alice now remembered, and the boys were Henrik and Zane— pushed her hair back. "Oh, we're great. You know, so happy to be back in school. We were in Connecticut all summer, and they really missed their friends."

"School sucks," Henrik, the older boy, said. Katherine grabbed him by the shoulders and pulled him tight against her legs.

"He doesn't mean that," she said.

"Yes, I do! School sucks!"

"School sucks!" parroted Zane, in a voice three times as loud as the elevator required. Katherine's cheeks turned purple with embarrassment. The elevator dinged, and she shoved both boys out. The younger one would be applying for kindergarten this fall, which meant that Katherine would be visiting Alice's office again soon. There were several emotions visible in Katherine's face, and Alice diligently ignored them all.

"Have a great day!" Katherine called out in a singsong voice. The elevator doors closed again, and Alice could hear her whisper-shout at her children as they walked down the hall.

There were so many kinds of rich people in New York City. Alice was an expert, but not because she wanted to be; it was like being raised bilingual, only one of the languages was money. One rule of thumb was that the harder it was to tell where someone's money came from, the more of it they had. If both parents were artists or writers or maybe had no discernible jobs at all and were available for pickup and drop-off, it meant the money was trickling down from a very large source, drips from an iceberg. There were lots of invisible parents, both mothers and fathers, who worked constantly, and if they did wind up at school or on the playground, they were always taking phone calls, a finger shoved into the other ear to drown out the noise of real live life. Those were the families with help. The ones who were ashamed of their wealth used the term **au pair** and the ones who were not used the word **housekeeper.** Even if children didn't always fully understand, they had eyes and ears and parents who gossiped with each other at playdates.

Her own family's money was fairly simple: When she was a child, Leonard had written **Time Brothers,** a novel about two time-traveling brothers that had sold millions of copies and gone on to become a serialized television program that everyone watched, either on purpose or as a result of unwillingness to change the channel, at least twice a week between the years of 1989 and 1995. And so Alice had gone to private school at Belvedere, one of the most prestigious in the city, since she was in the fifth grade. On the spectrum from blonds-in-uniforms to no-grades-and-calling-teachers-by-their-first-names, Belvedere sat close to dead center. It had too many Jews for the WASPs, and too many cozy traditions for the Marxists.

If one trusted the literature, most of the private schools in New York City were the same—challenging, enriching, and superlative in all ways—and while that was true, Alice understood the differences: This one was for the eating-disordered overachievers, that one was for dummies with drug problems but rich parents. There was the school for athletes and the school for tiny Brooks Brothers mannequins who would end up as CEOs, the school for well-rounded normies who would become lawyers, the school for artsy weirdos and for parents who wanted their kids to be artsy weirdos. Belvedere had started in the 1970s on the Upper West Side, and so it had been full of socialists and hippies, but now, fifty years later, the moms at drop-off idled outside in their Teslas and the children were all on ADHD medication. Nothing gold could stay, but it was still her place, and she loved it.

Alice only really saw the different categories of families once she was an adult: the blonds who had toned arms and well-stocked proper liquor cabinets; the actors with television shows and another house in Los Angeles for when fortunes changed; the intellectuals, novelists, and the like with vague trust funds and houses bigger than they should have been able to afford; the finance drones with their spotless countertops and empty built-in bookshelves. There were the ones with last names from history books, for whom jobs were superfluous but could include interior design, or fundraising. Some of those rich people were very good—good at making martinis, good at gossip, good at complaining about problems, because who could be mad at them? Everyone was on a committee of a cultural institution. And almost always, one of these types would marry one of the other types, and they could pretend that they had somehow married outside their bubble. It was a farce, the contortions that rich people would make so as to appear less dripping with privilege. It was true of Alice, too.

Alice met them all when they walked into the admissions office at the Belvedere School, where she, a single, childfree woman with a degree in painting and a minor in puppetry, would decide whether their little darlings would be accepted or not. There were lots of kinds of rich people, but they all wanted to get their children into the school of their choice, because they saw their children's lives like train tracks, each stop leading directly to the next, from Belvedere to Yale to Harvard Law to marriage to children to a country house on Long Island and a large dog named Huckleberry. Alice was just one step, but she was an important one. There would be an email from Katherine later in the day, she was positive, saying how **very nice** it was to run into her. In the real world, and in her own life, Alice had no power, but in the kingdom of Belvedere, she was a Sith Lord, or a Jedi, depending on whether one's child got in or not.

4

MATT'S APARTMENT WAS ALWAYS CLEAN. He'd lived there for a year, and had yet to prepare himself more than one meal a day in it—Matt did as many things as possible via app. As a city kid, Alice had also ordered in food a lot, but at least she had picked up the telephone and spoken to other humans. Like many transplants from small towns around the world, Matt seemed to look at New York City as a set to walk through, not thinking too much about what had come before. Alice set her bag down on the long white counter and pulled open the fridge. There were three different kinds of energy drinks, a half-empty kombucha that she'd left there a month ago, a salami, an unwrapped hunk of cheddar cheese that had started to harden around the edges, half a stick of butter, a jar of pickles, several takeout containers, a bottle of champagne, and four Coronas. Alice closed the fridge again, shaking her head.

"Hello? Are you home?" she called, in the direction of Matt's bedroom. There was no answer, and instead of texting him, Alice decided to do the small pile of dirty laundry she'd shoved into her tote bag before going to the hospital. The very best part about Matt's apartment was that it had a dishwasher and a washer/dryer. The dishwasher was wasted on him, as he rarely ate off actual plates, but the washer/dryer was the love of Alice's life. Usually Alice lugged her bag of dirty clothes to the laundromat around the corner from her apartment, which she didn't have to cross a single street to get to, and where they would wash and fold her things and then return the clean clothes to her inside a giant laundry bag dumpling, but the ease with which she could wash her favorite jeans and three pairs of underwear and the shirt she wanted to wear to work tomorrow, that was something special. Standing in front of the open washing machine, Alice decided she might as well wash what she was wearing, and so she peeled off her jeans and T-shirt and threw those in, too. When the clothes started to spin and swish, she slid in her socks down the slippery floor to Matt's bedroom to find something to throw on. The front door opened, and Alice heard Matt's keys hit the kitchen counter.

"Hi! I'm back here!" she shouted.

Matt appeared in the door of his room, giant horse-shoes of sweat on his neck and armpits. He took out his headphones. "I swear, I almost died. Today was a Mash Attack, which is three circuits, including dead lifts and extra burpees. I drank, like, four beers last night, and I fully thought I was going to puke."

"That's nice," Alice said. Matt went to CrossFit enough to have a smaller beer belly than he otherwise might, but not enough to be able to complete a class without threatening to vomit. He said the same thing every time he went.

"Gonna shower." He looked at her. "Why are you naked?"

"I'm not naked," Alice said. "I'm doing laundry."

Matt opened his mouth and panted. "I still think I might boot it." He walked around Alice's body and pushed open the door to the bathroom. She sat down on the bed and listened to the water go on.

They weren't a great couple, Alice knew, not like some of her friends and acquaintances, the ones who posted rhapsodic Instagram paeans every birthday and anniversary. They didn't like all the same things, or listen to the same music, or have the same hopes and dreams, but when they'd met on an app (of course) and had a drink, the drink had turned into dinner, and the dinner had turned into another drink, and that drink had turned into sex, and now it was a year later and the doorman didn't ask for her name. A year was a decent amount of time. Sam—who was married and therefore knew how these things went—thought that Matt would propose soon. If he did, Alice wasn't sure what she would say. She examined her toenails, which were in need of some more polish and now had only tiny discs of red at the tips, like polka dots. Her fortieth birthday was in a week. She and Matt hadn't made any plans yet, but she thought that if something was going to happen, maybe it would happen then. Her stomach did a little flip thinking about it, as if the organ were trying to turn around and face the other direction.

Marriage seemed like a good deal, most of the time—you always had someone there, and when you were dying, they would be huddled next to you, holding your hand. Of course, that didn't count the marriages that ended in divorce, or the unhappy marriages, where hand-holding was a memory. It didn't count people who died in car accidents, or had fatal heart attacks while sitting at their desks. What was the percentage of people who actually got to die while feeling loved and supported by their spouse? Ten percent? It wasn't just the dying, of course, that made marriage appealing, but that was part of it. Alice was sorry for her father, that she was all he had, and she was afraid that she was too much like him to have anything more. No— she would have less. Leonard had a child. Not just a child—a daughter. If she'd been a boy, and not trained by society to be a good, dutiful caretaker, it might have been different. It had all just gone so fast—her thirties. Her twenties had been a blur, and ten years ago, her friends were just starting to get married and have children—most of them didn't have babies until they were thirty-three, thirty-four, thirty-five, and so she wasn't that far behind, but suddenly now she was going to be forty, and that was too late, wasn't it? She had friends who were divorced, friends who were on their second marriages. Those always moved along more quickly, so it was easy to see what had been wrong the first time—if a couple got divorced and two years later, one of them was married with a baby on the way, it was no mystery. Alice didn't know if she wanted to have children, but she knew that at some point in the very near future, her not knowing would swiftly transform into a fact, a de facto decision. Why wasn't there more time?

Matt came out of the shower and looked at her hunching over her feet like a worried golem. "Want to order some food? Maybe fuck around before it comes?" There was a towel around his waist, but it dropped, and he didn't bend to pick it up. His erection waved at her.

Alice nodded. "Pizza? From the place?"

Matt pushed a few buttons on his phone and then tossed it behind her onto his king-sized bed. "We have thirty-two to forty minutes," he said. Matt might not have been great at cooking, or other things, but he was good at sex, and that wasn't nothing.

5

BELVEDERE, LIKE MANY PRIVATE SCHOOLS
in the city, was not contained in a single building,
but over time had spread across a small patch of the
neighborhood like a virus. The lower school and admissions were in the original building, on the south
side of 85th Street between Central Park West and
Columbus—a compact six-story modern architec-
tural eyesore with excellent air-conditioning and
big windows and built-in projection screens and a
carpeted library with comfortable chairs in bright
colors. The big kids—seventh through twelfth
graders—were now in the new building, around
the block on 86th Street. Alice was glad not to have
to deal with teenagers on a daily basis. The seniors
spent the fall loping in and out of the college prep
office next door, and seeing their lanky bodies and

poreless skin from ten feet away was more than enough exposure. The admissions office was on the second floor, and if Alice craned her neck out the window, she could see the slope up the hill into Central Park.

The admissions office had an airy waiting room, with expensive but well-loved wooden puzzles on the low, child-sized wooden tables, waiting to be played with by anxious parents as their children met with Alice, her colleague Emily, or their boss, Melinda, a formidable woman with wide hips and a rotating selection of chunky, dangling necklaces that the children always wanted to touch. "Tricks of the trade!" she would say whenever a mother complimented them, the woman trembling like a greyhound in her exercise clothes. It was also what Alice and Emily would say when they snuck out for cigarette breaks during the day. Emily would lean her head around the half wall that separated their desks and say, "Tricks of the trade?" and they'd pop out the emergency door in the back of the school and smoke in the small gray square of pavement where the garbage cans lived.

"Did you see Bike Dad today? I fucking love Bike Dad," Emily said. She was twenty-eight and in the middle of wedding season, which was exactly like bar mitzvah season, only you had to pay for your own outfit and present. Emily had gone to eight weddings over the summer, which Alice knew because Emily was a drunk texter, especially when she was feeling sad. "I bet he's a Leo. Don't you think?" she said now. "He's got that Big Leo Energy. The way he pulls the bike up on the sidewalk with both kids still on it? You know that thing has to weigh, like, two hundred pounds, and he just, **raaarrrrrr.**" She extended a fearsome claw.

"Nope," Alice said, taking a drag. The cigarette was Emily's, a Parliament. It tasted like wet newspapers, if one could set wet newspapers on fire. Alice had mostly quit several times over the last decade, but somehow it had never quite stuck, despite the gum, the books, and the disapproving looks from strangers and friends. Thank god for Emily, Alice thought. Almost none of the younger staff smoked anymore—they didn't even vape! They smoked pot but could barely roll joints. They took edibles. They were babies. Alice knew that it was healthier, sure, it was better for their lungs and probably the planet, too, but it made her feel lonely.

"He was wearing a striped T-shirt, like Picasso, only hot and not creepy. I love him." Emily scuffed the sole of her shoe on the concrete.

"His wife does pickup," Alice said. "What about Ray? Saw him come in, what's going on with that?"

Ray Young was an assistant kindergarten teacher and played the ukulele, and he and Emily slept together once a month, give or take. Emily always swore that it wasn't going to happen again, it was just that he walked his dog by her stoop, which Alice thought of as a **Melrose Place** problem, but

Emily had never seen **Melrose Place** and so she kept her thoughts to herself. He was twenty-five and perfectly available, which meant that Emily found him boring.

"Oh, you know," Emily said, rolling her eyes. "He fucks like his parents are watching."

Alice let out a cough of smoke. "You are terrible."

Emily winked at her. "Let's go back inside before we get detention." She dropped her cigarette and crushed it. "Oh, by the way, how's your dad doing?"

"Not great," Alice said. She flicked her still-burning cigarette to the ground.

6

MELINDA GAVE THEM EACH A STACK OF file folders, each one with a child's name written in Sharpie on the front. There were two hundred applicants for thirty-five places, and that was just for kindergarten. Alice, Emily, and Melinda would each interview the applicants in her stack, then they'd put their notes in the shared admissions spreadsheet, with all the children ranked—whether they were siblings, legacies, had famous parents, had applied for scholarship, were students of color, were from international families, anything of note. Sometimes Alice thought about all the boxes these tiny children had already checked and it made her feel sick. She felt like a judge for the Miss America contest. This one could play the piano! This one could read in two languages! This one had won a regatta! But the children were mostly wonderful, of course, weird and sweet and awkward and funny like all children were. The children were the best part of the job. Sometimes she thought that she would like to be a child psychologist, though it seemed late for that. She loved meeting the kids, and talking to them one on one, hearing their crazy thoughts and their high voices and watching their shyness melt away.

The plan had not been to work at her alma mater forever.

The plan had been to be a painter. Or an artist, of any kind, who got paid to make art. Or an art teacher who was beloved by her students, and had walls full of gorgeous things made by small children, and made her own art in her own time. The chances of her becoming a Famous and Successful Artist now were slim, but because she was still surrounded by people who had known her as an artsy teenager, they still looked at her that way, even though she hadn't touched a canvas or a brush in over a year. The friends of hers from Belvedere who had actually become artists had all left New York, which was too expensive. They had left five years ago, ten years ago, fifteen years ago. Alice had lost track. The ones she loved the most had even abandoned social media, except for some fuzzy landscapes or pictures of funny things in grocery stores once in a while. Alice missed them all.

"Earth to Alice," Melinda said, not unkindly.

They were sitting in a clumsy circle, their wheeled office chairs pointed inward.

"Sorry, I was just thinking about something. I'm here," Alice said. Emily winked at her.

"I'd love for us to get through this batch in the next two weeks—if you can reach out to the families on your list and set up times, I believe Emily's already made the sign-up spreadsheet. Great." Melinda nodded at them.

The pile of folders was heavy—each one had a child's photograph stapled to the outside and was filled with their application materials. Alice couldn't imagine it had been like this when her parents had sent her—they never would have filled out more than a single piece of paper. Alice shuffled the deck of folders on her lap, looking for names she recognized. There were always a few. The classmates of hers who had stayed in New York had procreated at astonishing rates—some were on their third babies, and the private school recycling mill was an effective one. Sometimes Alice thought it was strange, how many people stayed within the zip code where they'd grown up, but then she thought about how many people in small towns and cities across the country did it, too. It only seemed strange because this was New York, a place that regenerated every few years, populated by newcomers and transplants. It was usually nice to see the people she knew—mostly they were women who Alice hadn't known very well, but who were all perfectly friendly and seemed on very solid ground. More solid ground than she was. Much more rarely, Alice would come across the name of someone she'd known better.

Like little Raphael Joffey. How many Joffeys could there be? The boy in the photograph had olive skin, dark brown hair, thick eyebrows, and one missing tooth. He looked so much like his father that Alice knew what she would find before she opened the folder. There it was, on the second line—Thomas Joffey. The address listed was on Central Park West— the San Remo, where Tommy had grown up. He was nearly two years older than she was, and a grade level ahead. Alice couldn't remember the apartment number, which was comforting, but she could remember his landline number. If this information was true, he lived just a few blocks from school, and was still in the neighborhood where they'd both grown up. It was odd that Alice hadn't seen Tommy on the street, not ever, but that was the way it worked sometimes. There were some people who were just on your circuit, people who lived around the corner or across the borough, but for whatever reason, you and they were on the same track and would bump into each other again and again. Then there were the people who lived next door and were on a different schedule, and you never saw them at all. Different paths, different subway lines, different timetables. Alice wondered what Tommy did for a living, if anyone in his life still called him Tommy. If he'd just moved back, or if he'd been right down the street the whole time. If he and his family lived in the apartment he'd grown up in, or on another floor, with little Raphael taking the elevator up or down to see his grandparents. She wondered what Tommy's face looked like now, if his hair had started to gray, if his body was still as beautiful as it had once been, tall and willowy in his clothes, like there was always a breeze blowing against him. She hadn't even heard his name since her twentieth high school reunion the spring before last, which he had not attended, but where Alice had overheard several people asking if he was coming. That was the real power move—to be missed.

Alice closed the folder and left it on top of the pile. Alice wondered what they called the boy—if they said his whole name, or if he was Rafe, or Raffy, or Raf. She would send his email first, addressed to both parents. Alice would say what she always said to alumni in her stacks: **Hello! This is Alice Stern, class of '98!** At the end, after her copied-and-pasted message about setting up an interview and a tour, with a link to the sign-up page, Alice typed and then deleted a postscript. **Hello,** she wrote. **Hi!** No. **Hi—looking forward to seeing you and meeting Raphael.** It was always best to focus on the children. When she'd started in the admissions office, Melinda had explained that to her—sometimes the prospective parents were movie stars, or musicians who played at Madison Square Garden. It didn't matter. They didn't want you to fawn or to stutter. They wanted you to look their kids in the eye and be astonished, just like all parents did. They wanted you to recognize their special flower. The famous people didn't flummox her, not more than they would if she saw them walking down the street, but there were people she had known as a teenager whose names still made her stomach tighten. Alice didn't know what she'd say to Tommy if she saw him on the street, or in the back room of a dark, crowded bar—she might not say anything at all— but she knew what to say to him in her office. She would pull open the door and smile, nothing but sunlight and confidence. He would smile, too.

7

LEONARD'S HOSPITAL ROOM WAS ALWAYS cold, as all hospitals room are cold, in order to keep infections at bay. Germs love warmth, where they can zip into weak host after weak host, only the doctors and nurses with immune systems strong enough to battle them back into the dusty corners. Alice sat in the pleather visitor's chair—easy to clean, with a squishy seat for long hours in one place—and pulled her hands inside her sweater's sleeves. Lately she'd been trying to remember conversations she'd had with her father. One of her friends, a woman whose mother had died a few years earlier, had told her to record her conversations with her father, that she'd want them later, no matter what the conversations were about. Alice had felt embarrassed to ask, but she had recorded one conversation in the hospital the previous month, her phone facedown on the small table between her chair and his bed.

LEONARD: . . . and here comes our lady, here's the queen of the whole place.

(Nurse, unintelligible)

LEONARD: Denise. Denise.

DENISE: Leonard, I've got two pills, these are your afternoon pills. It's a present for you.

(Shaking sound)

ALICE: Thank you, Denise.

DENISE: He's my favorite; don't tell the other patients. Your dad, he's the best one.

LEONARD: I love Denise.

ALICE: Denise loves you.

LEONARD: We were talking about the Philippines. About Imelda Marcos. So many nurses come from the Philippines.

ALICE: Is that racist?

LEONARD: You think everything is racist. There are a lot of nurses from the Philippines, that's all.

(A machine beeps)

ALICE: You working on anything?

LEONARD: Come on.

Why did she ask? Who knew how many conversations she had left with her father, and that's what she wanted to know, the same thing that any hack journalist would have asked him at any point in the last twenty years? It was easier than asking him something personal or telling him something about herself, and also, she wanted to know.

• • •

When Alice closed her eyes and pictured her father, her father as he would live in perpetuity in her mind, it was an image of Leonard sitting at their round kitchen table on Pomander Walk. There were a few streets like it in the city: Patchin Place and Milligan Place in the West Village, and a few in Brooklyn, near where Alice lived, but Pomander Walk was different. Most mews streets were carriage houses, or had been built as housing for some grand building being constructed nearby, and were now expensive but still dollhouse-sized, for the rich people who wanted exclusivity and quaintness more than they wanted storage space. Pomander was a dash straight through the middle of the block, cutting from 94th to 95th Street in between Broadway and West End. It had been built by a hotel developer in 1921, and what Leonard had always loved about it was this:

it was a real street inspired by a novel-turned-play about a small town in England. It was a facsimile of a facsimile, a real version of a fictional place, with two rows of tiny houses that looked straight out of "Hansel and Gretel," locked behind a gate.

The houses were small, two stories high each, and most were split into two floor-through apartments. Tiny, well-tended garden patches sat in front of each door, and at the 95th Street end, a guardhouse no bigger than a phone booth held shared equipment—snow shovels and cobwebs and the occasional cockroach doing the backstroke. When Alice was a child, Reggie, the superintendent, had told her that Humphrey Bogart had once lived on Pomander, and his private security guard had used the guardhouse as his post, but she didn't know if it was true. What Alice did know was that Pomander Walk was a special place, and that even though the front windows were only about ten feet from their across-the-walk neighbors and their back windows faced their neighbors in the huge apartment buildings next door, it felt like their own private universe.

The scene was always exactly the same: Leonard at the kitchen table; the floor lamp on behind him; a book or three on the table in front of him; a glass of water, and then a glass of something else, sweating from the ice inside; a legal pad; a pen. During the day, Leonard watched soap operas, he walked in Central Park, he walked in Riverside Park, he took trips to the post office and to Fairway, he went to

City Diner on Broadway and 90th Street, he talked to friends on the telephone. At night, though, Leonard sat at the kitchen table and worked. Alice tried to put herself inside the frame, to watch herself walk through the door, drop her bag on the floor, and settle into the chair opposite her father. What had she said to him after school? Had they talked about homework? Had they talked about movies, about television programs? About answers they knew on **Jeopardy!**? Alice knew they had, but her memories were all pictures without sound.

• • •

A nurse came in—Denise, whose voice she had recorded. Alice scooted back in her chair, sitting up straight. Denise waved a hand. "Be comfortable," she said. Alice nodded, and watched while Denise inspected various machines and replaced bags of opaque fluids on the poles next to Leonard's bed.

"You're a good girl," Denise said on her way out, and patted Alice's knee. "I told your father already, but I loved **Time Brothers**—when I was in nursing school, my roommate and I were Scott and Jeff for Halloween. I told your father. I was Jeff, when he had a mustache. Very good costume, everyone knew who I was. **Until the future!**" That was their catchphrase, three words that Leonard found mortifying but that were often shouted to him while he walked down the street, or written in pen on his check at restaurants.

"I bet you looked great," Alice said. The **Time Brothers** characters made good costumes—not as snug as a spandex **Star Trek** uniform, not as collegiate as a Gryffindor robe, and easy enough to pull together out of normal clothes. Jeff had his tight jeans, his yellow raincoat, and in the later seasons, his blond mustache. Scott, the younger brother, with his long hair, plaid shirt, and work boots, had long ago become a lesbian fashion icon. Her father hadn't known what would happen when he published the novel. He'd had no way of seeing what was ahead. The book still sold, would always sell. It wasn't on the bestseller lists anymore, but there wasn't a bookstore that didn't have it on the shelves, or a teenager who didn't have a paperback copy in their bedroom, or an adult nerd who hadn't once dug around for a raincoat and a fake mustache, like Denise. Leonard had had nothing to do with the television show, but he did get paid every time it aired, and he had been an answer in the **New York Times** crossword puzzle more times than he could count. He hadn't ever published another book, but he was always writing.

When she was a child, Alice had sometimes thought of the **Time Brothers** brothers as her actual siblings—it was one of the lonely games she'd played in her tiny bedroom. The actors who played Scott and Jeff had been young and handsome, barely out of their teens when the show began to air. She hadn't read her father's book at the time, but she understood the gist—these two brothers traveled through time and space and solved mysteries. What more did she need to know? Now the actor who played Jeff was in commercials for vitamins for seniors, winking at the camera about how even his mustache had gone silver, and the actor who played Scott was living on a horse farm just outside Nashville, Tennessee, which Alice knew because he still sent her father a Christmas card every year. Would she have to tell him about her father? Would she have to figure out how to tell the actor who played Jeff, too? He had always been a true asshole, even when she was a kid, and Alice hadn't seen him in decades. He would send something extravagant and useless, a room-filling bouquet that he hadn't chosen with a note that he hadn't written. She wanted to tell her father that she was thinking about them, those two morons, one sweet and the other a buffoon.

Every time she left the hospital, Alice worried that it would be the last time she would see her father. She'd heard people talk about how their loved ones waited until they left the room. Alice stayed until visiting hours were over, and told her father that she loved him on her way out the door.

8

MATT PICKED THE RESTAURANT IN advance, which was a welcome surprise. They had a reservation, he texted, and sent her the info. It was a place they hadn't been before, or at least Alice hadn't, and she put on lipstick.

Matt made reservations for dinner, she texted Sam. **Some fancy place in midtown with a** Top Chef **chef.** Sam wrote back instantly—**Hot diabetic or sexy Japanese woman? I love them both equally.** Alice shrugged, as if Sam could see her, and then called her on FaceTime so that she could.

"Hi," Alice said.

"Hey, sweets," Sam said. It looked like she was driving.

"Samantha Rothman-Wood, are you driving? Why did you pick up FaceTime? Please don't die."

"I'm in the parking lot of Evie's ballet class, relax." Sam closed her eyes. "Sometimes I take a nap sitting up." Evie was seven, the oldest of three. There was a loud squawk from an unseen mouth. "Fuck, the baby's awake."

Alice watched as Sam nimbly climbed to the back seat, unbuckled Leroy from his car seat, yanked down her nursing bra, and settled the baby onto her breast. "Anyway," Sam said. "What's up?"

"I'm on my way to meet Matt for dinner, and it's at this fancy place, and I don't know, I think it might be an early birthday surprise thing, or . . ." Alice chewed on a fingernail. "I don't know."

Baby Leroy kicked his legs and slapped his tiny hand against Sam's chest. "Okay," she said. "I think this is it. I think he's going to ask you to marry him, and it's going to be quietly public. Like, no mariachi band, no flash mob, but, like, a ring hidden in dessert. And your waiter will know before you do."

Alice sucked in a whistle. "Okay. Yeah. Maybe."

Sam looked at her. "Are you breathing?"

Alice shook her head. "I'll call you after, okay? I love you." Sam blew a kiss and waved Leroy's tiny hand for him. They both looked so small in the back of Sam's SUV, a big hulking thing with one baby seat facing toward the back and a booster seat facing toward the front and Cheerios crushed into the floor mats. Alice pressed the button and made them vanish.

There had been a number of years—her twenties and early thirties—when Alice had been envious of her friends. Not only Sam, but Sam in particular. When Sam and Josh had gotten married, seeing Sam in her sleek white silk dress, dancing to Whitney Houston with all the Black women in her family and the Jewish women in Josh's family, Alice had thought: This is what real happiness looks like, and I'm never going to have this. She had cried when Sam got pregnant the first time, and the second. Alice wasn't proud—she'd talked it through in therapy. But then, years later, Alice had looked around and realized that while all of her friends from college had kids and couldn't stay out late, or couldn't sleep late, or could only meet her between the hours of 10:30 and 11:30 a.m., depending on someone else's nap, she could still do whatever she wanted, whenever she wanted. She had come out the other side of her jealousy. Alice was free to travel, free to go home with strangers, free to do anything.

It didn't help that her father had always treated marriage like a horrible disease he had overcome. Being a divorced single father suited him—he loved Alice and her friends, he loved going to the playground, he loved eating in front of the television, all in equal measure to the way he had hated all the things that marriage had once made him do. He didn't like buying Christmas presents for relatives he didn't otherwise speak to. Leonard could not abide dinner parties, or making small talk with parents he found boring. He was eccentric in a way that private school parents were not used to, meaning he was not exactly like everyone else. There had been women, at various points, whom Alice had imagined might be her father's girlfriends, but they never stayed the night or so much as kissed her father on the cheek in front of her. The hardest thing for Alice to picture was her father and mother together, in the same room, touching. Not even in an intimate way—touching in any way. A hand on a shoulder. Arms, side by side. They'd been married for almost ten years, four years before Alice was born and six after. When Alice was in first grade, Serena left for California, and they were separated by the entire country.

She had known happy married couples, of course—friends' parents whose lives she got to inhabit during sleepovers and on holiday weekends—but it always felt like watching a nature documentary. **Here is a heterosexual American couple in the year 1989—watch as they prepare a tomato sauce for dinner while occasionally touching each other's posteriors in a playful manner.** It wasn't real life. For the first time, Alice wished that her father had been some other kind of dad, a boring one with a set of golf clubs in the trunk of his car. With a car, period. And someone kind sitting in the passenger seat. If he'd been a dentist instead of an artist, if he'd been an accountant, a veterinarian, or a plumber, like his own father had been, maybe his life would have worked out differently. If her parents had stayed married, they would have been miserable. Surely this was what they had discussed at the time—which misery was the most important, which sadness was the heaviest? Was it the lack of whatever unknown happiness might still be ahead of them? Was it Alice's feelings? She doubted they had thought quite this far ahead.

The evening had begun to cool, and Alice shivered, wishing that she'd thought to wear another layer. The restaurant was in the lobby of a hotel on Central Park South. She walked along the park, passing the horses hitched up to hansom cabs, their drivers lazily trying to wave down tourists with money to burn. She narrowly avoided a pile of dog shit, and then a pile of horse shit. The leaves of every tree in Central Park shimmered in the last gasp of sunlight. People who didn't love New York could just fuck all the way off. Look at this place! Look at these benches, at these cobblestones, at these taxicabs and horses side by side! Whatever happened, she had this. Alice exhaled, stepped off the curb, and waited for a break in traffic before running across the street.

9

THE RESTAURANT WAS SO DARK THAT
Alice had to put her hand along the wall as she
walked down the two steps and toward the hostess
stand, where three tall women in identical black
dresses stood stone-faced, and for a moment Alice
thought that it might be so dark that they actually couldn't see her, but then the woman in the
middle said, "Can I help you?" Alice cleared her
throat and gave them Matt's name, and one of the
other women silently turned, holding out her flat
hand like a mime delivering an invisible cocktail.
She turned a corner into the dining room, and
Alice followed.

The floor was black, glossy as a marble, and Alice
stepped gingerly, afraid she might slip. All of the
chairs were covered in what looked like draped

tablecloths, the way furniture is covered in period piece films, to be whipped off by a fleet of servants just before the rich family arrives. Matt was sitting at a table along the far wall, handsome in a suit.

"Hi," Alice said, kissing him on the cheek before settling into her chair. It felt like sitting on a badly folded fitted sheet.

Matt picked up his glass and took a gulp. "Hey," he said. "Isn't this place crazy?"

Alice looked around. The waitstaff were all wearing silk pajamas, which seemed like a terrible idea, in terms of stains and dry-cleaning bills. The restaurant was new. Alice hadn't worked in food service, but she was a native New Yorker, which meant that she knew the statistics for how many restaurants failed. Her hopes were not high. At least nowadays gorgeous celebrity chefs could always turn back to television.

A silk-pajamaed server came over and deposited menus on the table—each one a leather-backed tablet nearly two feet long. As far as Alice could tell, the food items were described only by their ingredients and not by their final form: **pea shoots, kabocha squash, handmade ricotta. Sage, egg, brown butter. Oyster mushrooms, sausage.** "Can I have a large glass of wine, please? White? Nothing sweet?" Alice said before the woman walked away.

Matt was bouncing his knee under the table, shaking the surface slightly, like a minor earthquake. He looked handsome and sweaty, and Alice knew what was going to happen. She could see it all on fast-forward—the meal, Matt getting more and more anxious, them eating tiny, delicious things off plates that looked like painted compositions, a pause before dessert, and then Matt putting a small velvet box in front of her, right on top of a small drop of soy sauce.

"I've been thinking," Matt said. "What if you moved in?"

The server brought over Alice's wine, and she took a big sip, feeling the cool liquid slide across her tongue. "Why?" she asked. "Don't you like having your own space? Time alone?" Alice had never introduced Matt to her father. Sam thought it was weird, but Alice thought it was weird that Sam liked being pregnant. It was obvious that Leonard and Matt wouldn't particularly like each other, and so it had never seemed worth it. One upside to having a single parent was not rushing to get married, like so many people she knew had, just because they were trying to be adults. It was embarrassing, if you slowed down long enough to think about it, how many major life decisions happened because they looked like the model you'd been given.

"I don't know," he said. "I was just thinking, you know, if you moved in, we could get a dog, maybe? My friend from college just adopted this Siberian husky, it's so badass. It looks like a wolf."

"So, you want us to move in together just to get a dog?" Alice was trolling him—Matt was trying.

She could see it, still, and she wasn't sure if she wanted to step out of the oncoming traffic or just let it flatten her. Who knew how she would feel once he actually said the words? Maybe it would feel different than she thought it would, and maybe it would feel good knowing that someone once had wanted to ask her the question, because maybe no one else ever would.

Matt used the corner of his napkin to dab his forehead. He was beginning to look ill.

The server came back and asked if they knew what they'd like, and then launched into a ten-minute explanation of the menu. Alice and Matt both listened and nodded. When he was done, Alice asked where the bathroom was, and walked down another pitch-black hallway to an unmarked door that led to a large communal sink surrounded by stalls. It felt like a bunker, like she was now deep underground. She splashed water on her face and a woman appeared out of nowhere to hand her a towel.

"This would be a great place to murder someone," Alice said. The woman recoiled. "I'm sorry, it's really nice, it's just so dark. I'm so sorry, I didn't mean it. My boyfriend is going to propose, I think."

The woman smiled nervously, perhaps weighing exactly how likely it was that Alice was actually a murderer.

"Anyway, thank you," Alice said. She pulled two dollars out of her wallet and put them in the woman's tip jar.

Back upstairs, they ordered, then ate. Each dish tasted like it had taken a very, very long time to make. Alice was still hungry. When the table had been cleared, Matt looked up at Alice as she leaned back in her chair. "It's so good," she said. "Everything was so good."

"Okay," Matt said. The train was leaving the station. He pushed back his chair and bent over slowly, until his hands were on the floor, and then lowered one knee, and then the other. Alice watched in horror as he actually crawled a few steps before straightening his back and scooching forward on his knee. He reached for her hand, and Alice extended it. "Alice Stern," he began. "Will you order takeout with me and argue about Netflix for the rest of our lives?" Did that even sound good to him? He was still talking. "You are so smart and so funny and, just, really funny, and I want to marry you. Will you marry me?" Had he even mentioned love? Was she funny? What if she wanted to do something other than order takeout and watch television? She had actually thought it was going to be harder to say no. There was a ring in his hand— a beautiful ring that Alice had no interest whatsoever in putting on her finger.

"Matt," Alice said. She leaned down so that their faces were nearly touching. The restaurant was loud and dark enough that only the people at the closest tables saw what was happening, which made Alice want to go back to the bathroom and apologize again to the woman, and to say, **Oh, thank god for this dark, murderous place.** "I can't marry you. I'm so sorry, but I can't." He blinked a few times and then pushed back onto his heels and maneuvered awkwardly back into his chair.

"Shit, really?" he said, though his face looked more relaxed. Alice didn't think he wanted to get married any more than she did. His mother called him on the phone every single day—his older sister did, too. Alice could imagine the pressure on a young, successful man. It was the plot of most novels, wasn't it? To take a bride? It was the plot of most novels and most people in her socioeconomic stratum: college, job, marriage. Matt was on the tardy side, but still well within normal. Men had more time, of course.

"Really," Alice said. There was a plate of a mysterious dessert on the table—she hadn't noticed. It was green and round, wetter than a cake. Flan, maybe, or some sort of pudding. Alice dug in. It tasted like creamed grass. She took another bite. "I think you'll find the right person. I think it's great that you want to get married, I do. It's just not me."

"There was this girl—this woman—from high school who keeps writing me on Facebook. We went to prom together. She just got divorced." Matt picked up his spoon and dragged it around the edge of the pudding. "This is kind of weird."

"I think she sounds perfect." Alice took one last

scoop, straight from the middle, where the grass was deepest. All her life, Alice had wondered if she was doing things wrong, if she was in some way defective, or backward, but maybe it was just that she was exactly like her father, and better off alone. Maybe, she thought, cheering to the notion, her mistake had been assuming that somewhere along the line, everything would fall into place and her life would look just like everyone else's. At the center of the pudding, hiding, was a dollop of cream. "Ooh, look," she said. "I won!"

10

AS USUAL, ALICE HAD SET UP APPOINTMENTS back-to-back all day—there was no way around it. There were too many families on her list to spread them out; it would have taken months. But she did schedule Raphael Joffey as the last child of the day, because that way, if the interview ran long, no one would complain or feel slighted. Alice had also observed over the years that for appointments scheduled in the middle of the day, there was a much higher percentage of absent fathers, whereas if the appointments were either at the very start or end of a day, both parents were more likely to participate.

Tommy hadn't emailed—it was the wife, of course. The mother. Hannah Joffey. It was always the mothers. There had been no acknowledgment of a personal connection, that Alice was a human whom her husband had once known, and that they had known each other inside these very walls. So many things were automated these days, maybe his wife thought that she was corresponding with a computer, some sort of virtual assistant. Hannah had used the word **we,** though, and so Alice was expecting all three of them, the whole family. Her office was mostly tidy—after each child and set of parents left, she had a few minutes to finish her notes and put away the puzzles and games and paper and crayons.

Emily knocked on their shared door and then poked her head in from the hallway. Alice had told her the basics (high school friend, big crush, some sloppy make-out sessions, early and devastating heartbreak), which was probably a mistake, because now Emily was too excited.

"They're here. Want me to bring them in? Or do you want to get them? He's hot, just so you know. I mean, old. Older than me. I mean, he's your age. But he's hot. Would do him, for sure. Okay." Emily widened her eyes. "Want me to bring them in?"

Alice exhaled. "I'll get them. You go sit in a corner somewhere and be quiet." Emily nodded.

Alice was wearing a dress, which she didn't often do. It was burgundy, vintage, and made for a disco queen. No mother at Belvedere wore anything like it—they all wore the same things, the same brands of jeans, the same brands of shoes, the same workout clothes, the same puffy down coats in winter.

Alice wasn't interested in that. She wanted Tommy to look at her and think, Oh fuck, what did I miss? She wanted that almost as much as she wanted to see him and not have the exact same thought. Alice wanted him to be in a suit, boring, with doughy cheeks and receding hair. He wasn't anywhere on the internet—Thomas Joffey barely existed, except in the file she held in her hand. Alice smoothed out the skirt of her dress and walked out to the waiting room, already smiling.

•   •   •

The child was facing her, on the far side of one of the low tables. He was driving a car around the perimeter of a puzzle and making exploding noises. His parents were both kneeling in front of the table, their backs to Alice. It looked like they were praying at the altar of a tiny god. The boy looked up at her through his long dark bangs and froze.

"Hi, Raphael," she said. "I'm Alice. Can I see your car?"

The boy didn't move, but his parents did. Alice watched in slow motion as the Joffeys turned their heads toward the sound of her voice.

Hannah was beautiful, of course. Alice had found her Instagram, and had already scrolled through enough pages to have seen her from many different flattering angles. She wasn't what Alice had expected, which of course made it worse. Hannah had an interesting face—a large nose, slightly off-center, as if maybe she'd broken it once, and eyes wide-set enough to imagine that she'd been teased as a child. Her hair—dark brown, with gentle waves—hung to her waist. She did not smile.

"You must be Hannah," Alice said, walking toward her with an outstretched hand. She found that she couldn't actually look at Tommy, who was standing up to meet her. Alice was watching him out of the corner of her eye, just a shape and shadows, and her heart was beating fast. She shook Hannah's skinny palm, feeling all her tiny bones, and then turned on her heels.

Raphael had scooted around and was hiding behind his father's legs. Tommy had one hand on the boy's head, and the other flat against his stomach. Alice put out her hand, but Tommy raised his arm and tipped his head to one side, inviting her in for a hug. Alice closed her eyes and stepped into his body, her face grazing his shoulder. Her mouth was near enough his cheek to kiss it, but she didn't.

"Good to see you," Tommy said. She was finally looking right at him.

There was nothing doughy, nothing soft. His hair was still curly, still dark, though there were threads of silver at his temples. Alice didn't know if she still loved him, somewhere deep inside her body, or if it was only that she remembered him, which felt the same, a tug at her core. Tommy smiled.

"So, Raphael, are you ready to come and play with me? Or should we go talk with your parents first, and then we can play after?" Alice had worn her best necklace—a gift from Melinda. It was extra-tiny matchbox cars and toy airplanes, all dangling like a charm bracelet. She bent down to show it to the boy. He reached for the necklace with one hand and gently put the other one on Alice's forearm. She looked up at Tommy and winked. If the boy got in, then the power balance would shift, and she would just be someone he went to school with who for some reason had stayed locked into this one place, someone who was stuck in high school forever, but right now, Alice was fully in charge, and it felt good.

11

EMILY LOVED THE STORY ABOUT THE restaurant. She loved that Alice had said no. Emily still wanted to make everyone happy, and her breakups were always drawn-out, tear-soaked misery cakes with a smattering of sidewalk arguments sprinkled on top.

"I just think it's, like, the most badass thing I've ever heard." They were outside smoking. "And I cannot believe how hot that guy you went to school with is. What's his story, anyway?"

The information had come piecemeal, teased out as it was through conversations with and about a five-year-old. They had just moved back to New York from Los Angeles, where Hannah was from. Rafe—that's what they called the boy—had allergies, severe ones, and they were seeing a doctor in

New York, the best doctor in the field. They hadn't moved back to be near Tommy's parents, but the Joffeys owned a small apartment in the building, and so it's where they were. Hannah made jewelry and short films. Tommy said he was a philanthropist and when he did, Hannah had touched his leg, her hand gently stroking his thigh.

"What the fuck does that even mean?" Emily asked, flicking her cigarette.

"I have no idea," Alice said. "Last I heard, he went to law school."

• • •

When they got back to their office, Melinda was waiting for them.

"Are we grounded?" Emily asked. She popped a mint in her mouth. It was nearly five o'clock, and everyone except the security guard and the middle school volleyball team had gone home.

Melinda shook her head. "Sit." They sat. Emily and Alice looked at her expectantly, like musicians waiting for their conductor's baton.

"I'm retiring. At the end of the semester." She'd been talking about it for years—an empty threat most often leveled just before the holidays, or in the spring, when angry parents began to complain that their perfect, special child had not been accepted. "It's time."

"Melinda!" Alice said. She looked around to make

sure no one else was in the suite of offices. "Did they fire you? Those assholes! This is ageism. Sexism? Probably both!"

Melinda clucked her tongue. "No, no, my dear. It was my choice. I was going to do it last year, and the year before, and the year before, but the timing was never quite right." Everything about her was soothing. Children came to the office just to say hello to her and to hug her. On Emily's and Alice's birthdays, Melinda would produce over-the-top treats from the bakery around the corner and thoughtful handwritten cards that would invariably make them cry.

"I don't want you to go," Alice said.

"I'm seventy," Melinda said. "It'll be fine."

"Well," Emily said, "number one, sad, and number two, does this mean that Alice is the boss now?" She raised her thumbs.

Alice blushed, surprised. "Oh, I hadn't even thought about that." It would be a good balance to breaking up with Matt, a bigger job. She felt a chill run through her when she thought that she might soon have more hours to fill, if she wasn't going up to the hospital anymore. That was what people did with grief, wasn't it? Poured themselves into work? She could imagine it more than she could imagine learning how to knit, or downloading a meditation app and really sticking with it.

Melinda cleared her throat. "That would be

wonderful, but no. The school is bringing over the head of admissions from Spencer Prep." She paused, considering how much to say. "I believe they are looking to go in a different direction with their goals." Emily turned her thumbs toward the ground. Melinda patted her knee.

"Oh," Alice said. "Of course."

"That's fucking stupid," Emily said. "Excuse my French, Melinda."

"Oh, girls, stop that," Melinda said. "Let's not be dramatic. I've met the woman they're hiring. She's very smart, very sharp." None of this was reassuring, and she knew it.

If someone had asked her, Alice wouldn't have said that she hoped to take over Melinda's job someday. Melinda was irreplaceable, a singular force, and what qualifications did Alice even have? Belvedere had sent her to some administration courses, but she didn't have a master's degree. She hadn't thought about doing the same job at a different school. What did she know about those people, about those kids? The idea of some Professional Person coming over from Spencer Prep felt all kinds of wrong, as if the job—selecting kids, building classes, forming the community—were a business decision. Alice was so used to Melinda, to doing everything as it had always been done, that she couldn't actually imagine sitting in the office with someone else at the helm. Emily would be fine, she was still young.

She would leave soon, to go to graduate school for something or other. Most people did.

When Alice had been fresh out of art school, working at Belvedere had seemed quirky and amusing, a punch line. Belvedere often hired recent graduates for low-level jobs, a gentle tide of nepotism that never seemed to cause much harm because people never stayed long. But Alice had stayed. She had stayed in New York, she had stayed in the same apartment, she had stayed at Belvedere.

It had always been one of her best qualities, she thought—steadiness. Reliability. The last time she'd gotten a promotion was when Emily was hired, four years ago. Before that, she'd been Melinda's only assistant, and before that, she'd been moved around the school, temporary help for whatever hole needed to be patched. The time had passed quickly, five years, then ten, and so on. Now she'd worked at the school longer than she'd been a student, and some of her favorite colleagues had once been her teachers. For the first decade Alice had been on staff, she'd been a human Band-Aid: someone was on maternity leave; someone broke their leg and couldn't get on the subway—and Alice was there, reliable and familiar. She had always been happy at Belvedere, as happy as one could be. Sometimes she felt like a doll that had been left behind, with too much obvious sentimental value to just throw away, but most of the time, yes, she was happy.

"You'll like her, Alice," Melinda said. "I think she'll be a good mentor, actually. Better than me." Melinda cocked her head to the side, and Alice saw that her eyes were teary. "I was always just making it up as I went along." Alice and Emily both cried, and Melinda swung the tissue box from one to the other, always prepared.

12

HAVING A BIRTHDAY FALL ON A SATURDAY as an adult was a little bit like having a summer birthday as a kid. In one's twenties, of course, it was great, and meant not being hungover at an office job, but after that, the appeal dulled. Weekday birthdays had impromptu office parties, maybe a dusty bottle of champagne opened at lunch, if the mood was right. On the weekend, though, adults were less likely to reach out to friendly coworkers to wish them a happy birthday. A short text or a comment on a social media post, that was about the extent of it. Alice was actually sorry that her birthday was on a Saturday, but then feeling sorry about it made her feel pathetic and so she pushed her coffee table against the wall and pulled up a ten-minute yoga video on YouTube, though she abandoned it halfway through, when the instructor started breathing quickly through her nostrils while pumping her stomach in and out like a cat about to vomit.

The doorbell rang. A delivery—the package had her mother's PO box as its return address. Serena hadn't been to Brooklyn for a decade, and had visited Alice's apartment only once or twice in all the time she'd lived on Cheever Place. Serena didn't always send presents, but this year was significant, and when Alice opened the box, she was not surprised to find several large crystals and a metal singing bowl inside. Serena had never met a healing modality she didn't like, and Alice understood that these gifts, and all the ones like them that she'd ever received, were their own form of silent apology, the only kind she was ever going to get.

• • •

When Alice had imagined her fortieth birthday, as much as one imagines things like that, it had not been like this. She had attended a handful of swanky fortieth birthday parties, catered affairs in Brooklyn Heights town houses, and she knew she wouldn't have something like that, something with hired waitstaff passing around tiny quiches. Maybe Peter Luger, or some other ancient New York restaurant where the waiters were not would-be actors and models but grumpy old men in waistcoats, a place that felt nicely frozen in its fustiness. When

Sam turned forty a few months ago, her husband had gotten her a hotel room, where she spent the night alone, in silence. Alice's parents were already separated by the time her mother was forty, and Serena was out the door and on her way to a new life. So many of Alice's father's doctors were younger than she was—people who would come into the room and talk to her with confidence, their advanced degrees and professional expertise. Some of them were probably a whole decade younger. While they'd been dissecting cadavers and memorizing names of bones, what had Alice been doing? Her father read three books a week, sometimes more, and responded to every fan letter he received. She had tried to take up running, once. For a couple of years, she had joined a mentoring program, but the little sister she'd been assigned had then gone to college and they'd lost touch.

• • •

It was always hard to make a dinner date with Sam, because she had children and lived in New Jersey, each of which on their own would have been tricky odds to overcome. They were supposed to meet at a restaurant in the West Village, which wasn't exactly convenient for either of them but meant that they both had to travel, which at least felt fair. An hour before dinner, though, and soon before Alice would start walking to the F train stop, Sam called to say that Leroy had a fever, and that she could still come but wouldn't be able to stay long, and would it be possible if they met closer to the Lincoln Tunnel? The tunnel emptied out onto 39th Street, just above the Javits Center, perhaps the least appealing corner of Manhattan. "Of course," Alice replied, because she wanted to celebrate, and it didn't matter where it happened, not really.

• • •

They settled on a place on the lower level of a much-maligned shopping mall just south of the tunnel. If they were going to do it, why not go all the way? Not only were they going to go somewhere with hot dogs on the menu, but the hot dogs cost twenty dollars. On the way, Alice redownloaded a couple of dating apps and did a little scrolling. The blessing and the curse of the dating app lifestyle was that you could tell the app exactly what you were looking for, and, more or less, that's all you would see. Men? Women? Under thirty, over forty? All the men and women whose pictures showed up looked fine. They either went to the gym or had cats. They were either snobs about cooking or snobs about music. Alice closed the app and put her phone in her pocket. On the screen, everyone seemed equally unappealing, even the good-looking ones.

When she got off the train, there was a message waiting from Sam—she was running late. Alice wasn't surprised. When they were in high school, Sam would often show up an hour late, still loitering around her parents' Columbia faculty housing in Morningside Heights when Alice was waiting by the pay phone outside the Barnes & Noble on Broadway and 82nd Street or holding up a diner table and refusing to order more than one bottomless cup of coffee. Hudson Yards, the giant mall that held the restaurant, was still open, and so Alice wasted time by wandering in and out of empty shops. She nodded at salespeople, who looked back at her hungry for interaction, and then Alice pointed to her phone, pretending that she was listening to someone talk. Emily texted; Melinda sent an email. Alice took a photo of her hands making a peace sign and posted it with the caption **4-0.** Four-zero. Was that four wins, zero losses, or zero wins and four losses? Alice wasn't sure. One store full of beautiful sweaters was having a sale, and Alice tried one on in the aisle. It was two hundred dollars—on **sale**—but she bought it anyway, because it was her birthday. Sam texted, finally, to say that she had found a parking spot, and that she'd meet her in ten minutes.

• • •

Alice had already gotten a table when Sam hurried in, holding an enormous shopping bag. Sam always looked beautiful, even when she was exhausted and wearing sweatpants. Her hair, which had been relaxed in high school, she now wore naturally, and her enormous head of curls surrounded her face like a halo. Sometimes, when Alice complained about the lines around her eyes or her thin, flat hair, Sam would laugh gently and say that aging well was a Black woman's legacy, and that she was sorry for Alice's trouble.

"Hi hi hi," Sam said, throwing her arms around Alice's neck. "I'm so sorry, I know that this is a nightmare, and that this is never in a million years where you would want to come for your birthday, and I'm sorry. Also, hi! I miss you! Tell me everything." Sam crashed into the opposite side of the booth and started taking off layers of clothing.

"Hi hi," Alice said. "Oh, you know, nothing much. Broke up with Matt, didn't get a promotion that I didn't know was even a possibility at work, my dad is still dying. Everything is great."

"Yes, okay, **but,**" Sam said, "look at what I got you for your birthday." She reached into the shopping bag and pulled out a pretty box with a wide silk ribbon wrapped around it. Sam had always been crafty. On the table, Sam's phone vibrated. "Shit," she said, and picked it up. "I swear, Leroy is our **third** baby, and sometimes I feel like Josh is worse than a teenage babysitter. He just texted me to ask where we keep the baby Tylenol, as if it would be somewhere weird, you know, like the garage, or in my underwear drawer."

Alice slid the box closer to her. "Can I open it?"

"Yes, open, open!" Sam said. "Also, I need a very

large drink, but just one, or two at the most, so I can pump and dump when I get home." She looked around for a waiter and flagged down the first one she saw.

Alice slid the ribbon off the box and pulled off the lid. Inside was a tornado of tissue paper, and nestled inside the paper was a tiara. The diamonds weren't real, but it was heavy, not some plastic bridal shower nonsense. "Keep going," Sam said, and so Alice set the tiara on her head and took out another crumpled sheet of tissue paper. At the bottom of the box was a framed photograph. She lifted it out carefully. In the photo, Alice and Sam were both wearing tiaras and slips and dark lipstick. Sam had a beer bottle in her hand, and Alice was taking a drag off a cigarette. They were both staring at the camera, eyes like knives.

"We were so grunge," Alice said.

"We were not **grunge,**" Sam said. "Please. We were sixteen, and glorious. This is from your birthday, do you remember?"

The party had been on Pomander Walk. It was a risk, having people over, since Alice knew every single one of her neighbors, but as with all risks she'd taken at the time, Alice had been totally unable to foresee any consequences. She had made sure all the curtains were drawn, and she'd only invited fifteen people, and when nearly twice that number showed up, it was okay, as long as the house stayed quiet. Leonard was spending the night downtown at a hotel, at a science fiction and fantasy convention he attended every year, coming back the next evening. Alice could remember the party in flashes—the Calvin Klein underwear she'd been wearing, the smell of the empty beer bottles that littered every available surface, all the bottle caps filled with long cylinders of cigarette ash. She and Sam had both thrown up that night, but not before the picture was taken. It was widely appreciated as a very good party. Alice had ended the night heartbroken and sobbing. It was a long time ago.

"I love it," Alice said, and she did. It also made her feel profoundly sad.

The waiter brought over Sam's large glass of wine, and a second one for Alice. They ordered more appetizers than they needed, fried chickpeas and roasted cauliflower, bread and cheese, ham fritters, tiny shot glasses of gazpacho. "I'm paying," Sam said, "and I want to eat things that would make my children hide under the table." They ate octopus and olives and anchovies on toast. Sam asked about Leonard, and Alice told her. It wasn't that she was afraid that he was going to die—he was dying, she knew that. It was that she didn't know when it was going to happen, or what it would feel like when it did, and she was afraid that she would feel relieved, and afraid that she would feel too sad to go to work, and afraid that she'd never have another boyfriend because she was going to be too sad to meet anyone, and she was already forty, now she was **forty,** which was really different from thirty-nine, but then Sam's phone buzzed and buzzed again and Leroy had rolled off the couch and hit his head and maybe needed stitches, Josh wasn't sure. Sam paid for everything and kissed Alice on both cheeks and then on the forehead and was out the door before she even had her arms through the coat sleeves. The table was still full of food, and so Alice ate as much as she could, and then asked for a box to take things home.

13

BEFORE HE'D CHECKED INTO THE HOSPITAL, Leonard had called Alice a few times a week. They'd talked about whatever they were watching on Netflix, or the books they were reading, or what they'd eaten for lunch. Leonard was a terrible cook, capable only of boiling water for pasta or hot dogs or frozen vegetables. Like so many New Yorkers, Alice had learned to cook by dialing the telephone—Ollie's for Chinese, Jackson Hole for burgers, Rancho for Mexican, Carmine's for pasta with meatballs, the deli for bacon, egg, and cheese sandwiches. Sometimes they would talk about Alice's mother, about whether or not she believed in aliens (she did), about whether or not she was an alien herself (potentially). Leonard liked hearing about the kids at school. It wasn't that Alice and her father weren't having honest conversations—they were, and better conversations than many people had with their parents, to be sure—but they were conversations that skimmed happily over the surface, like a perfect flat rock.

Leonard had been in pain for months, and once he'd finally agreed to go to the hospital, the nurses on duty would help lessen the anguish by attaching his IV to a bag of diluted fluid, the strong stuff, and in the minutes before he got too stoned and fell asleep, Alice and her father started to really talk.

"You remember Simon Rush?" Leonard had asked. This was when he was in a room with a view, the mighty Hudson River and the George Washington Bridge right out the window. Alice watched boats go up and down the water, even Jet Skis. Where did people get Jet Skis in New York City?

"Literally your most famous friend? Of course I do." Alice could picture him standing in the doorway on Pomander, and remembered sometimes coming across him and her father smoking cigarettes on the corner of 96th Street and West End Avenue when she and some of her friends were climbing back up from Riverside Park.

"He always had stuff like this. Was too trippy for me, usually, but sometimes, yeah. Sometimes we'd get so zonked and just sit in his apartment on Seventy-Ninth Street and listen to Love's **Forever**

Changes on vinyl. He had everything on vinyl, plus the best speakers money could buy." Leonard pointed at her. "You have that, on your phone? Can you play it?"

Leonard had never gotten a smartphone—didn't see the point. But he liked that Alice could immediately conjure anything he wanted to listen to, like it was magic. She pushed a few buttons and then music came pouring out of the tiny speakers. Guitars like dancers. Leonard raised a thin hand and softly snapped his fingers.

"It's amazing, Alice, the way you were always just perfect. I was doing my thing, like always, and you were so **solid,** always. Like a bulldog. Terrestrial, you know."

Alice laughed. "Thanks."

"What? Am I not supposed to say that? I was great when you were little, man, and we could play, and just use our imaginations, and make up stories, but by the time you hit puberty, I should have called in someone who knew what they were doing. Sent you to some boarding school. Moved you in with Sam and her parents. But you were just such a good kid, you didn't seem to notice."

"You let me smoke in my room." Alice's bedroom had shared a wall and a fire escape with her father's.

"You didn't smoke, not really, did you? Cigarettes?"

"Dad, I smoked a pack a day. When I was fourteen." Alice rolled her eyes. They had smoked together, at the kitchen table, sharing an ashtray.

He laughed. "No, seriously? But you never even got in trouble. You and Sam and Tommy and all your friends, you were such funny, good kids."

"When I was in high school, you treated me like a grown-up. And so I thought I was a grown-up. But not, like, a square grown-up. I thought I was Kate Moss or Leonardo DiCaprio or something, one of the movie stars that was always stumbling out of nightclubs. That was my goal, I think."

Leonard nodded, his eyes starting to close. "Next time, we'll have more rules. For both of us."

It was true—she had always been just fine. So fine that no one ever checked to see what was happening underneath. There were kids with problems—Heather, who got sent to rehab for shooting up between her toes like she was in **The Basketball Diaries,** and Jasmine, who ate only one hundred calories a day and had to be held back because she spent four months in inpatient treatment, being fed through a tube. That wasn't Alice. Alice was fun, she was normal. She and her dad were like a comedy team, and she always laughed the loudest. If she'd had rules, or a curfew, or a parent who grounded her when he found drugs instead of just taking them away, maybe she could have gone to Yale, maybe she could have had test scores high enough that she could even have said that out loud without the college counselor laughing. Maybe she'd be wearing white in the fall, her hair long, and she would have left town and moved to France and done something, anything. Maybe she'd be talking to the hospital's nurses' station from her house in Montclair, watching through a window as her husband and kids splashed in the pool on the last seasonable days. When Sam had gotten too drunk as a teenager, she came to Pomander, and Leonard let her sleep it off in Alice's bed. Maybe parents were supposed to be narcs. Alice had always assumed that he knew everything and trusted her enough not to get in trouble, but maybe he just had never been paying attention, like everyone else. Now it was harder for him to pay attention, and he had to ask her the same question over and over again. Leonard remembered Sam and Tommy but couldn't have named anyone Alice worked with. Alice understood—this was how it worked. When she was young, she'd thought he was old, and now that he was old, Alice realized how young he'd been. Perspective was unfair. When Leonard was fully asleep, Alice left.

14

ALICE HAD ONE LARGE SHOPPING BAG IN each hand—her fancy sweater in one and her doggie bag in the other. She had never, in her life as a New Yorker, been alone, at night, in the far west Thirties. She walked east until Eighth Avenue, when she found herself in a crowd of people with wheelie suitcases heading into Penn Station. Alice didn't feel drunk, not exactly, but the world had taken on a slightly goofier tinge, and she giggled as she walked against the current of bodies in the crosswalk. The subway was right there, but she didn't want to take it yet—the beauty of New York City was **walking,** was serendipity and strangers, and it was still her birthday, and so she was just going to keep going. Alice turned and walked up

Eighth, past the crummy tourist shops selling magnets and keychains and I ♥ NY T-shirts and foam fingers shaped like the Statue of Liberty. Alice had walked for almost ten blocks when she realized she had a destination.

She and Sam and their friends had enjoyed many, many hours in bars as teenagers: they'd spent nights at the Dublin House, on 79th Street; at the Dive Bar, on Amsterdam and 96th Street, with the neon sign shaped like bubbles, though that one was a little too close to home to be safe; and some of the fratty bars farther down Amsterdam, the ones with the buckets of beers for twenty dollars and scratched pool tables. Sometimes they even went to some NYU bars downtown, on MacDougal Street, where they could dash across the street for falafel and then go back to the bar, like it was their office and they were running out for lunch. Their favorite bar, though, was Matryoshka, a Russian-themed bar in the 50th Street 1/9 subway station. Now it was just the 1 train, but back then, there was also the 9. Things were always changing, even when they didn't feel like it. Alice wondered if no one ever felt as old as they were because it happened so slowly, and you were only ever one day slower and creakier, and the world changed so gradually that by the time cars had evolved from boxy to smooth, or green taxis had joined yellow ones, or MetroCards had replaced tokens, you were used to it. Everyone was a lobster in the pot.

There was nothing else like Matryoshka—subway stations often had tiny, closet-sized bodegas with bottled water and candy bars and magazines, and some in midtown had shoe repair shops that also sold umbrellas and various other things commuting businesspeople might need, and there were a few barbershops, but nothing came close. All bars were dark—that was part of the point, of course— but Matryoshka was literally subterranean, on the left side of the turnstiles, at the bottom of the flight of stairs that led up to the street. Its entrance was a black doorway with a red **M** painted at eye level and no other discerning marks. Alice hadn't been in fifteen years. She knew it was still there—it was famous, an underground landmark, the sort of place that **New York** magazine liked to send reporters and movie stars to for some real ambiance. Alice pulled out her phone to text Sam, but then she thought about what it would sound like—**It's my birthday and I'm ending the night by going to a bar in a subway station. Alone!** It was a joke tweet, a cry for help. But Alice didn't want help, she wanted to have one last drink in a place that she had loved, and then she would go home and wake up forty and one day and she could start all over again.

A clump of people were walking up the stairs in the station, and for a moment, Alice worried that Matryoshka had gotten too popular, that there would be some sort of a line to get in, which she obviously wouldn't wait in, but it was just people getting off the subway. The door was propped open, and the familiar, yeasty darkness of the bar was exactly the way Alice remembered it. Even the stool that was propping open the door—black, with a cracked leather seat—looked like one she'd clocked some hours on, her skinny teenage elbows on the sticky bar.

The bar was two rooms long: the narrow space where patrons entered, which contained the bar itself, and a small seating area with black leather couches that looked like they'd been loved, abandoned on the curb, and dragged down the subway stairs to their final resting place. There were a few aging pinball machines at the far end, and a jukebox, one that Alice and Sam had always loved. Alice was surprised to see it—there had been jukeboxes everywhere when she was in high school, at bars and diners, sometimes tiny individual table-sized ones, but it had been years since she'd seen one like this, up to her shoulders and enormous, the size of a New York City closet. The bartender nodded at her, and Alice startled. It was the same guy who had worked there ages ago—which was normal, of course, he probably owned the place—but he looked exactly as she remembered him. Maybe there were a few white hairs sprinkled throughout, but he didn't look as much older as she did, Alice was sure. The darkness was flattering to everyone.

She nodded hello back and took a lap of the bar,

walking into the second, larger room. It was where she and her friends had mostly spent their time, because it had more couches, and room to sprawl and flirt and dance. A photo booth took up space in the back corner, where sometimes people posed for photos but mostly people hooked up, as the machine was usually broken but there was still a curtain and a small bench and the titillating feeling of somehow being caught on film anyway. Pockets of people sat around drinking and laughing, their knees pointed toward each other's laps, their mouths open and beautiful. Alice didn't know if she was looking for someone she knew, or pretending to look for someone she knew, or just half-heartedly looking for the bathroom. She circled back to the bar and sat down, her enormous shopping bags on the floor next to her.

"It's my birthday!" she said to the bartender.

"Happy birthday," he said. He put two shot glasses on the bar and filled them with tequila. "How old are you now?"

Alice laughed. "Forty. I. Am. Forty. Hoo, really not sure about how that sounds." She accepted the glass that he pushed across the bar and clinked it against the other, which the bartender drained effortlessly into his mouth. The shot burned. She'd never gotten into real alcohol—not in quantity, like the drunk housewives in movies, and not in quality, like the people she'd gone to college with who now had well-stocked vintage bar carts and fancied themselves amateur mixologists. "Wow," she said. "Thank you."

There was loud laughter coming from the corner by the jukebox. A trio of young women—younger than Alice, younger than Emily even—were taking pictures of themselves and then showing each other their phones.

"I used to come here when I was in high school," Alice said to the bartender. "I had a fake ID that I got on Eighth Street that said I was twenty-three, because I thought it would be too obvious if it said I was twenty-one, but by the time I was actually twenty-one, my fake ID said I was almost thirty. But now I can't tell the difference between people who are twenty-one and twenty-nine, so maybe it didn't really matter anyway."

The bartender poured another shot. "On the house. I remember turning forty."

Alice wanted to ask if it was last year, or a decade ago, or yesterday, but she didn't. "Okay," she said, "but this is the last one." The liquid tasted better this time—less like fire, and more like a smoky kiss.

15

POMANDER WALK WAS SO MUCH CLOSER than home, and she had a key, somewhere. It was three in the morning when Alice's car pulled up to the corner of 94th and Broadway. She'd abandoned her leftovers at the bar, or maybe she'd shared them? In any case, she was down to one shopping bag, and instead of the new sweater, it held her old sweater, because she'd spilled a whole beer onto it and then changed into the new one in the bathroom. The girls at the end of the bar had been hilarious, and they were **smokers,** thank god, at least in the way that early hours of the morning will make smokers out of nearly anybody. It was a ten-minute ride uptown—she could have taken the train, of course, but it was still Alice's birthday, and so she pushed the button on her phone for the most luxurious car around. When she got in, the driver took one look at her, a bit sprawled on the back seat of his brand-new Escalade, and Alice just knew that he expected her to vomit. She would not.

The minute the car pulled away, she did, in the gutter. The sidewalks were empty. Alice shivered and looked in her purse for her keys. She always carried a key to her father's house, just in case, but she hadn't been in several weeks. Often she would stop by to pick up mail or to feed Ursula, but one of the girls who lived on Pomander was getting paid to feed and pet the cat, and so Alice never felt too bad if she stayed away. She scraped the bottom of the bag with her fingers. The keys had to be there somewhere.

The main entrance to Pomander was on the 94th Street side, a small gated door next to the long list of names and buzzers. Tourists would sometimes stand at the gate and wait to be let in. During the day, it was mostly harmless. Pomander Walk must have been on some German travel websites or in some guidebooks, because it was almost always Germans, and the occasional Brit. No one rang the bells at three in the morning. The super didn't live on-site, and there was no doorman, just a part-time porter, someone you could ask for help with moving things in and out of the storage cave, a tiny closet with a mile-long waiting list. If Alice didn't find her key, she could always buzz Jim Roman, who lived at number 12, the closest to the gate—

if he was up, at least he wouldn't have far to walk, and he had a key to her father's front door, too. But the thought of waking up Jim Roman was deeply unappealing, as Jim was a dandy widower who had to be past eighty, and whom she had known since she was a small child. Exposing him to this iteration of her drunk and possibly still sticky self was too depressing to stomach, and so Alice leaned against the gate to further devote herself to excavating the contents of her bag. When she pushed her weight against it, the heavy black wrought-iron behemoth that had once crushed her ankle so hard that she'd needed an X-ray, the gate swung open. "Oh, sweet Jesus, thank you," Alice said. Who else had a key to her apartment in Brooklyn? She had an extra set of keys at school, but what good was that? Her landlady had a key. Matt had a key, despite the fact that he had never once used it to get into her apartment—she would need to get that back.

Alice climbed the steps to the walk itself and then steadied herself at the top. Pomander Walk was the most beautiful place she would ever live. The houses were doll-sized, almost, with ginger-bread details, like something out of a Hallmark Christmas movie, only with the ever-present New York City soundtrack of honking horns and jack-hammers. Because it was fall, people already had pumpkins sitting on their front steps, pretty ones that came from some farm upstate, ones too expensive to be carved. Those would come later, just before Halloween. There were always enough kids on Pomander for a good Halloween party—tiny little humans in costumes waddling from one door to the next, all the grown-ups drinking wine or apple cider in masks and funny hats. Her dad had lots of funny hats, and a few fake mustaches, and they had always enjoyed themselves, both when she was small enough to trick-or-treat herself and when she was too big and helped him give out candy.

She still couldn't find the key. One of the windows was a little bit wobbly, Alice knew, and it might be easy enough to open from the outside. Or she could just wait a few hours, until it was properly morning, and then Jim Roman could let her in, or the super. That was probably a better idea. Alice was just starting to sit down on her dad's front step when the little guardhouse caught her eye. It was one of her father's treasured domains—the way Alice imagined men in the suburbs felt about their garages, his own realm of domesticity, more orderly than the house itself. It belonged to all of Pomander equally, whoever needed dirt or a shovel or one of the shared tools inside, but Leonard loved it the most, and took care of it.

Close up, the guardhouse was nearly empty— there was a broom standing upright in one corner and a few sealed bags of gardening dirt propped up against the opposite wall, but otherwise the tiny little shack was spotless. Alice closed the door behind her and sat on the floor. After a few minutes, she wadded up the shopping bag with her dirty sweater in it and used it as a pillow behind her head, with the dirt as back support. She fell asleep quickly, imagining herself as the tiny bunny in the Richard Scarry book, cozy in his tree all winter.

16

THE ROOM WAS DARK AND ALICE FELT creaky. She opened her eyes and blinked. It took several seconds for her to realize where she was. Somehow, in the night, she had made it all the way inside the house, into her narrow childhood bed. Leonard wasn't one of those parents who turned his child's bedroom into a warehouse for exercise equipment, but neither was he precious about Alice's things. Most of them were still there, but once, on an annual clean-out that he did not ask her about first, Leonard had thrown all of her issues of **Sassy** magazine into the recycling, a transgression about which she was still mad. She stretched her arms over her head until her fingers tickled the wall behind her.

Alice's body didn't feel terrible, but her mouth

was dry and a headache was on its merry way. She kept her eyes mostly closed as she reached onto the floor and felt around for her bag and phone. Instead, Alice's fingers touched only the thick, shaggy rug, which she didn't think had ever been vacuumed, and the crowded surface of the bedside table.

"Shit," Alice said, and sat up. Her bag had to be nearby. Without her phone, she had no idea what time it was. It was certainly morning, even though her room was still dark. The backs of the houses on Pomander were always dark, especially in the morning, and the window in her bedroom overlooked the back windows in all the big buildings that lined the rest of the block, a whole inverted cityscape—fire escapes and mostly unseen windows, as far as the eye could see. Alice started making a mental list of all the credit cards she would have to cancel if she couldn't find her wallet, and everything else she'd have to replace. How did one make an appointment at the Apple Store to replace a phone if one didn't have a phone? Her laptop was at home. Alice exhaled.

She swung her legs onto the floor and stood up. She'd feed Ursula and figure out how to get on the train with no MetroCard. There had to be a few dollars somewhere in the house, enough to get home, and her landlady had a key to her apartment. The room was a mess—the floor absolutely piled with lumps of clothing, as if Leonard had been going through and getting rid of things before he went into the hospital. It was weird, but so was Leonard. Alice just nudged things out of the way with her bare toes, clearing a path to the door.

She shuffled into the bathroom and didn't bother closing the door. She sat to pee and closed her eyes. There was a thump in the living room, and then the sound of Ursula walking the hall. Her tiny black face appeared in the doorway, and immediately her body was against Alice's shins.

"Good kitten," Alice said. It was only then that she looked down at her own body. She was wearing boxer shorts and an enormous yellow Crazy Eddie T-shirt that pooled in her lap. Her thighs, even flattened against the toilet seat, looked narrow, as if she'd somehow lost weight in the night. Alice didn't remember changing clothes, and even if she had, she hadn't seen this shirt in decades, a relic from her childhood. She stood up and pulled the shirt taut to admire it, a real piece of New York City history. The television commercial began to play in her brain. There was no way that Alice was not going to wear it home. Ursula wound her body around Alice's feet and then ran off, no doubt to wait by her food bowl. Alice heard a noise from the other room—probably the tween cat sitter. Alice quickly pushed the door closed, not wanting to frighten the child.

Leonard's bathroom was like a time capsule.

Maybe it was that he still went to the same old-fashioned pharmacy he'd always gone to, or maybe it was that contemporary branding hadn't arrived on the Upper West Side, but everything in the bathroom—Leonard's toothpaste, his shaving cream, the towels that had once been beige and now just looked dirty, always—looked exactly the way it always had. Alice squeezed an inch of Colgate onto her finger and brushed her teeth. After she spat, she splashed some water on her face and dried off on the towel.

"I'll be right out," she called. "It's Alice!" Children probably didn't have heart attacks very often, but when she thought about her own childhood on Pomander Walk, there had been a lot of talk about stranger danger, and she had always been ready to kick and bite, like every good city girl. There was a quiet response, and so Alice straightened her T-shirt and walked out into the hall. She was a grown-up who worked with kids and could talk to anyone, even if she was wearing the kind of pajamas she'd worn as a teenager.

Ursula was perched in her favorite spot, the part of the windowsill directly above the heater vent, her black fur baking in the sun. She was the world's most ancient cat—no one knew exactly how old she was, but if Alice had to guess, she would have said she was twenty-five, or immortal. She still looked just as vital as she ever had.

"Hey, good morning," Alice said, turning the corner from the hallway into the kitchen. "Hope I didn't scare you."

"You're not that scary," said her dad. Leonard Stern was sitting in his spot at the kitchen table. There was a cup of coffee next to him, and an open can of Coca-Cola. Next to his drinks, Leonard had a plate with some toast and a few hard-boiled eggs. Alice thought she could see an Oreo, too. The clock on the wall behind the table said that it was seven in the morning. Leonard looked good—he looked healthy. Healthier, actually, than Alice could ever remember him looking. He looked like he could run around the block if he wanted to, just for fun, like the kind of dad who could play catch and teach his kid how to ice skate, even though he absolutely wasn't. Leonard looked like a movie star, like a movie star version of himself—handsome, young, and quick. Even his hair looked bouncy, its waves full and the deep, rich brown they had been in her childhood. When had his hair started to gray? Alice didn't know. Leonard looked up and made eye contact with her. He turned to look at the clock, turned back to Alice, and shook his head. "You are up early, though. A new leaf! I like it." **What was happening?** Alice closed her eyes—maybe she was hallucinating! That was possible! Maybe she had gotten beyond drunk, so drunk that she was still, many hours later, more drunk than she had ever been in her entire life, and she was seeing things.

Maybe her father had died, and this was his ghost. Alice started to cry, and rested her cheek against the cool wall.

Her father pushed his chair back from the table and slowly walked toward her. Alice didn't take her eyes off him—she was afraid that if she looked away, he would disappear.

"What is happening, birthday girl?" Leonard smiled. His teeth looked so white and so straight. She could smell the coffee on his breath.

"It's my birthday," Alice said.

"I know it's your birthday," Leonard said. "You've made me watch **Sixteen Candles** enough times to ensure that I wouldn't let this one slide. I did not buy you a boy with a sports car, though."

"What?" she said. Where was her wallet? Where was her phone? Alice patted her body again, looking for anything that belonged to her, that made this make sense. She pushed her enormous T-shirt against her body and felt her flat stomach, her hip bones, her body.

"It's your sixteenth birthday, Al-pal." Leonard nudged her leg with his toe. Had he always been able to stretch like that? He hadn't moved his body that easily in years. It felt exactly like when she saw her friends' children for the first time in a few years and all of a sudden they were full-on humans who could skateboard and came up to her shoulders, but in reverse. She'd seen her father every day, then every week or so, for her entire life. There was never a gap, a time when she could see him with fresh eyes. She'd been there for every gray hair's arrival, so of course she hadn't noticed when the balance had shifted, when it was more salt than pepper. "Want an Oreo for breakfast?"

PART TWO

17

ALICE STOOD IN HER BEDROOM DOORWAY.
Her heart was doing things that hearts weren't supposed to do, like beating in time to a Gloria Estefan
song. She wanted to go and sit with her dad, but
she also needed to understand if she was alive, if he
was alive, if she was asleep, or if she was, in fact,
sixteen years old instead of forty and standing in
her bedroom in her father's house. Alice wasn't sure
which option seemed the least appealing. If she was
dead, then at least it hadn't hurt. If she was asleep,
she would wake up. If her father was dead, and this
was her body's response to the trauma, fair enough.
The most likely option, other than this being the
most lucid fucking dream of her life, was that Alice
had had a mental health break, and that all of this
was happening inside her own brain. If she had

traveled back in time and her forty-year-old consciousness was once again inside her teenage body, and outside, it was 1996 and she was a junior in high school, that presented some major problems. It was unlikely that her bedroom would contain the answers to any of these questions, but teenage girls' bedrooms were full of secrets, so anything was possible. Alice had grown up with two imaginary time-traveling brothers as her only siblings, after all.

She turned on the light. The piles of clothing that she had nudged aside weren't things her father was dealing with; they were mountain ranges of her own making. The room was exactly as she remembered it, but worse. It smelled like cigarette smoke and Calyx, the sweet and bright perfume that she'd worn all through high school and into college. She closed the door behind her and then stepped gingerly over the piles of clothes until she had crossed the floor and reached her bed, the bed that she had woken up in.

Her flowered Laura Ashley sheets were in a tangle, as if a tornado had touched down just here, on top of her twin mattress. Alice sat down and pulled her squishiest pillow, the one with the Care Bears pillowcase, onto her lap. The room was small, and the bed took up nearly half the space. The walls were covered with pictures cut out of magazines, a collage that Alice had worked on continually from when she was about ten until the day she left for college. It looked like psychotic wallpaper—here was

Courtney Love kissing Kurt Cobain's cheek on the cover of **Sassy,** here was James Dean sitting on a tractor, here was shirtless Morrissey, here was shirtless Keanu Reeves, here was shirtless Drew Barrymore, her hands covering her breasts and daisies in her hair. There were lipstick kisses throughout, where Alice had blotted her lips on the wall instead of a tissue—Toast of New York, Rum Raisin, Cherries in the Snow. A giant **Reality Bites** poster, bought from a bin at the video store for ten dollars, was now the centerpiece, with other things taped to it and over it, leaving only Winona totally untouched. There were words written behind the movie stars—**movie, trust, jobs**—and Alice had added her own: **high school, art, kissing.** Someone had tagged over Ben Stiller's face—Alice's friend Andrew, her brain supplied a second later. Almost every single one of her male friends in high school had had a tag and pretended to write graffiti, even if most of them only wrote it on pages in their notebooks, not on the walls of the subway. Alice turned toward the nightstand and pulled open the small, rickety drawer: her diary, a lighter, a pack of Newport Lights, a tin of Altoids, a few pens, some hair elastics, some loose change, and a package of photos. It was like she'd just woken up in a museum where she was the only exhibit. Everything in her room was exactly as it had been when she was sixteen.

Alice opened the flap and lifted out the stack of photos. They weren't from any particular event, as far as she could tell—it was Sam sitting on her bed; Sam talking on the pay phone at school; pictures of herself that she'd taken in the mirror, a black hole where the flash had gone off; Tommy in the student lounge at Belvedere, covering his face. She thought it was Tommy. So many of the boys at Belvedere had dressed identically: enormous jeans, tops that would have looked preppy if they'd been three sizes smaller. Alice could hear her father turn on the radio in the kitchen and start to wash dishes.

"I'm just going to take a shower, Dad!" she called out. Alice had turned on her heels and escaped, which must have seemed enough like her teenage self that Leonard just shrugged and sat back down to finish his breakfast. What did her voice sound like? Did it sound the same? Alice caught her reflection in the cheap full-sized mirror that hung on the back of her closet door.

Every second of her teenage years, Alice had thought that she was average. Average looks, average brain, average body. She could draw better than most people. She couldn't do math for shit. When they had to run during gym, Alice had to take breaks to walk and clutch her side. But what she saw in the mirror now made her burst into tears. Sure, Alice had complained about getting older— she'd made self-deprecating remarks to Emily on her birthdays, things like that, and she'd felt it in her back and her knees and seen it in the lines by her eyes, but on the whole, she'd felt exactly the same as she had when she was a teenager. She'd been wrong.

Alice stood in front of the mirror and put a finger up, E.T. style, to greet herself. Her hair was parted in the middle and hung past her shoulders. There was a small pimple growing on her chin, threatening to break through the surface, but otherwise, Alice's face looked like a Renaissance painting. Her skin was creamy and smooth, her eyes were bright and big. The apples of her cheeks were comically pink.

"I look like a fucking cherub angel baby," Alice whispered to herself. She looked down at her flat stomach. "What the fuck was wrong with me?" She started to hyperventilate. Her pink cassette player was at the foot of her bed, its antenna extended. Alice hugged it to her chest. The little marker was just past the 100—Z100, 100.3, a terrible radio station she had listened to probably every day of her childhood. She had made so many mixtapes for boys she had crushes on, boys who she hadn't thought about in decades—and for Tommy Joffey, and for Sam, but also for a thousand other people, each song a secret message, and at least half of them Mariah Carey, who wasn't even subtle. The radio had gone on to live in the bathroom for a little while, where Leonard would sometimes listen to music while he was in the bathtub, but Alice hadn't seen it in more than a decade. She pulled it tighter, as if just holding it, she could hear every song she'd ever loved.

The Time Brothers had rocketed back and forth across the space-time continuum in a car. Marty McFly had the flux capacitor. Bill and Ted had their phone booth and George Carlin. The sexy lady in **Outlander** just had to walk into some ancient rocks. Jenna Rink had some fairy dust in her parents' basement closet. In **Kindred** and **The Time Traveler's Wife,** it just happened, out of nowhere. Alice ran through every scenario she could remember. What was it in **The Lake House**? A magic mailbox? Alice had gotten drunk and passed out. She took deep breaths, watching her cheeks fill and empty.

At her feet, Alice saw another familiar object— her clear plastic telephone, its eight-foot coiled cord long enough to go anywhere in her room. She'd gotten it for her fifteenth birthday—her own line. Alice sank to the floor and pulled the phone into her lap. The dial tone was as familiar and comforting as a kitten's purr. Her fingers traced a number— Sam's. Sam's pink phone, in her pink bedroom in her parents' apartment. It was still so early, and and while grown-up Sam would be up and feeding her kids breakfast and bribing them with cartoons, teenage Sam would be sleeping on her face, dead to the world. Alice dialed anyway.

Sam picked up after a few rings and groaned. "What?"

"It's Alice."

"Hi, Alice. Why are you calling me at the ass crack of dawn? Are you okay? Oh, fuck, it's your birthday!" Sam cleared her throat. "Ha-appy birthday to you . . ."

"Okay, okay, yes, thank you. You don't have to sing." Alice watched her reflection as she talked. "I was just checking to make sure of something. Can you come over? When you're up? Or can I come there? Just call me when you're up, okay?" Her chin was as sharp as a knife. Why had Alice never written poems about her chin, taken photos of her chin, painted portraits of her chin?

"Okay, birthday bitch. Whatever you say. Love you." Sam hung up, and then Alice did, too. Her closet shared a wall with the bathroom, and she heard her father go in and flick on the light and the whirring fan. The tap turned on—he was brushing his teeth. She hadn't heard the door close, which, with a shoddy lock, was the only way for the two of them to communicate to each other that they needed privacy. Alice listened to her father brush and rinse and spit and knock his toothbrush against the lip of the sink before settling it back into its glass cup with a jangle as it knocked against hers. It had been so long since she'd thought about those sounds—the coffee grinder, the slippered shuffle down the hall. Alice rooted around on the floor and in her closet until she found clothes that smelled clean.

18

LEONARD WAS SITTING IN HIS SPOT again, reading a book. Alice walked gingerly, like she might fall into a manhole at any second. Her father turned a page and stuck out his chin to let Ursula rub her face against it. Alice watched Leonard out of one eye while she opened the fridge and took out the milk. The cereal lived in the cabinet next to the plates and glasses, a collection of boxes beside the jars of peanut butter and the cans of soup and tomato sauce. Alice took out the box of Grape-Nuts, her father's favorite.

"Are you okay, Dad? You feeling okay?" She watched Leonard's face for any sign that he knew what was happening, that he recognized that something was amiss. But it was his face that was amiss—tiny crinkles around his eyes, but a full beard, a full smile. He was young, he was young, he was young. Alice did the math in her head—if she was sixteen, it meant that Leonard was forty-nine years old. Less than a decade older than she was. Alice was used to thinking of life as a series of improvements—high school to college, college to adulthood, twenties to thirties. Those had all felt like laps in a race she was doing well in—but Alice could see in her father all the ruin that was to come. The trips to the hospital, the endless doctor's visits, once he agreed to go. The hearing aids, after years of yelling **What, what, what?** across the table in restaurants.

"Sure, why?" Leonard narrowed his eyes at her.

"No reason." Alice looked at the cereal box. "I don't know anyone else who buys this," she said. "In my whole life, not one other person."

Leonard shrugged. "I think you need to meet some more people."

Alice laughed but also doubled over her bowl so that Leonard couldn't see that tears had appeared in her eyes. She blinked them away, finished making her cereal, and finally went to sit next to her father.

He had the **New York Times, The New Yorker, New York** magazine, and an issue of **People** with JFK Jr. and Carolyn Bessette's wedding on the cover. "Oh, man," Alice said. "So sad."

Leonard picked up the magazine and inspected it. "I see, yes. I, too, thought that there might be a chance for you, an old-fashioned child bride. Could have been great." He let the magazine fall back to the table and gave her upper arm a squeeze. Alice's breath caught in her throat. It felt real. The kitchen felt real, her body felt real. Her dad felt real. And John-John was newly married, and alive.

"No, I mean. Oh," Alice paused. "Right." She spooned some Grape-Nuts into her mouth. "These are so weird," she said. "It's like the parts that got left over when they were making good cereal, the crumbs, and they decided not to be wasteful and just repackaged them." When she was sitting next to her father in the hospital, so badly wanting him to open his eyes and talk to her, she had not imagined them starting with Grape-Nuts.

Leonard snapped his fingers. "Resourceful **and** delicious. So, what's the big plan for the day? You have your prep class at ten, hang out, do whatever, and we'll have dinner with Sam, right? And then I'm heading down to the convention hotel, and I'll be back tomorrow night, after my panel. You sure you don't mind?"

Alice put her elbows on the table. Being a kid was wild—it was someone else's job to buy the milk and the cereal, to make sure that there was toothpaste and toilet bowl cleaner and cat food, but everything you did—an SAT prep course on Saturdays, going to high school—was in service of some ambiguous, soft-focus future. Ursula walked across the open newspaper and sniffed at Alice. Like many black cats', Ursula's eyes sometimes looked green and sometimes looked yellow. She nosed up at Alice, who lowered her face to the cat in response.

"How old is Ursula?" Alice asked. The cat sniffed Alice's cereal and then jumped back down to the floor.

"One cannot simply assign a number to a creature like that," Leonard said. "I was not present at Ursula's birth, and so I can only make a sorry human guess. She was already full grown when we found her. She was in front of number eight, remember? After we brought her home, I thought someone must be missing her—a cat this good you don't just let go missing."

Alice nodded. "I remember." Maybe Ursula had traveled, too, from some point in the future when cats lived forever. Or maybe there was a new Ursula every year. "So, where is the test prep class?"

"At school. Same place as it was last week."

"At Belvedere?"

Leonard snapped the paper in half, folding it neatly down the middle. Why did they make newspapers so enormous, so that you needed to hold them like that? "Yes." He tilted his head to the side. "Are you okay? Is this birthday brain fever?" The back page had the TV listings, and Leonard had circled things that he wanted to watch so that he wouldn't forget. There was a Hitchcock marathon, and the new episode of **Early Edition.**

"I guess so," Alice said. The idea of going into school—into her building, the original building— actually sounded good, like she might walk through the door and just bump into Emily and Melinda and ask them to take her straight to the hospital for a psychological evaluation.

"You know it doesn't really matter, right? Your SAT scores?" Leonard had gone to the University of Michigan, which was in his hometown and cost his parents almost nothing, which is why he hadn't even been allowed to apply anywhere else. Alice did know this, now, but at Belvedere, there had always been pressure. Alice felt like she was part of that pressure now—the parents who brought their kids into her office had to say where they went to school, as if it had any bearing on their children's lives, whether they went to Harvard or community college or no college at all. Being a parent seemed like a truly shitty job—by the time you were old and wise enough to understand what mistakes you'd made, there was literally no chance that your children would listen. Everyone had to make their own mistakes. Alice had been one of the youngest students in her grade—some kids were a full year older. By junior year, some of her friends already knew where they wanted to go—Sam wanted to go to Harvard, and Tommy had already applied to Princeton, where his entire family had gone, back at least three generations, but swore he would rather die than go. Alice wasn't sure—she hadn't been sure then, and even decades later, she thought she could have chosen a hundred different things and had a hundred different lives. Sometimes she felt like everyone she knew had already become whatever they were going to become, and she was still just waiting.

"I guess so," Alice said. Her stomach rumbled—she was still starving. The test prep class had been a giant waste of time—she remembered it now. Or part of her did. Alice felt aware of simultaneous thoughts, sort of like when you were driving cross-country and the local radio stations kept flipping back and forth as you moved in and out of range. Her vision was clear, but it was coming from two different feeds. Alice was herself, only herself, but she was both herself then and herself now. She was forty and she was sixteen. She could suddenly see Tommy leaning back in his chair, chewing on a pencil, and her stomach began to bubble. It wasn't the cocktail of emotions she'd had when Tommy had brought his kid into Belvedere, a mixture of anxiety and embarrassment. It was the old feeling—absolutely delusional lust. "What's your panel about, at the convention tomorrow?"

"Oh," Leonard said. "It's a celebration of the **Time Brothers** show. Someone is going to ask me questions. Tony and Barry are coming, too. Everyone is very excited to see them." His mouth was a flat line. He had never liked the actors, especially not Barry. "I'm sure Tony will have some fascinating anecdotes from his time on the movie set with Tom Hanks." Tony had had a small role in the section of **Forrest Gump** set in the 1970s, as if no casting director knew where in time to place him. Alice thought that was probably the reason he would abandon acting altogether and spend the rest of his days with horses, who only knew him in the present, holding an apple in the flat of his palm.

"Do you have to do it?" Ursula jumped back onto the table and began to lap up the remaining milk in Alice's bowl.

"Everyone is very excited to see them. It sells tickets, sells books, buys the Grape-Nuts. It's fine." Leonard waved a hand in the air, shooing away Alice's concern. "Where do you want to have dinner?"

"We're still eating breakfast," Alice said, petting Ursula. "Let me think about it." Her father took a sip of his coffee. His arms looked strong. If she was hallucinating, she was doing a really terrific job. There was a loud noise, and Alice thought, Oh, that must be my alarm going off, I'm going to wake up any second, but no, it was her telephone blaring from her bedroom.

"Aren't you going to answer it?" Leonard asked. "Usually when your phone rings, you're like a streak of lightning across the sky. A human blur."

"I'm sure it's just Sam. I'll call her back in a minute." Outside, on Pomander, the Headricks were sweeping. Alice had always loved them—they were the kind of neighbors who reminded other people to move their cars on street sweeping days, or would let the gas company in, or would help get leaves out of gutters. They had every tool, somehow, even though their house was as small as everyone else's and equally lacking in storage space. Kenneth Headrick was wearing a Mets hat and khakis, and he put a hand up to say hello when he saw Alice staring through the window.

"Wow. Can we call this maturity, Al?" Leonard shook his head. "I guess sixteen really is different."

19

SAM CALLED AGAIN AND SAID THAT she'd meet Alice at Pomander and they'd walk to the class together. Ten minutes later, Alice called Sam and asked her what she was wearing. Half an hour later, Sam called to say that she was going to be running late, and that Alice should just go ahead without her. It was like texting, but only with her voice. It hadn't been this easy to get Sam on the phone in over a decade. The one time that morning Sam didn't pick up, her answering machine did, with a muffled exhortation to "hit my pager." Alice remembered it all: *911 for emergencies, *143 to say **I love you.** *187 to say **I'll murder you if you don't call me back right away.** Alice wanted to keep calling, just to hear Sam pick up every time.

20

ALICE ASKED LEONARD TO WALK HER TO
Belvedere for the prep class. She didn't need him
to, obviously—she could have walked there in her
sleep, which maybe she was doing, although whatever was happening was starting to feel much more
real. Alice had pooped, which she had never once
done in a dream, and showered, and she'd eaten
three meals in rapid succession, two of them standing directly in front of the open fridge. The class
was only an hour long, and seeing Sam in person as
a teenager was irresistible, and so even though Alice
was a little afraid to let Leonard out of her sight,
she decided that she would go. If Leonard walked
her there.

Belvedere was close—twelve and a half blocks.

Down Broadway to 85th, then left and up the hill, or one could zigzag according to holes in the traffic. Alice had always been proud of her stride and speed as a walker. There was nothing like the satisfying feeling of stepping into a street as a car zoomed past, the daily ballet of a well-timed jaywalk. Jaywalking, Alice's only professional sport! Leonard was on the slow side, for a New Yorker, but Alice couldn't believe how fast he was moving now, practically dancing down Pomander like Cary Grant with an umbrella. The last time Alice had seen her father walk down the street, it had been June. They'd met for dinner at Jackson Hole, the glorified diner at the end of Belvedere's block, on 85th and Columbus, which made it easy for Alice to meet after school before getting on the train and going back to Brooklyn. Leonard loved Jackson Hole because the burgers were enormous, like hockey pucks for giants, and the onion rings were, too. Alice had gotten there first and grabbed a table near the window, and she'd watched her dad struggle to hurry across the street, narrowly avoiding the downtown M11 bus. Since then, she'd seen him walk up and down hospital hallways, and then not at all.

Leonard was wearing a jean jacket, as he had most days of most years since Alice was born. "Can't believe you're sixteen, Al." He had brought a can of Coca-Cola for the road, which he now opened with that satisfying release of sugary bubble air. On their way out, Alice had glanced at the guardhouse, which looked filled with stuff, as it always had been. The end of last night was blurry except for the barfing, which had been very pink and very gross. Where else had she been for sure? Alice tried to piece it together, like doing a complicated math problem in reverse. "Me neither," Alice said.

After talking to Sam, Alice had found what she suggested on the floor of her closet: a pair of woolen black sailor pants that had a thousand buttons and a tie in the back, and a silk top that had once been underwear, back when people wore extra layers for no reason and WonderBras didn't exist. "When you take walks, where do you go?" Alice asked.

She was as tall as her father already—Serena was the taller parent by a few inches, and Alice would end up an inch taller than Leonard, too, but it hadn't quite happened yet. Her mother hadn't called to wish her a happy birthday, but it was still early on the West Coast, and who knew what the moon was doing, or the rest of the planets. The planets controlled a lot of Serena's interactions with the world. The air was cool. Climate change had gotten Alice used to T-shirt weather in October, but now it was still chilly. Had the blizzard already happened? She couldn't remember, but Alice could see the snowdrifts in her mind, the thick white blanket that had stopped the city for a few days.

"I walk everywhere," Leonard said. "I walk up-town, I walk downtown. Once I walked all the way around—circumvented the whole island of Manhattan. Did you know that? Why are you asking?"

Alice tried to shrug. "Just curious, I guess." She was thinking about Simon Rush and the rest of Leonard's friends—well-read dorks, all, even the ones who were rich and famous. She had so few memories of her father during daylight hours, out-side of Pomander Walk. The Sterns had never gone hiking, they'd never gone camping, they didn't like the beach or national parks or whatever it was that normal families did. All they had done was this—talk. Be in their neighborhood, their tiny king-dom. That was the stuff that Alice wanted to soak up, to absorb as much as she possibly could. What did it feel like, to have their strides match, to both hurry in the face of an oncoming taxi? What did it feel like to have her father next to her, to hear him grumble and hum, make the noises just beneath language? What did it feel like to see him and not worry if it would be the last time?

Leonard put a hand on her shoulder. "That's very nice."

She hadn't touched him until then—she had wanted to hug him when she first walked into the kitchen, but they weren't really a hugging family, and Alice was pretty sure that she had smelled at best like dirt and at worst like dirt and alcohol and so she had scooted quickly back into her bedroom, too afraid that one of them would vanish into thin air or turn into a pile of dust. Alice put her hand on top of her dad's. She didn't remember him ever being younger than this. "What age do you think I was best at?" Alice took her hand back and stared at the ground. "Like, if you had to pick me being one age forever, what age would you pick?"

Leonard chuckled. "Okay, let's think. You were a terrible baby. Screamed one hundred percent of the time. Your mother and I used to worry that the neighbors were going to call the police. You were very cute after that, to make up for it—say, three to five. Those were good years. But no, I'd say now. I can swear as much as I want to, and you don't need babysitters anymore. And plus, you're good company." Every block they walked had something that Alice had loved and forgotten: the spandex party dresses at Fowad and Mandee, the brightly lit challah bread at Hot & Crusty, the bohemian rich lady shop Liberty House, where Alice had spent her allowance on Indian printed tops and dangling earrings. Tasti D-lite, Alice's one true love. Were there still Tasti D-lites? Once, in her early twenties, Alice had seen Lou Reed and Laurie Anderson at Tasti D-lite, both of them with small cups, no sprinkles. She started to tell her father that, but stopped. The only Lou Reed song she'd actually owned was on the **Trainspotting** soundtrack, and she wasn't sure if it had come out yet. Without the internet, how would she even check? Mr. Moviefone's voice sprang into her ears, a robotic memory that she hadn't thought of in a decade, and Alice laughed. It was another century. It hadn't felt like it at the time, but it was. New York City did this over and over again, of course, a snake shedding its skin in bits and pieces, so slowly that by the time the snake was brand new, no one would notice.

"Thanks," Alice said. Maybe that was why. Maybe he was right, and this was the best she ever was, and even though this version of her dad hadn't seen her barely graduate from art school, and have dumb boyfriend after dumb boyfriend, and never really make art, and still work at Belvedere, he knew that this was the apex.

Leonard grabbed Alice's elbow and pulled her back from the curb. A boxy gray sedan swung close, taking the corner tight and fast. "Not on my watch," he said. They walked until they got to French Roast, the coffee shop that was open twenty-four hours a day, and then turned left, toward the park.

21

THERE WERE A FEW PEOPLE STANDING
outside Belvedere. Alice was so used to the route,
and the block, which had hardly changed, except
for the hairdresser that had become a dog-grooming
parlor and the frame shop that had become a Pilates
studio, that she didn't actually feel anxious until
she and her father were close enough to recognize
the faces of the people assembled on the sidewalk.
Alice froze. She had thought about seeing Sam, who
would still be just Sam Wood, without her married hyphen, but Alice hadn't thought about seeing
everyone else. Her life was so full of Belvedere that
she hadn't thought about all the people who had
vanished from it. Leonard tossed his cigarette to
the sidewalk and stepped on the filter.

"What's going on?" he asked, though Leonard had never needed a reason to avoid people.

There was Garth Ellis, who played soccer and had the cutest, roundest butt. Alice had kissed him one time, her freshman year, and then pretended that it never happened. There was Jessica Yanker, who curled her bangs into a perfect tube every morning—Alice and Sam used to prank-call her, pretending to be representatives from a hair spray company, but then *69 came along and you couldn't take the risk. There was Jordan Epstein-Roth, whose tongue was always hanging out of his mouth just a tiny bit; there was Rachel Hymowitz, whose name sounded too much like "hymen" for her to escape unscathed. Everyone was gorgeous and gangly and slightly undercooked, like they'd been taken out of the oven a little bit too early, even kids that she'd never really looked at too closely, like Kenji Morris, who was taking the SAT class a whole year early, like he was Doogie Howser or something. Some people's arms and legs looked too long, some noses looked too adult. They were people Alice hadn't thought of in twenty years, and whom she hadn't given much thought to even at the time. She cringed a little, thinking about what these forgotten classmates would think of her now, still at Belvedere at forty, still alone, still weird. Alice looked up at the building, and to the window of her office. Leonard leaned against a parked car and lit another cigarette.

"Just high school, I guess," Alice said. It wasn't **Time Brothers,** whatever was happening to her, and it wasn't **Back to the Future.** It was **Peggy Sue Got Married.** Alice tried to remember the plot. She'd fainted? No, that had been a dream, hadn't it? Mostly? Kathleen Turner had woken up in the hospital, still married to Nicolas Cage.

The front door pushed open, and Alice watched as her boss, Melinda, attached the little metal hook to the side of the building so that the door would stay open. Alice's breath caught in her throat, the same way it had when she saw her father at the kitchen table. She'd known Melinda for so long that she hadn't thought of her as having changed— she looked the same, she wore the same clothes— but no: Melinda, like her father, had been young. Alice had just been too young herself to notice.

The other kids started to funnel in. Alice walked over to her father and leaned beside him.

"If you could go back in time, what would you do?" Alice asked. "Back to high school, I mean. Or college."

"Oh, no, thank you. Wouldn't want to change too much, because then I wouldn't have you. And if you're not going to change it, you don't want to see it, trust me." Leonard elbowed Alice gently.

"Mm-hmm." Alice had to get back to Matryoshka. They probably didn't open until at least five o'clock. She couldn't think of anything she would ruin, any- thing she would lose, but she also did not want to live her entire life over again starting at sixteen. She had to figure out how she had ended up here, and how to shake herself out of it.

"Happy birthday, Al," someone said behind her. Alice turned.

Tommy had his hands in his pockets. He was wearing a ringer T-shirt and had a plain brown cord tied around his neck, a homemade choker. Most of the boys at Belvedere had already moved on from the Jordan Catalano school of fashion, but not Tommy. His hair was long, and he tucked it behind his ears. He was a senior, still trying to get better SAT scores, even though his were almost perfect. Parents at Belvedere were still like this, willing to spend time and money focusing on **almost** instead of **perfect.** He looked better than she remembered, and what she remembered was heavenly. Her stomach squished in a way that it hadn't when she'd seen him as an adult. It was like there were two of her, the teenage Alice and the grown-up Alice, sharing the same tiny patch of human real estate.

"Thanks," Alice said. He wouldn't touch her in front of her father.

"Hey, Tommy," Leonard said. He nodded his head in greeting.

"Hi, Leonard," Tommy said. "I read that book you told me about, the one with the monsters. Cthulhu."

"And? What did you think?" Leonard dropped his cigarette and crushed it under his heel. He pushed himself off the car and took a few steps closer to Tommy, so that they were all standing in a little circle.

"Oh, it was tight," Tommy said. "So tight."

Alice laughed. Being at the mercy of one's teenage slang was humiliating, and it made seeing Tommy in this state easier.

Tommy turned and started up the stairs. "See you later, Alice," he said. "Tonight?"

It was the night of her party. Alice had forgotten. The picture from Sam, of the two of them, positively drunk on their own immortality. That was tonight.

22

IT WAS TEN BEFORE TEN WHEN A CAB
pulled up in front of school and Sam hopped out
of the back seat, her mother behind her. Sam's
mother, Lorraine, taught in the Africana Studies
department at Barnard, and always wore pearl
earrings and elaborately tied scarves beneath her
close-cropped hair.

"Happy birthday, happy birthday," Sam was
chanting, and before Alice could respond, Sam had
wrapped her arms around Alice's neck, tight. She
was playing, like they were kids. Which Alice knew
they were, but it certainly hadn't felt like it at the
time. Sam was wearing a giant polo shirt and baggy
jeans, her tiny body swimming inside her clothes,
and a cowrie shell necklace tight against her skin.
Alice kissed Sam's cheek, and then the other cheek,

like they always did, who knows why. There were so many customs, so many codes, so many habits. Teenage girls' skeletons were half bones and half secrets that only other teenage girls knew. Sam smoked weed out of a blown-glass bowl that she hid in a fake book on her bookshelf, a book that had been part of a magic kit that her parents had bought her for her tenth birthday.

"Hi there, Leonard, Alice—" Lorraine gestured toward the door. "Can you make sure she gets inside? I'm running to a meeting downtown."

Leonard nodded and tossed his cigarette. Lorraine was a vegetarian and a yogi, a serious woman, but even she was not immune to **Time Brothers,** and she liked Leonard well enough. Well enough to let Sam sleep over as much as she wanted, even though she knew that he'd never once fed her child a vegetable. "Course."

Lorraine folded herself back into the taxi and waved as it drove off. Sam jumped up and down, dancing.

"I'll leave you to it, young scholars," Leonard said. "Just come home after, okay, Al?"

"Sure, Dad," Alice said. "I'll come right back."

"Lenny! Come on! It's our girl's birthday! Finally! I feel like I've been sixteen, like, forever." Sam had turned sixteen five months ago, which had been at the tail end of the previous school year, on the other side of a whole summer, which did feel like forever ago. Leonard nodded and started to walk away. Alice lingered on the sidewalk, not wanting him to go, like in preschool when she had cried and clung to his legs until her teacher had to pry her off with a death grip.

"Come on," Sam said. They linked their arms and walked into school.

• • •

If Alice'd had to guess how much Belvedere had been renovated since she was in high school, she would have said hardly at all—maybe now and then a floor had been redone, or some classroom chairs replaced, but by and large the place had felt exactly the same as it always had. Walking in through the front doors, though, Alice could see immediately that she was wrong. The lobby of the school was painted a very pale peach, with a paisley carpet to match, no doubt a holdover from the 1980s. The receptionist's office was walled off with square glass bricks. Alice paused to take it in, but Sam reached for her hand and pulled. "Let's go," she said. "I have to pee before it starts."

Sam led them down the hall to the bathroom just before the swinging doors to the gym, where Alice could see the test prep class already assembled. There were several rows of chairs and a large chalkboard that had been wheeled out to half-court.

"Do you think this is to underscore the idea that standardized tests are a game for us to beat, or did they just not want us to go upstairs and be, like, running wild inside the school on a Saturday?" Sam asked. She pushed open the door to the bathroom and Alice followed her in.

It was the biggest bathroom in the school, with three stalls and a shower—the visiting teams used it as a locker room. Sarah T. and Sara N., two juniors who were best friends, were at the mirror, reapplying their lip gloss, and someone was in one of the stalls.

"Hey, Sarah," Alice said. Sarah was pretty and heavily freckled, with curly hair cut short enough that it bounced out from behind her ears. She always had extra tampons in her bag and she had died of leukemia before she was thirty. They hadn't been friends except in the way that everyone was friends when you had biology homework to talk about. She was the second person in their grade to die, after Melody Johnson, who died in a skiing accident during spring break of their senior year. God, Melody would be walking around, too. Alice wondered if she could warn her, tell her that she had a premonition, tell her about Sonny Bono, tell her to insist that her family go to the beach instead. But there was nothing that Alice could say to Sarah, who was smiling at her in the bathroom. "Hey, Al. How wack is this shit? I am so tired of talking about college and we haven't even applied yet. Yesterday my mom went on a ten-minute rant about how women's colleges weren't just for lesbians, but guess what? It's all lesbians." Sarah was a lesbian, too, as her mother no doubt guessed, as were half a dozen other girls in their grade, but no one would come out until college or years after.

"So, what time is your party tonight?" Sara asked.

"Tonight?" Alice looked at Sam.

"We should be done with dinner by eight thirty?" Sam supplied. "What did we tell people, to come over to chill at nine? That seems good."

Sarah and Sara tucked their lip glosses back in their bags. "Dope. See you later."

There was a flush in the occupied stall. Alice pushed Sam into the shower stall and drew the curtain. "Are you going to pee in here?" Sam whispered. Alice shook her head. She didn't know how to explain, where to start.

Suddenly, a hand pulled the curtain aside. "Thought I heard my ladies." Phoebe Oldham-O'Neill was wearing jeans so long with bells so big that it looked like she didn't have any feet. Alice was the tallest of her friends but it was true for her, too; her pants were so long that they dragged on the ground, creating a seismograph of filth along the raw bottom edge. Phoebe kissed them both on the cheeks, her oversized nylon jacket shushing itself every time she moved her arms. Phoebe's breath smelled like Newports and every other inch of her smelled like the first floor of Macy's, like an entire bottle of CK One was being sprayed out of her pores. Alice felt drunk on the idea of how many of her friends smoked, how adult they had all seemed and felt. How the cigarettes had been giant flashing signposts, to themselves and each other. You could never trust someone who smoked Marlboro Lights, the Diet Coke of cigarettes—those were for the girls with pale lipstick and overplucked eyebrows, the girls who maybe also played volleyball and had sex with their boyfriends in their beds which were still covered with stuffed animals. Girls who smoked Parliaments were neutral—it was as close as you could get to not smoking, but still, you could flick your thumb against the recessed filter, and you could bum one to anybody, the type O negative of smoking. Girls who smoked Marlboro Reds were wild—those were for girls who had no fear, and in their whole school, there was only one, a tiny girl with brown, wavy hair to her waist whose parents had been in a cult and then escaped. Newport girls were equally harsh but listened to hip-hop, and those girls, like Phoebe, wore lipstick and nail polish like vampire blood, rich and purple. Newport Lights girls were like that, only virgins. The girls who smoked American Spirits were beyond everyone—they were grown-ups, with keys to their boyfriends' houses. Alice had to laugh at the secret rooms of her brain, where this information lived and had been sleeping. She had smoked Newport Lights, and yes, she was a virgin.

Sam looked at Phoebe. "Did you get it?" She batted her eyelashes.

"I did. My brother was being super stingy, but he finally caved." Phoebe's older brother Will was a freshman at NYU and Belvedere's main source for drugs that weren't just weed.

"What did you get?" Alice asked, even though she knew the answer. She felt like she should close her ears, like she was a teacher who had just walked in on these girls, and if she wanted to, she could get them all thrown out of school. They shouldn't be saying any of this in front of her—sometimes, in her real life, Alice would walk to the corner and see some of the high school students smoking a joint and she would spin around and go the other way.

"Birthday surprise," Sam said, and kissed the air. "Thanks, Pheebs. We'll meet you out there, okay?"

Phoebe nodded, as serious as a marine. She would get expelled in the spring, and vanish for a decade before resurfacing in the Catskills as a potter who charged her crystals in the moonlight.

When the door clicked shut, Alice took a deep breath.

"What's up? Did you talk to Tommy? He's coming tonight, right?" Sam asked. They moved out of the shower stall to the sinks. Alice shook her head slowly. "I can't believe we have to do this stupid class, it's so annoying. And on your birthday!"

"Can I tell you something that is very strange and will sound like I'm making it up?" Alice asked.

Sam shrugged. "Obviously."

Alice watched them in the mirror. Even in the unforgiving fluorescent light of the bathroom, she and Sam looked glorious.

"I came from the future." Alice looked at Sam when she said it.

"Sure, okay." Sam nodded, waiting for the rest. Once, when they'd shared a six-pack of Zima, Alice had told Sam that she felt like her head wasn't actually connected to her body, like they were totally different organisms that just happened to be roommates. Another time, on a field trip to Rye Playland, Sam had told Alice that sometimes she had dreams that she had a twin sister but ate her when they were small children. It was important to have friends who could listen to you say what you needed to say and not burst into laughter.

"Not, like, the distant-distant future. Not, like, two hundred years in the future. But when I went to sleep last night, it was the night before my fortieth birthday, and then I woke up on Pomander Walk, looking like this." Alice chewed on her thumbnail. "You know, like Peggy Sue?"

Sam leaned back against the wall, whirring the automatic hand dryer awake. "Shit!" she said, and repositioned herself with her back to the lip of the sink.

"I know it sounds crazy, and it is crazy, but that's what happened. So I'm me, but I'm like, **this** me." Alice put her face in her hands. "I know, it doesn't make any sense."

Sam crossed her arms. "Did you take drugs, Alice Stern, and not tell me?"

Alice shook her head. "No, Sam. I know how it

sounds, but that is what happened. I think! I mean, I don't know! I thought maybe I was asleep, but, like, it's been a while, now, and I don't really think I am. I mean, I am here. Right? Like, you're real, right? And so I have to figure out what the hell is going on. And I have to figure out how to get back to my regular life, if that's a thing that still exists. Because I've seen enough episodes of **Time Brothers** to know that shit is not supposed to last."

"Or like in **Back to the Future.** You could erase yourself." Sam was nodding. She lifted a finger to her lips and tapped it there, thinking.

"Well, I think that happened because Michael J. Fox was messing up his parents' relationship, which then made him and his siblings potentially not exist, which is not the same, but yes, I take your point."

Sam crossed her arms. "Alice, are you fucking with me? Are we on **Candid Camera**? Because honestly this is kind of creeping me out."

Alice thought about it. "I get it." When the Time Brothers rocketed around, they never had to tell people. They showed up in their time-traveling car and helped housewives in the 1950s, or medieval princesses, or space women of the future living in a moon colony. They never went back two and a half decades and had to look at their own friends and family and say, **Hey, guess what we can do?** It sounded objectively unhinged.

Sam nodded. "But listen, if that's what we're doing today, then okay. I can't say that I totally believe what you're saying, but I want to be supportive, especially since it seems like you don't totally believe it either? Is that a fair assessment of the situation?"

Alice wanted to burst into tears. "Yeah."

"God, and you still came to SAT class?" Sam rolled her eyes. "If I thought that maybe I had time-traveled, I think I would skip the SATs. Like, even the actual test. Do you have children? Are you married? Am **I** married? Oh my god, I don't want to know. Do I want to know?" Sam put her hands on her stomach. "How do I look? Am I happy? We're friends, right? Still?" She quickly closed the gap between her and Alice and hugged her tightly. "I still don't actually believe you, but just in case."

"Yes, Sam," Alice said. "That's why I told you. And yes, you're married, and you have kids, and you're happy, and we're friends. But no specifics, okay? I don't want to Michael J. Fox you or your beautiful family. But can you help me?" Alice felt herself tear up. "I just, you know, haven't been sixteen in a while and I don't really remember how this goes, and I just need your help." Sam smelled like herself, like Love's Baby Soft and cocoa butter and Herbal Essences shampoo.

Sam held both of Alice's hands. "I promise to try to help. Even if it means helping you talk to someone. You know, like a doctor."

23

EVERYONE WAS ALREADY SITTING IN their seats when Sam and Alice walked into the gym, and so everyone turned around to look at them when the door squeaked open. There were a few empty chairs in the last row, and Alice and Sam ducked into them quickly. Jane, who had been Belvedere's college counselor when Alice was a student, stood at the front holding what looked like about five hundred loose pieces of paper, which she was no doubt about to distribute among the students, who were either bored, anxious, or both. Jane was not beloved at Belvedere for many reasons, but the biggest reason was that she often told students that their dream schools were well out of reach and spent most of the counseling sessions asking questions about their parents' finances. In retrospect,

Alice got it. Jane was pragmatic and understood how the machine worked.

"I have no memory of this," Alice said to Sam under her breath. "I barely remember taking the actual SAT, but for sure, I have zero memory of this."

Jane handed the giant stack of paper to the kid sitting in the front corner—Jessica Yanker, with the tubular bangs—who took a few pages and handed the rest to the person next to her. Tommy was in the row ahead of Alice, leaning so far back in his chair that it looked like his clothes were going to melt onto the floor. Alice suddenly felt like she couldn't breathe. "I'm going to get some water, just get me whatever they're giving out, okay?" Sam nodded, and Alice hunched over and ran back out the gym door.

There was a water fountain on the second floor, down the hall from what Alice thought of as her office, though right now, of course, it wasn't her office at all. Being in the school building on a Saturday always felt transgressive, even as an adult. Unlike the first floor, the second floor looked remarkably the same as it had the last time she'd left the office. The wood floor was exactly the same, and so were the ornate doorframes, the only part of the building that still resembled the brownstones that had once stood on the spot. Someone was chatting and laughing in one of the offices. Alice would have recognized Melinda's big, throaty laugh anywhere—it sounded like a happy oak tree, full and broad and dappled with sunshine. Alice started down the hall and immediately tripped over a bench outside the college prep office.

"Shit," Alice said, clutching her shin. "Shit shit shit."

At the end of the hall, Melinda's head poked out of the doorframe. "You okay out there?"

Alice straightened up and tucked her hair behind her ears. "Hi, yes," she said. "Fine. Just walked into something."

"Need a Band-Aid? Ice pack?" Melinda had a nice husband, grown children who didn't seem like ax murderers, and adorable grandchildren who made her lumpy ceramic sculptures. In 1996, she wouldn't yet have grandchildren, but her kids would already be older than Alice, maybe even out of college already, she wasn't sure. What a very long time one had to be an adult, after rushing through childhood and adolescence. There should be several more distinctions: the idiocy of the young twenties, when one was suddenly expected to know how to do adult things; the panicked coupling of the mid- and late twenties, when marriages happened as quickly as a game of tag; the sitcom mom period, when you finally had enough food in your freezer to survive for a month if necessary; the school principal period, when you were no longer seen as a woman at all but just a vague nagging authority figure. If you were lucky, there was the late-in-life sexy Mrs. Robinson period, or an accomplished and powerful Meryl Streep period, followed, of course, by approximately two decades of old-crone-hood, like the woman at the end of **Titanic.** Alice hadn't ever thought about how Melinda might want to be around her and all the students in part because it was nice to be surrounded by young people. She felt it, at Belvedere. It wasn't fair to call it a fountain of youth—nothing could make you feel ancient and crumbling faster than a cruel word from a teenager—but even so, being around young people kept the heart healthy and the mind open.

"No, I'm okay," Alice said. She walked closer, unable to keep herself from the office that she thought of as her own, but which now belonged only to Melinda.

"Are you looking for something?" Melinda asked. She sat back down in her giant, cushioned rolling office chair in front of a desktop computer the size of a Fiat.

"Does that have email on it?" Alice asked. The computer looked, like, prehistoric. She didn't know how to explain how she was feeling to Melinda, other than that she'd been brought to her door by muscle memory honed over years that hadn't happened yet.

"You mean AOL?" Melinda looked around her desk and produced a CD. "I haven't installed it yet. I have it at home. Do you want it?"

Alice closed her eyes and tried to imagine her life without a soul-crushing number of unread messages in her inbox. "No thanks," she said. Alice couldn't remember coming into this office as a student, not really—there was no reason she could manufacture for needing to be there, but she also knew that Melinda wouldn't push if she couldn't provide one. It was often impossible to get kids of any age to talk about something directly, and so all school administrators were used to a sort of backward dance into conversation. "I just mean, are you here to make sure that the kids—that we—don't destroy everything?"

"Something like that. But I like coming in on Saturdays. Schools are noisy animals, and sometimes it's nice to have the run of the place." Melinda was wearing a necklace that Alice recognized, a fat string with dangling wooden fruit. There was a stack of paper on the long desk, and it felt nice to see Melinda's familiar handwriting—strong, slanted generously to the right—on Post-it notes stuck to her computer monitor. Melinda pointed to the couch in her office, used by many students as a chattier nurses' station, a place to crash. Alice scooted over, past the space where she usually sat, and where Emily sat, straight to the couch, where she gingerly lowered herself down.

Melinda crossed her legs at the ankle and let her knees splay out to the sides, creating a tent of mouse-colored corduroy. Alice rubbed her hands together and thought about how to put into words the fear that she was having a breakdown, the fear that she had time-traveled, and the fear that she might have to live her whole life again, starting now.

"I guess, downstairs . . ." she started. "I guess I just don't really know what my plan is, you know? Like, my life path?" The light in the room was so familiar, the stripes of sunshine that would slice through the air and land on the computer screens, making them impossible to read. What Alice wanted to ask was: **Is it crazy if I try to do my whole life differently, and my dad's, too? Is it possible to make things better, starting now?**

Melinda nodded. "You're an artist, aren't you?"

Alice didn't want to roll her eyes, but she couldn't help it. "I mean, I don't know. Yeah?"

"What kind of art are you interested in?" Melinda knit her fingers together. She looked just the way she did when she was talking to five-year-olds—open, patient, and kind. Alice had seen this happen before, Melinda talking down an angsty teen. Eventually she would send the child back to class, but first, she listened.

"Who even knows anymore. I used to be into painting. I guess I still am." Alice frowned. She couldn't ask what she wanted to ask, which was what the hell was happening, and why. Anyone who had ever read a book or seen a movie about time travel knew that it was never pointless. Sometimes it was to fall in love with someone born in a different century, and sometimes it was to do your history homework. Alice had no idea why she'd woken up on Pomander, or what she was supposed to do now. "I guess my real question is how do you know which choices matter, and which ones are just dumb?"

"Alas," Melinda said, "that can be hard. But a decision like which college to go to, and what to study, those matter to an extent, but they're not face tattoos. You can always change your mind. Transfer schools. Start over. I studied art, too," she said, which Alice hadn't known. Melinda's hair was thick and dark, held back in a French braid. She and Leonard were the same age, more or less, but Melinda had always looked so much older, so much softer than Alice's father. "I studied painting and drawing. And after I graduated from college, I moved to New York and worked for some galleries, but then I needed a job that gave me health insurance, and that's when I started working here. And it made me happier than anything else, and I could still make art, and I could make art with kids. And I didn't have to pay for my two C-sections."

"So college does matter."

"Everything matters," Melinda said. "But you can change your mind. Almost always."

Alice nodded. She looked around the office, searching for a reason to linger. "I should get back to the class. But thank you."

"Of course," Melinda said. "Anytime."

On her way out, Alice ran her hand over the desk, half-heartedly hoping for a secret button to push.

When she didn't find one, she stood in the open doorframe. "Can I come back another time?"

"I already told you! Yes! Winter, spring, summer, or fall," Melinda said, another one of her favorite phrases. "But I will tell you, in terms of a life plan, you don't need one. That's my advice. It's real life. It's **your** real life. Plans don't work. Just go with it."

Alice wanted to stay, to give Melinda a hug, to tell her what was happening, but the more people she told, the crazier she would sound. Melinda would (rightly) call Leonard and tell him what she'd said. In real life, in real time, Melinda was her friend, but right now, Melinda was an adult and Alice was sixteen. Someone squeaked on the wooden floor outside, and Alice turned to look. Sam had come to fetch her, and stood at the end of the hall, beckoning. "Okay," Alice said. "I'll be back."

24

THE TEST PREP CLASS WAS ENDLESS—
Sam was hunched over her paper, scribbling as if it
would make any difference. Alice ducked back into
her chair and looked around. Tommy caught her
eye and did his patented single chin raise, a move
that never failed to make Alice's heart rate double. The sheet was a page of multiple-choice math
problems—trigonometry. Alice had barely passed
trig in high school, and now the concepts of sines
and cosines were as far away from her consciousness
as Pluto. Which wasn't a planet anymore. Except
maybe it was now, again? Alice reached into her
pocket for her phone, which of course wasn't there,
and then checked the watch on her wrist. The class
was only half over. She tried to listen, but Jane's

voice was so monotonous and the gymnasium was so warm that Alice felt herself just getting sleepy. She rested her cheek on her palm and felt her eyelids begin to droop. Alice shook herself awake, worried that if she did fall asleep, she would vanish out of Belvedere in a puff of smoke and wake up forty again. It was what she wanted, she thought, but not like this—she needed to get back to her dad. She wanted to have Gray's Papaya with him for dinner and make him quit smoking. She wanted to make him learn how to cook vegetables—she knew how! She could show him! Alice started making a list of things she knew how to cook on the back of her worksheet and before she knew it, chairs began to squeak against the floor and people were stuffing papers into their bags and Tommy was standing in front of her.

"Wanna smoke?" Tommy asked. He ran a hand through his hair and it all immediately bounced back into place. Everything in Alice's brain was telling her to say no, to grab Sam and head back home as she'd told her dad she would, but the word that came out of her mouth was "Yeah." Sam looked annoyed but Alice couldn't stop herself. "I'll beep you," Alice called out as she and Tommy pushed open the door and stepped into the sunlight.

They ran across Central Park West, crossing against the light, Tommy reaching for Alice's hand to pull her out of harm's way. They walked up the path that led to a small playground, one with only a few dinky swings. Because it was a Saturday, there were parents with small children all around and a line of strollers parked just outside the heavy iron gate of the playground.

"Here," Tommy said, pointing with his head farther down the path.

Belvedere used the park regularly, for the baseball diamonds on the Great Lawn and for annual winter outings to the Lasker ice-skating rink, and for gym classes when the weather was great and spring fever had felled them all and so if they were going to jump rope, they might as well do it outside. Several members of the faculty and staff used the park as a gym as well, carrying jogging clothes in their bags and going for runs before or after school. Not Alice.

Central Park wasn't made for exercise. It was made for this, for tucking away into a shady grove of trees and sitting on a bench. It was made for low voices and secret affairs. The size of the park— 840 acres, she'd had to memorize it for a middle school project—sounded antithetical to intimacy, but that's what it was, intimate. There were hidden pockets at every turn, as many corners of privacy and quiet as there were of Rollerblading showboats and people breakdancing for tourists. Alice loved the park—loved that there was something so glorious, so seemingly endless, that belonged to her as much as it belonged to anyone else.

Tommy sank to the grass and leaned back against

a tree. He pulled a pack of Parliaments out of his jacket pocket and started smacking them against his palm.

"Why are people always slapping something?" Alice said. "Cigarettes, Snapple bottles. It's so weird." She sat on the ground next to Tommy and hugged her knees to her chest. Alice's body felt like it was made out of rubber, like she could kick her leg all the way over her head if she wanted to, or do a handstand. Alice hadn't had her first orgasm until she was in college and had her first real boyfriend, but it didn't matter, not when her body felt this good all day every day. Just looking at Tommy, sitting this close to Tommy, made her whole body feel like it was made out of an electrical current. She could still feel his hand in hers from when they ran across the street, even though he'd let go when they reached the other side. Alice had forgotten how much she'd been in contact with her friends' bodies, how much she and Sam were always sitting in each other's laps and touching each other's faces.

"Yeah, it's kind of wack," Tommy said, and stopped. "I don't know. I just like it, I guess." He unwrapped the cellophane and threw it on the ground.

"Whoa, whoa," Alice said. "Let's not be litterbugs." She scooped up the plastic and put it in her pocket.

"Are you okay?" Tommy asked. "I have seen you do that about one thousand times."

"Oh, sure, yeah," Alice said. She felt like an

imposter, like she was wearing a costume made with her own face. The wind stirred up a pile of leaves near them and twirled them into a tiny cyclone, and Alice watched. Maybe she'd just gotten **loose** somewhere, slipped through a crack. There was one episode of **Time Brothers** where Jeff had fallen through a portal in the middle of the Golden Gate Bridge, and Scott had to go after him to bring him back, time travel within time travel. That was what happened when TV writers got bored of solving the same problems over and over again. Alice could be lost, or she could be stuck, or she could be lost **and** stuck. The one thing she was sure of, finally, was that whatever this was, it was really happening. It was the wobbly nerves in her stomach, like the drop on a roller coaster; it was the hyperawareness of everything around her. Alice felt like Spider-Man, except all of her powers were just being a teenage girl.

She and Tommy were friends. They had never been boyfriend-girlfriend, not even close. There were a few solid couples at Belvedere: Andrew and Morgan, Rachel Gurewich and Matt Boerealis, Rachel Humphrey and Matt Paggioni, Brigid and Danny, Ashanti and Stephen. Alice had always thought of them as several levels beyond her, in terms of human development. They kissed on the mouth in the hallways, knowing everyone could see them. They held hands in public, on the sidelines at soccer games. They freaked during school dances, knees clamped together like extras in **Dirty Dancing,** and nobody started whispering. Alice had had a few boyfriends, but none of them lasted longer than a month and they were all variants of the Canadian boyfriend scheme, except instead of being pretend humans in Canada, they were real humans whom she hardly knew in her math class. All it took was several weeks of negotiations between various lieutenants and then one awkward phone call. It was basically exactly like the sixth grade, except that sometimes, rarely, she and a boy were alone and they clumsily reached into each other's pants.

Alice and Tommy were different. He had girlfriends sometimes. Fellow upperclassmen, girls who weren't virgins. He was the cutest boy in their grade, and so when the older girls got bored of their options, they all picked him. He'd even gone out with girls from other schools, girls who would walk across the park in their uniforms to pick him up, girls who lived on Park Avenue and whose parents owned whole islands. Alice was his friend, and she was in love with him. Sometimes he would sleep over at her house and they would spoon all night and Alice wouldn't sleep at all, just listen to his breath and sometimes, sometimes, in the middle of the night, they would start kissing, and Alice would think, Oh, it's really happening, he's going to be **mine** now, but in the morning, he would always act like nothing had happened, and so nothing ever changed. It wasn't that different from all the men she'd met in bars in her twenties and on dating apps in her thirties.

Tommy held out the pack, and Alice slid out a cigarette. "Thanks," she said.

"So, what's up?" Tommy asked. "Who's coming to the party?"

"I have no idea," Alice said, truthfully. "Sam's in charge."

There were things that Alice remembered from her birthday party: She remembered helping Sam throw up, and half-heartedly trying to clean up after people while the party was still going. She remembered Tommy sitting in the corner of the couch, his head back, eyes closed. She remembered taking whatever it was that Phoebe's brother got them, tiny little pills that looked like aspirin, and she remembered sitting on Tommy's lap and his hands going under her shirt. She remembered Danny leaning out of the window so far that he fell four feet to the ground, fracturing his wrist. She remembered closing the blinds so that Jim and Cindy Roman wouldn't call the police, and then wishing they had.

"Did I tell you that I'm going to write a screenplay?" Tommy said. "Brian and I were talking about it yesterday. We're going to write a screenplay, kind of like **Kids** but without it being just skaters, you know, and less depressing, and then we're going to star in it, too, and direct it."

"What about college?" Tommy had gone to Princeton, just like his parents.

"No way," Tommy said, and took a drag. "I'm not going to do just what my parents want me to do. No way." Something buzzed, and Tommy unclipped his pager from his belt. "It's Sam, at the pay phone at school."

"I'll go back in a second. What's up?"

"Is Lizzie coming? To your party?" Lizzie was a senior and not remotely Alice's friend except for the one time she had gone with Alice and Sam to buy weed at a bodega that wasn't really a bodega. Tommy and Lizzie would have sex at Alice's birthday party, right in her bed, and after that, Tommy and Alice would never speak again, not until he walked into his office with his wife and his child.

"I have no idea," Alice said. She stood up and dusted off her pants. "Let's go back."

25

SAM WAS STANDING IN THE PHONE BOOTH
at Belvedere, biting her fingernails. The phone
booth was on the first floor, next to the teacher's
lounge at the back of the building, its wood well
carved with decades of students' initials and various profane messages. The little door was shut, but
when Sam saw Alice through the scratched glass,
she slid it open, and Alice squeezed in.

"What did pretty boy want? Just to have you
admire him for a little while?"

"To know if Lizzie was coming to the party."

Sam rolled her eyes. "He asked you that on your
birthday? That is so irritating. I'm sorry."

"Honestly, I have other things to worry about
right now." Alice picked the phone up off the hook
and stared at it. "How do I call information again?"

Sam showed her, and handed Alice the phone.

"Hi," Alice said. "Can I have the number for Matryoshka Bar, please? In the subway station?" After she made the call and set the receiver back in its cradle, Alice turned to look at Sam, whose face was pale.

"You're serious, aren't you?"

"I'm afraid so." Alice felt her eyes starting to well up with tears.

"Fuck," Sam said. "So you're, like, old?"

"I'm not **old,**" Alice said. "I'm forty."

Sam laughed. "I respect the fact that you think there's a difference."

"It's just all relative. Like, my dad . . ." Alice wasn't sure how to explain how young Leonard was, today, in 1996. But she had to admit that Sam was right—forty did suddenly sound ancient. Twenty-five sounded old, and forty was too much to comprehend. Twenty-five was a guy who might hit on you at a bar, and you'd be both flattered and creeped out. Forty was strictly parental. Authority figure. The president.

"Did he, like, **Time Brothers** you here?" Sam made a hand motion like a car zooming through space. In the credits, which were ridiculous, Barry and Tony drove in front of a background of asteroids, their rust-colored sedan bouncing over the stars.

"No," Alice said. She pictured Leonard in his hospital bed. "Definitely not. But let's go, I have an idea."

"Wait," Sam said. "Just tell me something, okay?

Just tell me one thing so I know you're not making this up. You know I fucking hate pranks."

Alice thought about it. Sam wouldn't care about sports statistics or which famous person was actually gay. She would care too much about her own wedding, and that seemed dangerous, in terms of **Back to the Future**-ing things.

"The thing with your dad," Alice finally said. They hadn't talked about it until they were in college, miles away from each other, relying on the phone to stay in touch. Walt had always traveled a lot for his job, to DC and back, DC and back, and he'd often stay for a few nights. Lorraine had finally divorced him when Sam went to college, which was when they told her that he had another woman. A whole other life. Sam had been suspicious for years, but she'd never said a word to Alice. "It's true. I'm really sorry. But it is what you think."

Sam swallowed a mouthful of air. "Damn, man. I thought you were going to say, like, Arnold Schwarzenegger is president or something."

Alice pulled Sam in for a hug. "I'm sorry. I'm really sorry." Sam cried into her shirt, but when she took a step back, she smiled.

"I fucking knew it," she said. "Okay, let's go."

• • •

Matryoshka didn't open until 5 p.m., but the guy on the phone said that if she was just looking for something she lost, she could come by whenever.

Alice was sure that it had happened at the bar—dark, subterranean, and always a little bit sticky underfoot. If there was any secret pathway to the past and the future, it made sense that it would be underground, running alongside the 2/3 train tunnels, places where no one ever went if they didn't want, in one way or another, to disappear.

Alice had read about homeless people who lived in the tunnels, and there were abandoned train stations, she knew, there was one right on 91st Street, you could see it if you were on the 1/9 train, if you were paying attention. That had to be it—someone who had dug too far, crossed through some boundary, messed some shit up. Alice wished that she had paid attention when Leonard and his friends talked about science fiction novels, instead of just making fun of them for being grown men who spent all their time talking about parallel universes.

"So, what's it like, being a grown-up?" Sam asked.

"It's okay, I guess. I can do whatever I want. I can go wherever I please."

Sam started singing, "And nothing compares to you . . ."

Alice laughed. "Yeah. I guess right now I just feel like if I had made different choices, then everything would be different. And everything is okay, you know; I'm not dead, I'm not in jail. But I can't help wondering if things could be better." She thought about Leonard, and all the tubes and machines, and the frowning doctors.

According to Sam, they had only been to the bar once or twice—all the times that Alice remembered spending there must have happened later than Alice remembered. The summer after they graduated, maybe, or even during college, when they were both home for Thanksgiving and seeing friends. Alice thought they looked too young to just walk in, especially during the daylight hours—they would have to make something up.

"What are we looking for?" Sam whispered.

"Something," Alice said. "We are looking for something. A doorway, a tunnel. A light switch? I don't know. I think we'll know it when we see it, if we see it. Just think about any time travel book or movie you've ever seen, okay?"

"Got it," Sam said. "I mean, I will try." Their dynamic was already different, Alice could feel it. It wasn't that Sam didn't trust her—clearly, she did. But Sam understood that the Alice she was talking to wasn't just her Alice; she was like a chaperone Alice, a babysitter Alice. She hadn't even told her that she worked at Belvedere yet. Then she'd be Professional Administrator Alice, and what fun would that be?

The door of Matryoshka was propped open, and the girls walked in slowly, waiting for their eyes to adjust to the dark. It was empty, with rows of bottles lined up on the bar and a half-seen person bent over on the other side, counting. Sam gripped Alice's elbow, clearly freaked. Alice understood—her friend's greatest powers were in situations she could control and organize, like studying for the LSATs or marrying a boy who worshipped her.

"Hello?" Alice said. She clutched Sam's arm back, holding tight.

The bartender stood up straight—the one who had overserved her in such a friendly manner only the night before. "Oh, hi!" Alice said, relaxing. "Hi. Nice to see you again!"

"Girls," the bartender said, both a greeting and a wary identification. He gave no indication that he recognized her.

"I lost something here, I think," Alice said, and cleared her throat. "I called earlier. Can we just look around for a minute? We're not going to drink anything."

He started moving bottles back into the racks behind the bar. The whole place smelled terrible, like the cumulative regret of a thousand strangers with a soupçon of vomit and Lysol. "Okay," he said as he worked.

Alice pulled Sam into the corner by the jukebox. "Okay, so I was here, and he was here, and I told him it was my birthday, and he gave me many free shots, and then I got drunk and I spilled something on my sweater and I think I handed out some tapas to some sorority girls."

"When was this?" Sam asked. Their noses were almost touching, skin orange from the light of the tiny bulbs behind the songs.

"Last night. **My** last night."

"Got it, got it. So we're just looking for something weird? Like . . . a door? A creepy hallway?" Sam looked at the room around them—an ancient pinball machine, a sagging couch that probably held DNA to solve half a dozen crimes, the jukebox.

"The photo booth!" Alice said. She pulled Sam by the hand past the bar and into the next room.

The photo booth curtain was open and the seat empty. Alice scooted in, and Sam slid in beside her.

"It looks normal to me," Sam said.

"Me too," Alice said. "I just wish I could Google this."

"Are you talking future to me?" Sam pursed her lips. "If you're going to do that, then I'm going to need to know more about who I married, and whether it's Brad Pitt or Denzel Washington."

"They are both too old for you. Even grown-up you. But fine! Fine. Okay, I know I said I wasn't going to, but in the future, there's this thing called Google, and you just type something in and it spits back thousands of answers. And there's this website called Wikipedia that does the same thing, basically. And I really wish that I could just type in **'time travel help please'** and get some answers."

"So you just type in anything? And it tells you everything you need to know? Does anyone do their homework?" Sam asked.

"I don't think so," Alice said. She ran her finger around the instructions for how to operate the booth and the dollar slot. She stood up, pried her wallet out of her back pocket, and yanked out a crinkly dollar bill. She slid it into the slot, and the light started to flash. Alice and Sam posed once, twice, three times, four times, and then the whirring of the internal mechanisms began, and they slid out.

While they waited for the pictures to develop, Alice walked the perimeter of both rooms, feeling along the tacky walls, looking behind pictures that hadn't been moved in decades. There was nothing weird, or at the very least, nothing weirder than seeing a nighttime place during the day, the bizarro version of being in a school after hours. The machine finally spit out the photos and Sam and Alice hurried back over, holding the still-wet strip by its edges.

"Classic," Sam said approvingly. Kissy faces, tongues out, eyes open, eyes closed.

"I love it," Alice said. She could see herself in them—her sixteen-year-old face, of course, but the rest of her, too. It was something in her irises, in the tension in her mouth. It wasn't the exact same photo Sam had given her for her fortieth birthday, but it was close, like the difference between fraternal twins.

"You keep it," Sam said. "A birthday present, from me to you."

Alice felt slightly defeated. "Let's just go back to Pomander. I want to spend as much time as possible with my dad."

"Okay," Sam said. They waved goodbye to the confused bartender and went back through the turnstiles, flashing their school passes. They slid to the end of a row of empty seats.

"Tell me something else," Sam said. "Something good."

"You move to New Jersey," Alice said, and smiled.

Sam threw a fake punch. "You're just playing with me."

Alice nodded. Sometimes the truth was hard to hear.

26

LEONARD WASN'T HOME WHEN THEY got to Pomander, but Ursula crisscrossed through their legs as Sam and Alice walked through the house and back to Alice's room. There was a Post-it note stuck to her door that said **Back soon —Dad.**

"So what's the plan?" Sam asked, curling up on Alice's bed. She leaned over and picked up a copy of **Seventeen** magazine. "I can't believe you subscribe to this garbage."

"For tonight? Or for my life?" Alice sat next to her.

"Isn't that kind of the same thing, maybe?"

"I guess, if I think about it, tonight, I want to have a better time at this party than I did the first time. I want to figure out how to get back to my life. To my other life. I want to hang out with my dad." It felt shameful to admit it so plainly. Kids at

Belvedere were now open wounds of self-conscious vulnerability. They changed sexual orientations and genders, they experimented with pronouns. They were so evolved that they knew they were still evolving. When Alice was a teenager, the entire point of life had been to pretend that absolutely nothing had an effect on her. Technically, she still couldn't quite bring herself to tell Sam the truth—that if she could, Alice wanted to make sure that Leonard didn't end up where she'd left him. She wanted to save his life, simple as that. Just then, Alice heard the front door open and close, and Ursula leap off of some high-up place—the bookshelf, maybe, or the top of the refrigerator—to run to the door.

"Al? You home?" Leonard called out.

"Yeah! I'm here! With Sam!" Alice shouted back. She watched Sam flip pages in the magazine—all the pastel-colored ads for Maybelline Great Lash mascara and Swatch watches and Bonne Bell Lip Smackers and Caboodles jewelry boxes. Alice had truly believed that magazines were preparing her for the future, that **Beverly Hills, 90210** was a mirror, only with shorter dresses and more hats worn at school. Everything that she consumed told her that she was grown. She wanted to shake Sam by the shoulders and tell her that they were both still children and no one around them knew, like they were standing on each other's shoulders in a trench coat and everyone believed it. But Sam already knew, because Sam got in trouble when she stayed out late. Sam got grounded when her mother found the roach of a joint in her room. Sam got her beeper taken away for two weeks after Lorraine got a call from Belvedere saying that Sam had been caught kissing a boy—Noah Carmello—in the back stairs during class. One of the worst parts about being a teenager was realizing that life wasn't the same for everyone—Alice knew that at the time. What had taken decades was realizing that so many things that she had thought were advantages to her own life were the opposite.

"Are you going to go home before the party?" Alice asked.

"No, why? I'll just wear something you have," Sam said. Alice had forgotten about the transient nature of the clothing of teenage girls, about no longer being able to tell which item belonged to whom. She and Sam wore the same size, more or less, close enough to share almost everything.

In the photos Sam had given her for her birthday, they were wearing tiaras and slips, like beauty queens forced to hold a pageant in the middle of the night. "Let's wear regular clothes," Alice said. "Nothing fancy."

Sam shrugged. "It's your birthday."

The phone began to trill. It took Alice a minute to find it, underneath a pile of clothing.

"Hello?" she said.

"Happy birthday, Allie," said her mother, using a nickname that Alice had never liked. It was as if Serena were talking to someone else, which in a way she was. Serena was always talking to a version of Alice that she thought wanted to hear from her, or would be satisfied with irregular phone calls and irregular care. "I sent some things, did they arrive?"

"Hi, Mom," Alice said, and Sam went back to her magazine.

"You girls want lunch?" Leonard called, and they both called back, "Yes!"

27

GRAY'S PAPAYA WAS THE GREATEST restaurant in new York City, because it served only one thing: hot dogs. Hot dogs with ketchup, hot dogs with mustard, hot dogs with sauerkraut, hot dogs with relish. Behind the counter, there were large churning vats of brightly colored juices, but if you ordered something other than papaya, you were a narc. There were no places to sit, only high tables along the windows facing both Broadway and 72nd Street, perfect for people-watching. Alice and Sam jockeyed for a spot at the counter overlooking Broadway while Leonard went to order.

"Have you told him?" Sam whispered.

Alice shook her head.

"But he, like, knows stuff," Sam said. "About this."

"What do you mean? Like, **Time Brothers**? Sam.

That's a book. It's fiction. And, like, goofy fiction. It's literally about brothers who time-travel and solve low-level crimes."

"But maybe that, like, **made** it happen? Do you have a rusty car somewhere?" Sam's eyes got wide. "Maybe the car is disguised as, like, your bathroom."

"What are you even talking about?"

"Oh, now **I'm** the one saying something crazy, sure," Sam said, and rolled her eyes. Leonard squeezed past the people lined up behind them and set down four hot dogs, two with ketchup and mustard and two with sauerkraut and onions. "My favorite vegetables," he said.

"Dad, I have never seen you eat something green that wasn't, like, Blue No. 5 and Yellow No. 8 mixed together," Alice said. Leonard swiveled back to the counter to pick up their drinks.

"Just ask him," Sam said through gritted teeth.

"Not yet," Alice said, and then smiled at her dad as he set his elbows on the counter on her other side. She took a bite of her hot dog and it tasted exactly the same as it always had, like heaven. Leonard closed his eyes as he ate, clearly enjoying his lunch as much as she was enjoying hers. Maybe that was the trick to life: to notice all the tiny moments in the day when everything else fell away and, for a split second, or maybe even a few seconds, you had no worries, only pleasure, only appreciation of what was right in front of you. Transcendental meditation, maybe, but with hot dogs and the knowledge that everything would change, the good and the bad, and so you might as well appreciate the good.

• • •

When they were finished, they walked up Amsterdam toward Emack & Bolio's for ice cream, dodging other clumps of families and tourists coming from the Museum of Natural History up the block. It was a birthday celebration Alice could have had at five years old or ten years old or as an adult. Taxis swerved to collect passengers from the corners, and all the other cars honked in great choruses of displeasure, as if they didn't understand how things worked. Everyone on the sidewalk looked straight ahead, or at their friends, or at the clouds of pigeons descending to feast on some particularly delicious garbage in the crosswalk, someone's dropped lunch.

Inside the empty ice cream shop, Alice and Sam peered into the glass cases and chose elaborate concoctions—scoops of mint chip and double chocolate with hot fudge and rainbow sprinkles for Alice, scoops of pistachio and strawberry with whipped cream for Sam, and a large cup of cookie dough for Leonard. They sat at a small round table, their knees crowded together underneath.

"What do you write, at night?" Alice asked her dad. She dug her spoon into the massive heap of sugar in front of her. The sound of her father working—guitars wailing through the speakers, his slippered feet shuffling down the hall, his fingers punching away at the keyboard—was as comforting to her as a white noise machine. It meant he was there, he was writing, and that he was happy, in his way.

"Who, me?" Leonard asked.

"Yes, you," Alice said. The hot fudge had hardened into very slow lava, and it clung to the weak plastic spoon.

"Stories. Ideas. Different things."

Alice nodded. This was where she had always left it, before Leonard began to bristle, before she began prying. "So why not publish it? Obviously, any publisher in New York would buy it. Even if it was garbage."

Leonard put a hand on his heart. "You wound me."

"I'm not saying that I think it's garbage, Dad. I'm just saying that it's sort of no duh. Someone would buy it, and publish it, and give you tons of money. So why not?" Alice blushed.

"I think what Alice is asking, Leonard," Sam said, "is whether there is a **Time Sisters** in the works. You know, same general idea, just with girls instead of boys, because girls are smarter in every way."

Leonard nodded. "I hear you, I do. And thank you, Sam, for what is truthfully a million-dollar idea that I should have had years ago. But what's the fun in doing something again? If I wrote the same book again, just with different people in it, don't you think that would be boring?"

Alice and Sam shrugged.

"It's a bit like **Spider-Man,** if I may be so bold. When you have a successful book, you have the power to publish another, but the reason the book was successful in the first place creates a sense of responsibility to one's readers—they liked this, which is why I have that, and so on. There are some writers who write the same book over and over again, once a year, for decades, because their readers enjoy it and they can do it, and they do it well, and that's that. And then there are some writers, like me"—here Leonard smiled—"who find the whole idea so utterly paralyzing that they'd rather watch **Jeopardy!** with their teenage daughter and just write what they want to write and not worry about anyone else ever seeing it."

"**Jeopardy!** is a really good show," Sam said. "I get it."

Alice didn't think Sam got it. Sam had more academic and intellectual ambition in her toenails than most people had in their entire bodies, just like her mom. Sam had gone straight from undergrad to law school, bing bang boom, without so much as coming up for air. Alice got it, though. She saw it all the time at Belvedere—the parents who carried tennis rackets had children who carried tennis rackets. The parents with drinking problems and well-stocked home bars often were the ones called into the school counselor's office about the Olde English forty-ounce found in Junior's locker.

The scientists had little scientists; the misogynists had little misogynists. Alice had always thought of her professional life in perfect contrast with her father's—he'd had wild success, and she, none, just hanging on to something stable like a seahorse with its tail looped around some seagrass—but now she thought that she'd been wrong. He was afraid, too, and happier to stay close to what had worked, rather than risk it all on something new.

"I'm sorry, Dad," Alice said. "I know how you feel."

Leonard put his hand on her cheek and gave her a gentle pat. "You always did, you know that? It was very strange. Even when you were a very small child, and I asked you a question, somehow you always knew the answers. It was like someone was hiding in the bushes, and going to jump out and say, **Ha! You thought this child knew the difference between a marsupial and a mammal, and she's only three!** But no one ever jumped out. You just knew."

"You really should, though, Dad. What Sam said. It would be so good—you know it would, don't you? People would love it. Just because **Time Brothers** was, like, this world smash doesn't mean that another book would be a total flop or something. It's not a reason not to try."

Leonard dug his spoon into the bottom of his paper cup. "When did you two get so smart, huh?" The girls had already finished their massive quantities of ice cream, and Leonard stood up and collected the detritus and threw it in the garbage can, then swept all the errant, escaped sprinkles off the tabletop and into his palm and threw those away, too. Sam looked at Alice and cocked her head to one side. "I have an idea," she said. "I have to go home to look at something, but I'll meet you back at Pomander, okay? Page me if you need me. Thanks for the ice cream, Lenny."

Leonard bowed. "Anytime."

Sam scurried out the door, waving. She blew a kiss to Alice, who caught it, suddenly nervous to again be alone with the truth.

"Are you too old for the whale?" Leonard asked.

28

THE MUSEUM WAS ALWAYS CROWDED ON Saturdays, but no matter how busy it was, people crammed into the dinosaur exhibits on the upper floors, which Alice hadn't particularly cared about since she was five. That wasn't where they wanted to go. Leonard flashed his membership card at the entrance and they quickly turned to the left, passing by a bronze Teddy Roosevelt and a few dioramas that no doubt greatly underestimated the tension between the Indigenous people of the region and the colonizing pilgrims. Leonard and Alice crossed through a doorway into a room that felt like a jungle, complete with life-sized tiger and a clamshell that was big enough to swallow even the tiger. That was always how Alice knew they were close.

It had a real name, of course, the Milstein Hall, but no one called it that. How could you, with a whale the size of a city bus swimming overhead and the dark sounds of the ocean all around you? Being in that room felt like sitting at the bottom of the sea, untouchable by whatever was happening on the surface. The upper balcony had spider crabs and jellyfish, all sorts of creatures lining the walls, but the real action was down the stairs, under the whale, surrounded by enormous hand-painted dioramas. The manatee, sleepily floating as if witnessed forever mid-dream. The dolphins, jumping show-offs. The seal, recently clobbered to death by a gigantic walrus. In the corner, almost hidden by coral and fish, a pearl diver. Leonard and Alice walked carefully down the stairs without talking. The room wanted silence in the same way that a movie theater wanted silence, or a church pew.

The problem with adulthood was feeling like everything came with a timer—a dinner date with Sam was at most two hours, with other friends, probably not even as long. There was maybe waiting for a table, there was a night at a bar, there was a party that went late, but even that was just a few hours of actual time spent. Most of Alice's friendships now felt like they were virtual, like the pen pals of her youth. It was so easy to go years without seeing someone in person, to keep up to date just through the pictures they posted of their dog or

their baby or their lunch. There was never this—
a day spent floating from one thing to another. This
was how Alice imagined marriage, and family—
always having someone to float through the day
with, someone with whom it didn't take three
emails and six texts and a last-minute reservation
change to see one another. Everyone had it when
they were kids, but only the truly gifted held on to
it in adulthood. People with siblings usually had a
leg up, but not always. There were two boys from
Belvedere, best friends since kindergarten, who had
grown up and married a pair of sisters, and now
all four of their children went to Belvedere, driven
by one mom or the other in a little cousin carpool.
That was next-level friendship—locking someone
in through marriage. It seemed positively medieval,
like when you realized that all the royal families in
the world were more or less cousins. Even just the
concept of cousins felt like bragging—**Look at all
these people who belong to me.** Alice had never
felt like she belonged to anyone—or like anyone
belonged to her—except for Leonard.

He had walked to the center of the room and
lowered himself onto the floor. Alice watched as
he stretched out on his back, his scuffed sneakers
flopping out to the sides. He wasn't the only one—
a family with a small baby was also lying down,
staring up at the vast belly of the whale. Alice knelt
down next to her dad.

"Remember when we used to come here all the time?" she asked. They had visited weekly when she was a kid, if not more often—Alice even remembered being at the museum with her mother, who had preferred the hall of gems and minerals. Alice ran her hands up and down her thighs. Her sailor pants were dark and stiff. She'd bought them at Alice Underground, her favorite store, and not just because it shared her name. It was still so strange to see her body—her young body, a body she hardly remembered as it was, because she'd been so busy seeing it as something it wasn't.

"Only place in New York City where you would stop crying," Leonard said, a wide smile on his face. He slapped the floor next to him. "Come on down."

Alice flopped onto her back. Some of the stoners at Belvedere went to the light show at the planetarium right around the corner—the Pink Floyd one, with the flying pigs—when they were high, but Alice didn't know why anyone would want to be anywhere other than in this room.

"I don't know why I never come here anymore," she said. "I feel like my blood pressure just dropped."

"Since when do you worry about blood pressure? Man, sixteen ain't what it used to be." Leonard shifted his hands to his stomach, and Alice watched them rise and fall with his breath.

Alice thought about saying something right then. There were families pushing sleeping children in strollers and tourists lugging around shopping bags, but the room was quiet, and whatever Alice said, no one but her father would hear her.

Leonard had, of course, thought about time travel more than most people. Even though he routinely mocked terrible sci-fi novels and movies and television shows, even ones made by his friends, Alice knew that he loved it. The impossible being possible. The limits of reality being pushed beyond what science can fully explain. Sure, it was a metaphor, it was a trope, it was a genre, but it was also **fun.** No one—certainly no one Leonard liked—wrote science fiction because it was a tool. That was for assholes. Of all the writers in the world, Leonard's least favorite were the fancy ones, the ones from highly ranked MFA programs and award ceremonies where one had to dress in black tie, who had descended briefly to earth and stolen something from the genres—the undead, perhaps, or a light apocalypse—before returning to heaven with it in their talons. Leonard liked the nerds, the ones with science fiction in their blood. Some of those fancy writers were deep, true nerds under the surface, and Leonard was okay with them. But Alice didn't think that she could just start a conversation about nerds, or science fiction, or time travel, not without giving herself away, and she wasn't ready to do that just yet. It wouldn't be like telling Sam, Alice knew, who still had one eyebrow raised, like an agnostic who believed in **something** but not necessarily in God. Leonard had always trusted Alice—about which girl had pushed her off the slide in kindergarten, about which boy had teased her, about which teacher was grading unfairly. She wasn't worried that he would doubt her. Alice was afraid of what would happen next because Leonard would believe her right away, without hesitation.

The whale was the length of the whole room, its nose pointing down, poised to dive into the inky depths. The wide tail looked like it was about to push upward, maybe even through the ceiling, to help propel the giant animal down. Alice closed her eyes and concentrated on how solid the floor was beneath her back.

"Did I ever tell you about when Simon and I went to see the Grateful Dead at the Beacon Theatre?"

He had.

"Go ahead," Alice said, and smiled. She knew every word that was going to come out of his mouth.

"1976," Leonard began. "Jerry had this white guitar. I know a lot of people who saw the Dead a thousand times, but I only saw them that one time. The Beacon can feel so small, depending where you're sitting, and Simon had gotten tickets from his agent, who was this super hotshot, and somehow we were in the third row—the third row!—and every woman there was drop-dead gorgeous, and it was like being on another planet for four hours."

This was what Alice had been missing. Not just

the answers to questions that she'd never been brave enough to ask, and not just family history that no one else knew, and not just visions of her own childhood through her father's eyes, but also this: the embarrassing stories she'd heard a thousand times and would never hear again. She could see the whole concert, Leonard's sweaty, smiling face—before he was married, before he was a dad, before he'd published a book. She could see it as clearly as she could see the whale, even with her eyes closed.

29

WHEN THEY GOT BACK TO POMANDER, the phone was ringing. Leonard swung his body aside and gestured for Alice to answer it.

"It's for you," he said.

"How do you know?" Alice said, and picked up the receiver.

"Jesus, I have been calling, like, every ten minutes for **hours**," Sam said.

"Sorry, this is Alice, not Jesus." Alice wound the cord around her pointer finger. Why did people think that having cell phones was less tethered than this? She'd been floating in space all day, unreachable, and now, connection.

"Oh, shut up, grandma. Where do you want to have dinner? I'll meet you there."

"Where should we have dinner, Dad?" Alice

asked Leonard. He was standing over the kitchen table, looking through a stack of mail and magazines and who knows what.

"Let's go to V&T. Then Sam can just walk and meet us. Sound good?"

"Yes, Sam, did you hear that? Gooey pizza. V&T. Six o'clock." Alice turned her body away from her dad. "Anything else?"

"Yes," Sam said, slightly breathless, as though she'd been jogging in place for hours and not just redialing the telephone. "I think I figured it out. Maybe. Potentially. I'll tell you when I see you." Alice felt a flame in her belly, a flare of hope, or anxiety, that buried itself in her rib cage.

"Okay," Alice said, and hung up.

Leonard tossed the stack of mail back onto the table. "Why is it always just junk?" he asked.

The television was in an awkward place—perched on the end of the kitchen counter, where it could be swiveled one way to face the table and another to face the couch. The table was in the way of the couch, but there wasn't much space, and anyway, Leonard and Alice were both used to it. The VCR was tucked underneath, all the wires dangling off the counter. If they'd had a different kind of cat, a normal cat and not Ursula, the wires would have been an irresistible trouble, but Ursula was above such things. They had hours before dinner. Alice opened and closed all the cabinet doors until she found the microwave popcorn. She waved it at her dad.

"Want to watch a movie?"

Leonard opened the closet, which was where the VHS tapes lived, and started calling out titles. "**Wizard of Oz**? **Rebecca**? **Chitty Chitty Bang Bang**? **Bedknobs and Broomsticks**? **Mary Poppins**? **Stand by Me**? **Dirty Dancing**? **Back to the Future**? **Eraserhead**? **Prick Up Your Ears**? **Peggy Sue Got Married**?"

"**Peggy Sue**," Alice said. She stepped around the closet door so that she could see him. Leonard pulled the tape out of the box and handed it to her.

"Voilà," he said. "Now, are we the two most smartest people or what? Other people are jogging, for fun, and we're watching a movie in daylight hours."

The movie was just as good as always, except that it drove Alice crazy how little Peggy Sue seemed to notice her parents. Who cared about her lame friends, about her stupid boyfriend? She should have fucked everyone as quickly as possible and then just stayed home. And her grandparents? Peggy Sue had a charmed life. She got married and had kids and still had living parents and everything in her life was perfectly fine except maybe she wanted a divorce. It wasn't actually time travel at all, not really. Peggy Sue faints and has a dream. It seemed like one of those movies where they might have made three different endings because the test audiences didn't like the one they were shown. Alice wanted to see the ending where Kathleen Turner crawled around the floor of a bar looking for a rabbit hole but couldn't find one and so was trapped forever, making the same mistakes all over again. Alice wanted to see the horror movie version. But then again, she might be about to live it, so maybe she didn't need to see it after all.

Leonard nudged her. Alice had fallen asleep, her head leaning against the arm of the couch like the bottom half of seesaw. In her forty-year-old body, her neck would have been sore for days, but in this one, Alice just sat up.

"Pizza time," Leonard said.

• • •

V&T was on the corner of 110th Street and Amsterdam Avenue, across the street from St. John the Divine, where Leonard had taken Alice every year on Saint Francis Day, when they opened the enormous front doors and let an elephant walk in. As a family, the Sterns did not celebrate any religious holidays, but they celebrated lots of New York holidays: in addition to Saint Francis Day with the elephants, there was the Macy's Thanksgiving Day Parade, when they would go and watch the balloons get inflated the night before; there were the Christmas windows in the fancy department stores on Fifth Avenue; there were San Gennaro and Chinese New Year, for cannoli and dumplings; and there was the Puerto Rican Day Parade, when all of uptown was flooded with reggaeton, and the

St. Patrick's Day Parade, when it was equally bois-
terous, but with bagpipes.

The pizza wasn't the best slice in the city—it was
the gooiest. It was as if the pizza oven had a slight
dip in the middle, which caused every single pizza
to have a molten, liquid center, the vortex of a whirl-
pool. The cheese slid one way or the other, and the
first person to pick up a slice was bound to pull
the whole gooey mess off the slice's siblings and
have to rearrange the pizza with their fingers or a
handy knife. Alice loved it. When she and Leonard
got to the corner, Sam was pacing in front.

"Hi," Sam said. She clutched Alice's arm. "Come
pee with me."

Leonard waved them on.

The bathroom was small and empty. Sam flushed
the toilet and turned on the tap.

"Don't make fun of me, okay?" Sam asked. She
crossed her arms over her chest.

"Obviously I am not in a position to make fun,
nor would I ever!" Alice said. "Please. Tell me." The
bathroom smelled like Lysol and tomato sauce.

"Okay, so my mom loves **Time Brothers,** you
know that. So I was looking through it, and then
I started looking through some other books that
she has—it turns out, for a professor, that woman
has a lot of time travel shit on her shelf." Sam was
clearly filled with too many words she wanted to
say at once. "I think there are two main options,

in terms of what's going on. Not options as in you have a choice—two theories."

"Okay," Alice said. Sam was still like this, thank god—thoughtful and smart and willing. Alice wanted to tell her that it was these very qualities that made her a great mom, but didn't.

"Basically, I think you're either stuck here or you're not. So, Scott and Jeff, they have this car, right, and the car carries them around, just like Marty McFly, you know? That's not you. And the fact that you're inside your own body, no offense, seems like a bad sign. Like, if there were two of you, and you were watching yourself do things, like in **Back to the Future Part II,** then obviously you would be able to go back, because otherwise there would be two of you forever, see what I'm saying?"

"Yes?" Alice said.

"I think it's probably a wormhole. Scott and Jeff went through a wormhole once, do you remember? It's not in the book, but it was on the show— you know the episode I mean? When they were on Scott's family's farm in Wisconsin and it was all, 'Doop doop doop, guess we're not time-traveling this time,' like they were on vacation or whatever, and then Scott was helping his grandmother clean out an old barn and then all of a sudden it was 1970 and Scott was a baby? And spent the whole day as a baby? But he was with his grandmother and you got to see how his mother died? And then the next day, he was himself again, but different? I think it could be like that—like, you went into the barn."

"And now I'm the baby."

"Yes, but you know you're the baby."

Someone knocked on the bathroom door. It was the only bathroom in the restaurant. Alice turned off the faucet and shouted, "Be right out!" She and Sam made eye contact in the mirror. "I don't really know what to do, though."

Sam shrugged. "Let's start with pizza."

• • •

When they got back to the table, Leonard had already ordered them Coca-Colas, and a wan salad of iceberg lettuce and pale tomatoes sat in the middle of the red-checked tablecloth. Pathetic pizzeria salads were the only salads Leonard actually liked. The girls settled into their chairs across from Leonard and each took a long gulp of soda. Sam wasn't allowed to drink soda at home, and so she drank it like crazy when she was with Alice and Leonard.

"Are you sure you need to go to the conference tonight?" Alice asked.

Leonard raised an eyebrow. "Pepperoni? Mushroom? Sausage and peppers? Don't you already have something planned?"

Sam gasped. "Leonard! You aren't supposed to know!"

"It's fine, have a little party." He smiled. The waiter brought over a glass of red wine, and Leonard thanked him. "I trust you."

He'd brought his bag—a beat-up satchel from the army/navy store. It was hanging on the back of his chair. Leonard would go straight to the hotel in midtown for the convention. Alice had been so focused on herself, she hadn't even noticed.

"You're really going?" Alice asked.

"Oh, come on, you two don't want me around. You have fun. I'll call to check in tomorrow morning, but you have the hotel number if you need me. It's on the fridge." Leonard took a swig of wine and puckered. "That is . . . vinegar. But I love vinegar. Happy birthday, my baby." Leonard raised his glass.

Alice groaned, despite herself. "Dad."

"Happy birthday, Alice," he tried instead.

She nodded. "Thanks. Okay."

An hour later, Leonard slung his bag over his shoulder and headed out with a wave as the bell over the door tinkled. It wasn't yet eight o'clock. Alice couldn't remember what happened next, the first time.

30

THE HOUSE ON POMANDER SEEMED
smaller at night. Somehow the lack of sunlight,
meager though the sunlight ever was reaching over
the much taller buildings that surrounded their
narrow walk, made the space feel even tighter. Alice
and Sam had filled the fridge with beer, and they
put bowls of potato chips out on the kitchen table.
Alice smoked, nervous. Sam was rifling through
the closet, pulling out different options.

"Tell me something scandalous," Sam said.

Alice took a drag and thought about what she
would have been most impressed by on her sixteenth birthday. "I've had sex with a lot of people."

Sam stopped and held a clump of dresses to her
chest. "How many is a lot?"

She didn't know the exact number—college had

been fuzzy, as had large swaths of her twenties. Did blow jobs count, or times when she'd started having sex but gotten interrupted and then just given up? "Thirty? Or so?" There had been many years when she'd only slept with one person, and years when she'd spent six months without so much as a kiss. But there were a lot of years with a lot of people in between.

The look on Sam's face was somewhere between awe and horror, worse than when Alice had said she would move to New Jersey, but she collected herself quickly. "Okay," she said. "Tell me. What do I need to know that I don't know?" Sam and Alice were both virgins, and would stay that way until they were in college. Sam would have two boyfriends before Josh. Three people, total, as far as Alice knew—that was Sam's list. Alice remembered what it had felt like, their shared belief that they would never, ever have sex with another human, that they would stay virgins until they were old and gray. Alice had forgotten that worry, that she didn't know what to do with her body, that she didn't know how to produce pleasure in herself or someone else, but she could feel it right now, the panic and fear and desire all swirling together in her guts.

"Oh god," Alice said. "Probably a lot? Starting with understanding the clitoris?" It was easier to imagine a teenage boy at Belvedere solving world hunger than it was to imagine a teenage boy at Belvedere able to locate or stimulate the clitoris in 1996.

Sam's face turned purple. "Oh my god," she said. "Okay. Maybe just forget I asked. I feel like I'm getting a one-on-one health class, and that's kind of the only thing more awkward than a regular health class."

The doorbell rang, and Alice began to panic. "I should have canceled."

Taking her time to climb out of the closet, Sam tiptoed over to the bed, where she dropped the armfuls of clothes. "I'll get the door. You put something on. And if the party sucks, we kick everybody out and watch **Pretty in Pink.** Whatever you want."

Everything was already different—it had to be. Could one person do everything the same way twice, even if they were trying? Alice couldn't remember what she'd had for lunch the day before; how could she remember everything that happened on her sixteenth birthday? There were two open beers on her nightstand, and Alice drank the first one as quickly as she could, and then the second. The goal was to get back, wasn't it? Or to figure out what the hell was going on? Was the goal not to vomit, not to let Tommy break her heart, not to exist as she always had? Was the goal to make sure that Leonard took up running instead of pounding cans of Coca-Cola as his favorite exercise? Birthdays were inherently disappointing—they always had been. There wasn't a birthday she could remember truly enjoying. That was one way that social media had buoyed depression rates across the globe—now it was easy to see how much fun everyone else had on their birthdays, the elaborate gifts they received from their partners, the parties they were thrown, surprise! Alice did not want a surprise party, but still. More than not wanting a giant party, she didn't want to feel unworthy of one. This was the last big birthday party she'd ever had, the last one with people she hadn't invited swimming in and out of view.

• • •

If there was one thing that Alice felt like she'd done wrong, it was being too passive. She hadn't quit working at Belvedere like everyone else had, she hadn't broken up with people when she knew they weren't right for her, she hadn't ever moved anywhere or done anything surprising. She was just floating. Like a seahorse.

Seahorses were Leonard's favorite animal. There was an Eric Carle book about seahorse fathers, who carried their young, and Alice thought that was probably why. Raising children required a lot of conversations about animals, and favorites, and so every parent had to have an answer, and all the better if it was one on display at the museum blocks from their house. There weren't that many animals in the wild whose mothers treated them like Alice's had. There were lots of mothers who abandoned their young straight off the bat—snakes, lizards, cuckoos—but Serena hadn't done that. She'd stuck around long enough that it hurt, and after that, Leonard had carried Alice. There were good reasons and bad reasons to do anything. Her father had floated on purpose, holding fast, never going too far, and then Alice had done the same thing by accident. It was the worst fact of parenthood, that what you did mattered so much more than anything you said.

• • •

Alice pushed herself up to stand. She wasn't drunk, but she was certainly en route. She walked to the doorway of her room to survey what was going on in the rest of the house. There were already half a dozen people standing in the living room, each of them holding an enormous bottle of beer. Sarah and Sara, Phoebe, Hannah and Jenn, Jessica and Helen. Except for Sarah, they were all still around in Alice's adult life, more or less—Alice knew at least the broadest strokes of where they were living and what they were up to. Sara and Hannah were doctors and spent their time on Facebook, posting pictures of their kids on ice skates. Phoebe posted pictures of things she made out of clay, and sunsets. Jessica had moved to California and taken up surfing—all of her photos were old, but she had at least two kids, maybe more, and a hot husband with visible abdominal muscles. Helen lived up the hill from Alice in Park Slope, and had had a string of glamorous, low-paying jobs, but that was fine, because Helen's great-grandfather had invented some part in a machine that was used to make sneakers and so she could have made pot holders for the rest of her life and sold them for fifty cents apiece and she could still buy expensive clogs. Once or twice a year, Alice and Helen would run into each other on the street and hug and kiss each other's cheek and swear to make a plan for dinner, which neither of them would follow up on.

"Alice Stern, there are only girls at this party," Helen said, coming up to Alice and kissing her on the cheek. Her breath smelled like vodka. Maybe that's why everyone had thrown up—her friends had already been drunk when they arrived. The doorbell rang, and Alice excused herself to answer it.

The boys arrived in a solid mass. A forest of boys, a school of boys. Their bodies took up nearly the whole space in between the two sides of Pomander Walk. The boy in front, Matt B., put a hand to the side of his mouth and said, "We roll mad DEEP," which was probably supposed to sound tough but instead sounded like he was an effective camp counselor who had ferried his flock from one side of the street to the other. Alice stepped aside and they filed in. There were some she didn't recognize— boys always seemed to have cousins, or friends from other schools, which was fine, but boys from other schools existed somewhere outside real life, extras in the movie. Every boy kissed Alice on the cheek on his way through the door, even the ones she didn't know, like it was the price of admission. Tommy was in the middle of the pack, which meant that she had to accept his kiss and then stand there while strangers kissed her and walked into her house. She shut the door behind the last one—Kenji Morris, the tall sophomore who was handsome and quiet enough to hang with the older boys, with one sad eye peering out from behind a curtain of dark hair—and locked it. Alice had known most of the boys since she was in the fifth grade, but even so, only single facts about them came to mind: Matt B. supposedly had a crooked penis, James had barfed on the school bus on the way to a field trip in the seventh grade, Kenji's father had died, David had made Alice a mixtape with so many songs from musicals that Alice understood that he was gay.

Someone had put on music—her CD booklet was open on the kitchen counter, next to the boom box. It didn't matter that when she was alone, Alice listened to all different kinds of music: Green Day, Liz Phair, Oasis, Mary J. Blige, even Sheryl Crow if she came on the radio and no one was around to make fun. At parties, it was all Biggie and Method Man and the Fugees and A Tribe Called Quest. It wasn't that all the white boys in private school were pretending to be Black, it was that they thought that being from New York City meant they had a claim to Black culture that other white boys didn't have, even if they lived in a classic six overlooking Central Park. They were playing the Method Man/ Mary J. Blige version of "You're All I Need to Get By" and every single girl was singing along while the boys were just bobbing their heads and pretending not to notice anyone or anything. Phoebe pushed through the crowd and grabbed Sam and Alice by their wrists and pulled them both into the bathroom.

"Voilà!" she said, pulling three pills out of her pocket.

"What is that?" Alice said, though she knew the answer.

Sam looked nervous. "Phoebe said that her brother said that it's like ecstasy, but it's not made of chemicals, so it's like, natural?"

It wasn't natural. It was pure chemicals. It was a real drug, bought from a real drug dealer, and now it was in her bathroom, in the palm of her friend's hand.

"We don't have to do it," Sam said. "I don't think we should do it." She'd said this the first time, too. Sam was smarter than Alice—she always had been.

Alice thought about what she actually remembered from the night, which parts had calcified over time into fact: how big it had felt when Tommy turned his face away from hers and toward Lizzie's, how she had watched them vanish into her bedroom, Alice's hope for true love going up in flames, and on her birthday, no less. After that, Alice had been engulfed by rage, like a mobster's wife in an eighties movie. If she'd had clothing to dump out the window and set on fire, she would have. If Tommy didn't want her, someone else might. Alice had wanted to kiss **someone, anyone,** and so she'd gone up to one boy after another and kissed them, each mouth less appealing than the one before it, just wet and jabby and gross. It didn't matter, Alice kept going. She was going to die a virgin and Tommy had never belonged to her. Outside the bathroom, Kenji, the only sober person at the party, had said to her, "You don't have to do that, you know," and that was when Sam started to throw up and needed her help. Eventually everyone else left and it was just them and Helen and Jessica, all four of them asleep in Alice's room until noon the next day, by which time everyone who was not at the party had heard about Alice's orgy and Tommy and Lizzie's romance and from then on, it was Alice's thing, kissing and kissing and kissing and staying just shy of being called a slut because she didn't actually have sex with anyone, but she definitely wasn't anyone's girlfriend, either.

She hadn't understood it at the time—the difference between her and Sam, the difference between her and Lizzie, the difference between wanting someone to fall in love with her and wanting anyone to fall in love with her. Sam had never had time for the Belvedere boys—they didn't deserve her, it was obvious, and that was that. She could wait. Lizzie, and all the girls like her, understood that everyone was equally terrified all the time, and that all high school power required was confidence.

"I don't need it," Alice said. "I would like to, very much, but not tonight." Making out with lots of people actually sounded wonderful, but making out with a passel of teenage boys sounded disgusting, like being attacked by very large frogs. They—teenagers, the ones all around her—didn't look young to her, though, the way the Belvedere students did to her as an adult. They looked beautiful and sophisticated and fully grown, the way they always had. Alice realized that she wasn't seeing them as a forty-year-old—she was seeing them as she had, or rather, as she **was.** Part of her brain was forty, but another part of it was sixteen. Alice was fully in herself and of herself. The hindsight was there (**fore**sight?), but Alice didn't feel like a creep, or a narc.

"Okay," Phoebe said. "Sarah and Sara said they'd do it, if you didn't want to." She slipped back out, and once she was gone, Alice leaned against the door, the hanging towels behind her back.

"I'm going to do something wild. I probably shouldn't, but I'm going to, okay?" Alice shut her eyes tight and scrunched up her face, as if that would keep Sam's good sense from intervening with her plan.

"Like what?" Sam crossed her arms.

"God, you are already a better forty-year-old

than I am. Remember that part in **Peggy Sue Got Married** when Peggy Sue goes for a motorcycle ride with the poet and they have sex on a picnic blanket and then he dedicates his book to her, which is the only thing that happens in the whole movie that implies that the rest of the movie actually happened and wasn't just a dream?" Alice was talking fast, but she knew Sam knew what she was talking about.

"Uh-huh," Sam said.

"I'm going to go have sex with Tommy, if he wants to, and I think it'll change my life. Not the actual sex, which I am almost **positive** will be terrible, but I think that if I actually take ownership of my feelings, and act on them, instead of being afraid all the time, I think that will change my life." Alice opened one eye.

"Okay, here are my thoughts. Number one, he's eighteen, and so even if it's kind of weird, it's also not a crime," Sam said. "But number two, technically, you are sixteen. I don't know what the rules are for people who are trapped inside their own bodies at an earlier point in their life, but I do think it's okay. If he thinks it's okay. And you do. And you use protection."

Alice hadn't thought about her ovaries in years. She had an IUD that ruled her body with a copper fist, metering out only tiny periods that were supposed to remind her that her body could produce a child, if one were required. Before that, she'd been on the pill for fifteen years. Alice wanted to make changes in her life, but having a baby as a teenager was not one of them. "Those are all good points." She paused. "I know where to find condoms."

Her father's room was as spartan as Alice's room was messy—his full-sized bed was always made, and the stack of books on his bedside table was the only thing not put away. There wasn't so much as a sock on the floor. Alice had seen the package of condoms in his bedside table years ago—when she was in the seventh grade, she had stolen one and put it in her wallet, because she thought it made her seem tough, even though she never showed it to anyone else, not even Sam. She pulled open the drawer. Like hers, it held a pack of cigarettes, some matches, a notebook, a pen, loose change— but unlike hers, in the very back of the drawer, tucked in the corner, was a package of Trojans.

"This grosses me out," Sam said, watching from the doorway as Alice slid one into her pocket. "Majorly."

• • •

Tommy was on the couch, just the way Alice remembered. In the time that they'd been in the bathroom, more people had shown up, and now the counter was covered with beer bottles and makeshift ashtrays and CDs that had been pulled out of rotation, now stacked on top of each other like the leaning tower of Pisa. Lizzie was in the corner talking to some other girls, but she was eyeing him. She was wearing a skimpy tank top, and the end of her high ponytail swept her bare shoulders. Alice swooped in, collapsing next to Tommy on the couch.

"Hi," she said.

"Hey," Tommy said. He smiled and curled toward her.

"Can I talk to you for a second?" She put her hand on his chest. He had slept in her bed so many times. He had kissed the back of her neck. Alice had always thought that Tommy was playing hard to get, or just **playing** with her, period, but now she understood. He was a teenager, just like she was, waiting for someone else to tell him what to do.

Alice had been in love a few times, enough to know that soul mates were a myth and that a person's requirements and tastes changed as they did. Her first love, in college, was a sweet boy with red hair who'd studied film. Her second was a lawyer, a friend of Sam's from law school, who'd loved to take her to fancy restaurants, places that she'd only been for weddings and bar mitzvahs. Her third was an artist who liked to have sex with other people— Alice had tried and tried to make it work. She would have married him if he'd asked, despite everything.

That was it—despite everything, despite her life after tonight, after the rest of her life, Alice had always been sure that this was where she'd gone wrong. There was an infinite number of partners in the world, of lovers, of husbands and wives and significant others, but there was only a tiny number of people who set you on your path. Alice thought of Richard Dreyfuss's voice at the end of **Stand By Me**—did anyone have friends like when they were twelve? Once, when Alice was in college, one of her painting professors had gone on a long, meandering tangent about how Barbara Stanwyck was the start of his sexual profile, and though everyone in the room cringed, Alice had nodded in appreciation. There was a spark, a root. Tommy Joffey was her root. She didn't know what it would do to her life if she had him the way she had so badly wanted him, what it would do to **her,** but Alice wanted to find out. Even if she couldn't figure out how to get back to her real life, even if she was stuck.

Alice got up and pulled Tommy to his feet. A few of the boys covered their mouths and said, "Oh, shit," as they walked by. Alice could feel Lizzie's eyes on her back, but only for a few moments—she didn't know what she was missing, only what she'd wanted, and Alice knew all about that. The feeling would pass.

• • •

When they were in her room, Alice shut the door. There was a slim hook-and-eye latch that she'd made her father install, and Alice gently slid the metal hook into the hole, locking them in.

"You didn't clean up? Before everyone came over? Jeez, Al." Tommy gestured at the mountain ranges on the floor. He nudged a path clear with his boot. There was one chair in the room, in front of Alice's small desk, but it had a pile of sweaters on it and several textbooks and Tommy headed right for her bed. Her stomach was doing cartwheels being so near to him in this moment, touching his skin. Alice hadn't felt this way when Tommy had walked into her office—she had felt the much more familiar feelings, the ones that she'd been living with for decades: shame, incompetence, a basic geriatric millennial malaise. Now Alice's whole body felt combustible, on the verge of explosion. She wanted him.

"Why bother? I want people to know the real me. No putting on airs."

Tommy let himself collapse onto the bed. "Fine with me. It's cozy in here. I feel like I'm a hibernating bear." He pulled the comforter onto his head, like a veil with a long train.

"Here," Alice said. "Use this instead." She yanked her shirt off over her head and threw it at him. Tommy caught it and smiled at her, unable to mask his feeling of lucky confusion.

"Oh yeah?" Tommy said. "Is there any more where that came from?" He raised an eyebrow, but not an inch of him expected her to do it.

So many people had seen Alice naked—not just her sexual partners but also her friends and people at Fort Tilden Beach and in the locker room at the YMCA on Atlantic Avenue and a string of gynecologists and who knows who else. When she was a teenager, Alice had buckled and unbuckled her bra under her shirt, even when she was alone. But she didn't hesitate now—she undid her pants and slid them down, rocking side to side until they were in a puddle on the floor.

"Whoa," Tommy said. He pulled the comforter off his head and slid it onto his lap, where, Alice had no doubt, his body had noticed her. Part of her knew that she shouldn't, but a larger, momentarily stronger part of her knew that this was her chance, and she was taking it. She hadn't spent the last twenty-odd years wishing that she'd been with Tommy, that she'd married Tommy, but she **had** spent the last twenty-odd years learning that waiting was an inefficient way to get what she wanted. If Alice was going to do anything better, it was that— making her wishes known. She had wanted him, and she hadn't known how to say so. Now she did. Alice felt her adult brain recede to the back of her consciousness—it wasn't in charge anymore. She was looking away, and giving herself—her teenage self—privacy.

"You have no idea," Alice said, and walked toward him as slowly as she could, knocking him backward onto her bed with a single finger. She climbed on top of him and hovered her face half an inch above his, waiting for him to come up to meet her.

"Are you sure?" Tommy asked, and she was.

31

SOMETHING CRASHED TO THE FLOOR IN the living room. Alice could hear Sam shouting at someone to clean it up, and then the music got louder and all she could hear was the Fugees. Tommy was flat on his back, his face pink with exertion and delight.

"I'm going to go check on that," Alice said. "Actually, you know what, I'm going to kick everyone out. I'm done." She was wasting time. Teenagers were fickle, crazy beasts, and Alice suddenly felt she was chaperoning her own party—her own **body**—and she needed to get out. It felt a bit the way Alice imagined conjoined twins had sex—this part of her was over here, this part of her was over there. They were sharing oxygen but they weren't a hundred percent the same. The sixteen-year-old hadn't been raptured out in order for the forty-year-old to move in—they were roommates.

Tommy pushed himself up on his elbows. "Yeah, get them out of here. I couldn't agree more. Everyone needs to go, and then you need to come right back here so that we can do that one hundred more times."

Alice laughed. "Easy, tiger." Still, she slapped him lightly on his rib cage. "Okay. Time to get dressed and go home."

Tommy opened his eyes wide. "What? After that? I thought . . . you know."

"Oh, yes, I know," Alice said. She smiled at him. "And we will. But you know what? I have to go do something."

"Can I come with you?" Tommy asked, his voice plaintive. She hadn't heard that before.

"Maybe," Alice said. "Depending on how fast you can clear out the house."

Tommy leaped out of bed, tugged on his underwear and pants in one fluid motion, and yanked his shirt over his head. He vanished into the hallway before Alice even had her bra fastened. There were groans and laughs and high fives, but soon, they were followed by the satisfying clunk of the front door. Alice could imagine the looks on their faces—judgmental, annoyed, amused, put out—because they were the same looks they'd have at forty when they were standing outside her office, watching Melinda interact with their children.

People changed and they didn't. People evolved and they didn't. Alice imagined a graph that showed how much people's personalities shifted after high school on one axis and on the other, how many miles away from home they had moved. It was easy to stay the same when you were looking at the same walls. Layered on top would be how easy your life was along the way, how many levels of privilege surrounded you like a tiny glass object in a sea of packing peanuts. Elizabeth Taylor probably marked time based on her husband. Academics who moved from Ohio to Virginia to Missouri in search of a tenure-track job probably marked time by their shifting health insurance or the school mascots. What did Alice have to mark her time on earth? She was frozen in amber, just pretending to swim. But she was ready to try. Tommy jogged back a few minutes later and slapped his hands together, triumphant.

Sam stood at the door of Alice's bedroom, ready to go. She nodded. "I'm ready to solve this shit," she said. "I was thinking more about it, when you were, um, doing whatever you were doing, and in the baby episode, it's just a day. One day. And then he's back. Which would only leave you . . ."

"Not much time," Alice said. "I mean, if that's what's happening."

"What shit? What's happening?" Tommy asked.

"Don't even worry about it," Alice said. She grabbed the piece of paper with the hotel information from the fridge and led the way.

32

LEONARD'S HANDWRITING HAD ALWAYS been bad, largely indecipherable bumps and polka dots, but Alice was amazed to see how much more legible it had been. She could make it out clearly enough: **Marriott Marquis, Bway + 45th St., Room 1422,** with the phone number scrawled underneath. Both Sam and Tommy insisted on coming with her, even though Alice thought it would be better to go by herself, but they'd stood in the kitchen staring at her, unwilling to leave, and so off they all went. The house was a disaster, but it would still be a disaster when she got home, and Alice could clean up then. The night was clear, and the 2 train came quickly, whirring into the station with its metallic birdsong. Tommy grasped Alice's hand when they sat down, and nestled their shared fist in between their touching thighs. Things were already different.

Manhattan was best at two things: daytime and nighttime. The reasons were the same: the streets were always alive, always moving, always busy. Even when one felt lonely, it was nearly impossible to be alone in New York City. During rainstorms, there was always someone else dashing through puddles with a broken umbrella to toss in the trash can, a stranger whose pain and struggle were the same as your own, at least for a few minutes. The subway system was slow and filthy and Alice loved it anyway. The 2/3—which Leonard still called the IRT—was narrow, with long skinny cars, which made it terrible during rush hour, when Wall Street brokers would pack in on the Upper West Side and there was no hope of sitting down until just before the train crossed under the river into Brooklyn, and someone was always getting too close on purpose. It was lively at night, though, crossing from Harlem to midtown and then to 14th Street and below. Theatergoers, club kids, everyone rode the train. Sam was sitting on one side of Alice, and Tommy on the other. They could have been going anywhere—to the movies, to a party, to Madison Square Garden. Alice leaned her head against Sam's, and then against Tommy's. She closed her eyes and thought about falling asleep, just for a few minutes, but then she thought about waking up without talking to her father and she sat up straight.

"You were right, Sam. As usual," Alice said. "I should have just canceled the party. I shouldn't even have let him go. Like, what actually matters?"

"I'm always right," Sam said.

• • •

The hotel was enormous—nearly a whole city block, just north of Times Square, with a driveway cut through down the middle for taxis, and three revolving doors for everyone going in and out. On the train, Alice had tried to warn Sam and Tommy about what they were about to see, but their jaws dropped anyway.

Science fiction and fantasy conventions had guest speakers like Leonard, and Barry, and other famous writers and actors and movie directors and animators, but that's not who the conventions were for—conventions were for the fans. Conventions were for the most devoted, the most faithful—the people who spent their days and nights on message boards, arguing with each other over whether Han Solo shot first or which Doctor Who was the best, adults who had closets full of elaborate costumes and friends whom they'd met at other hotels in other years. Fans for whom normal life was insufficient. Tommy slowed to a complete stop.

Darth Vader was standing outside, smoking through a small hole in his mask. A woman with blond extensions and a glorified **Playboy** bunny costume with a giant fake gun strapped to her thigh joined him.

"Is she supposed to be, like, Army Barbie?" Sam asked.

"That's Barb Wire," Tommy said. "You know, Pamela Anderson?"

"That was fast," Alice said.

"Sorry," he said, blushing. "I liked **Baywatch**."

"Come on," Alice said, leading both Tommy and Sam by the hands through one of the main non-revolving doors. There were clumps of costumed people in the lobby, hordes of people moving around the space. Young people, old people, people of every color. Fandom knew no bounds. There were enormous vinyl signs hanging from every available surface, pointing one direction or another, to one ballroom or another. It was more nerds than Alice had seen in her entire life, all in one place, and all so, so happy to be arguing with each other about minute details that no one else in their lives took seriously.

Leonard always said that he hated conventions, and Alice believed that he hated his usual part, which was sitting at a folding table with a cheap tablecloth and signing autograph after autograph after autograph. Every third person who approached would ask a complicated question about **Time Brothers** television lore, to which Leonard would respond, "I didn't write the TV show, and

I think that's a very good question." He had written some episodes, though, which they knew, and so then he might reluctantly answer their original question, even though it pained him. Every tenth person would ask a question about the novel, and Leonard would answer those more cheerfully. Often people would take photos. He was paid to attend, and deep down, he enjoyed it, too, and would have gone anyway, just to see his friends who had flown in from out of town.

The hotel bar was the epicenter, especially after the official programming had finished for the day.

"I feel like I'm actually **in** the Mos Eisley Cantina," Tommy said. "Only I never thought it would be really over-air-conditioned."

"How nerdy are you, actually?" Sam asked, with a note of appreciation in her voice.

"Here," Alice said. Two handsome men—brutally handsome for the science fiction crowd, which meant that in the regular world, they were slightly above average—held court, both in leather jackets. One, who was white haired with a trim white beard, saw Alice and slapped a hand dramatically over his stout chest. The people assembled before him turned to look.

"Alice, darling," the man said. He was Gordon Hampshire, the Australian author of many, many books about elves and fairies who had a lot of sex. He was sixty and round of tummy, but still, if one looked through a certain science fiction convention filter, bore a passing resemblance to an older, hirsute Tom Cruise. Alice knew from her father that Gordon had slept with every woman he knew, actual scores of women—his friends, his fans, his friends' wives, other writers, countless hotel employees and cocktail waitresses. He was incapable of speaking to women without flirting.

"Hi, Gordon," Alice said, letting him pull her in for a hug.

"This is Alice Stern, daughter of Leonard Stern, the author of the incomparable and life-altering **Time Brothers**!" Gordon announced. The assembled crowd oohed, as cued.

The younger man in the leather jacket, who had been Gordon's performative conversation partner, nodded. "I love your dad. I'm Guillermo Montaldan, I wrote—"

"The Foxhole!" Tommy said from behind her. "I love that book, man! The part where the Fox—he's not really a fox, he's, like, a space thief—breaks into the soul vault and all the souls escape and he's surrounded, I love that! So fucking sick, man!"

Guillermo placed a hand on his heart and bowed slightly. "Muchas gracias."

"Gordon, have you seen my dad? Is he in his room?" Alice checked around the bar. She saw a few other writers she recognized, and Princess Leia, and a man with a glued-on push-broom mustache talking to Barry Ford, who scowled at the imposter from beneath his own real one.

"Yes, I believe he is," Gordon said. "You want me to take you up? Lot of escalators and elevator banks in this place, it's a maze."

The surrounding crowd looked apoplectic. "No," Alice said. Tommy was deep in conversation with Guillermo, and Sam waved her on. "Go ahead, Al, we'll be down here if you need us."

33

GORDON WAS RIGHT—THE HOTEL WAS A
mess, designed by a sadist. In order to get to the
top floors, you had to switch elevators and follow
signs, and Alice got lost a few times, only to have
Captain Kirk and Sailor Moon show her where to
go. She walked down a long carpeted hallway until
she found the right door, and knocked.

Simon Rush answered the door. He was sweaty,
and his white button-down shirt had spots of something on it—mustard? Mountain Dew?—and the
top few buttons were undone, letting out a small
patch of gray chest hair.

"Alice!" Simon said. He turned back to face the
room. "Everyone, Alice is here!" There was a small
cheer, and Alice stuck her head in. Howard Epstein

was inside, Leonard's favorite (and only) academic friend, who taught courses on science fiction; there was Chip Easton, a screenwriter; and John Wolfe, a Black actor who almost always played aliens. Howard stood beside the bed, his hands tucked behind his back; John sat on the bed, leaning against the headboard like someone reading before they turned out the lights, and Chip sat on the lone chair in the room.

"Is my dad here?" Alice asked. "Is this his room?"

"Oh, he'll be back, he was just—talking to someone, I think. Come in, come in," Simon said, stumbling a bit over his own feet. He was clearly drunk.

"Okay," Alice said, and stepped all the way into the room. It overlooked 45th Street, and down on the sidewalk, Alice could see people pouring out of the theaters—Minskoff, Schoenfeld, Booth. It was Saturday night in the world, and people were out in full force. Alice never went to plays. She never went to Times Square. She hardly ever went to see live music anymore, and she hadn't been to Madison Square Garden since she was twelve. Alice rode the subway. She went to Belvedere, and her four favorite bars and restaurants, and sometimes she took the train out to Jersey to visit Sam. Where were all these people going, with their young hearts? When she was a teenager, the 1980s had felt far away, a lifetime ago, but now, when she was so many more decades ahead, 1996 still felt recent. The first twenty years of her life had gone by in slow motion—the endless summers, the space from birthday to birthday almost immeasurable—but the second twenty years had gone by in a flash. Days could still be slow, of course, but weeks and months and sometimes even years zipped along, like a rope slipping through your hands.

"Alice, to what do we owe the pleasure?" asked Howard.

"Well," Alice said, considering how to answer the question honestly. "I guess I was just thinking about, you know, **Time Brothers,** time travel. That kind of thing. Understanding the family business, you could say."

"Alice, I love that you're finally interested!" Howard said. He and Leonard had met decades ago, when the former had interviewed the latter for **Science Fiction** magazine. Howard lived in Boston and had four cats, each of whom was named after a Japanese monster.

"Nepotism," Simon coughed into his hand, winking. Both of his adult sons worked at the publishing company that put out his books, and eventually, after Simon died, one of them would keep writing books and publishing them under Simon's name.

"I just want to understand the various theories, I guess. About how it works. How time travel works," Alice said. She tucked her chin between her knees.

"Well, you've got time loops, time circuits, stubs, multiverses, string theory . . ." Howard said.

"You've got wormholes, slow time travel, fast time travel, time machines . . ." Simon said.

"Did you ever read **A Wrinkle in Time,** Al? Tesseracts?" Howard said. "Basically, a scrunched-up place in the universe where space and time are sort of folded, and you can get through."

"Or like **Back to the Future,**" Chip said. "He had a time machine and just needed certain fuel, and to go eighty-eight miles per hour, and then he was in business."

"I was in **Back to the Future,**" John said. "I had one line."

"Oh, yes," Howard said. "'Wow, man!' Or something, wasn't it? I've always been partial to the Jack Finney model; that's where this guy gets drafted into this special time travel program, but all he actually needs is to be in a period-precise apartment in the Dakota, and then he sort of feels it change, and then he's there, a hundred years ago."

"What are the circuits?" Alice said. "Loops? Stubs?"

"Have you heard of the grandfather paradox?" Chip asked. "Sometimes people call it the Baby Hitler problem. You go back in time, you kill Baby Hitler—does that prevent the Holocaust? Or if you push your grandfather off a bridge, then your parents aren't born, then you aren't born; what happens to you, you know?"

"Shit," Alice said. "Okay."

"Basically, in some time travel, there's a loop in which things can change, and what you do affects everyone else: i.e., you kill Baby Hitler and then Hitler doesn't exist, and that could affect a million other things and change history entirely. Or there's a loop where nothing changes except the fact that you've done it before, like **Groundhog Day**." Alice hadn't considered the possibility that she would wake up the next morning and have to do the whole thing again. What was worse than turning sixteen once? Turning sixteen a hundred times in a row. Turning sixteen forever. She wondered what would happen to the part of her brain that was forty, if it would eventually fade to black, a room with no electricity.

"And then you're getting into the idea of the multiverse—if you go back in time and change something, are you changing the future, period? Or are you just changing one possible future, and the other future—the future you left—still exists?" Howard said.

"This is giving me a headache," Alice said.

"You know what time travel movie I always liked?" said John. "The one where Superman had to go back in time to save Lois Lane, and he just had to fly extra fast. Simple, effective."

"I like the ones where the person has no say and is just yanked back and forth, like **Kindred**," said Simon. He took out a cigarette and lit it, and then one by one, so did all the other men in the room. "My readers wouldn't go for it, but a lot of people would."

"The Time Brothers had a machine. You had one—maybe two?—with time travel, Simon?" Chip said. "The one with the paleontologist who goes back to the Triassic, what did he have? A magic bone?" He stifled a laugh.

"Yes, it was a magic bone, fuck you very much," Simon said. "That magic bone bought me a house in East Hampton."

"How nice for you and your bone," Chip said.

"What's it called when someone uses information from the future to influence the past? Like Biff and the almanac?" Alice asked.

"Well, that's just good thinking," Simon said, smiling.

"Right, so if I was, like, from the future, and I came back to tell you that at some year in the next ten years, the Red Sox will win the World Series, and then you all made a bazillion dollars by betting on the Red Sox, that's just good news, because it doesn't hurt anybody?" Alice asked. Everyone groaned, except Howard, the lone Bostonian. He cheered and pumped both fists in the air.

"Well, define **hurt**," Simon said. "I personally bleed Yankee blue, so it would hurt me. But sure, I see what you mean."

"Is this what you guys do at these things? You sit around and talk about books and movies and just make fun of each other?" Alice asked.

"Sometimes people bring margarita machines," Chip said. "Or drugs." Howard elbowed him. "She's sixteen! Come on! Alice, do you really walk through a crowd of grown-up people in costumes and think to yourself, 'I bet all these people are dead sober'?"

"No," Alice said. "I don't. But so how does a stub work? What's a stub?"

"Like a parallel timeline, one that doesn't affect the future that already happened. Sometimes people call it a continuum, or a continuing timeline, which I guess just means it can go on and on and not loop back in." Howard crossed his arms. "I think I've read more books than all of you."

"Oh, please," Chip said. "You're just the one who's used to lecturing large groups of students, and so you talk the loudest."

"But what about traveling back? Like, how do people get back? If there's no time machine or whatever?" John handed Alice an apple, and she ate it, wondering if everything she was eating in 1996 would be rotten inside her body when she got home. If she got home. As if **home** were a particular point in time as well as a place.

"Wormhole?" Simon said.

"Portal?" John said.

"Ancient ruins? Magic?" Simon said. "In addition to the dinosaur bone, once I used an owl pellet that had been taken apart in the future, and a third-grade teacher got sucked back in time, and he had to find that very same owl in order to get back."

"I cannot believe how much money you make," Howard said, shaking his head.

"Do you guys know where my dad is? I actually need to talk to him," Alice said. She felt her voice start to wobble. It was all too much, and she was wasting time.

Howard sighed and looked toward John, who tucked his chin toward his chest in a tight nod. "Come on, Al. I know where he is."

34

HOWARD LED ALICE DOWN THE HALLWAY,
past the elevators, and made a left turn. They were
standing in front of another hotel room.

"Is this where you murder me?" Alice joked. "Because there are a lot of witnesses."

Howard rolled his eyes and raised his knuckles to
knock. Inside the room, she heard a woman laugh, and
then her father pulled open the door. Leonard wasn't
naked—he wasn't even shirtless—but there was no
mistaking the situation. Over his shoulder, Alice
could see a woman putting on her earrings. Alice's
first thought was that it was exactly like when
Donna Martin had been following Color Me Badd
and instead found her mother in the midst of an
affair on **Beverly Hills, 90210,** but that wasn't

exactly like this at all. Her father wasn't married. Not to her mother, not to anyone.

"Look who I found," Howard said. "Good to see you, Al." He offered a small wave and got the hell out of the way, hurrying back down the hall.

"Hi," Alice said. Leonard was surprised, and ran his hands back and forth over his beard like he did when he was nervous.

"Al-pal, what's going on?" Leonard said. "Are you okay?"

Alice took a few steps back and leaned against the wall. "Who's your friend?"

Leonard sighed. "I did not anticipate this situation," he said.

"That is not an answer." Alice slid down the wall so that she was sitting cross-legged on the carpet.

"Her name is Laura, she's a magazine editor. She's thirty-four. She lives in San Francisco." Leonard put a hand flat against his forehead. "We've known each other for several years, and when we're in the same city, we—" He stopped. "I don't know why I didn't tell you."

"I can hear you, you know," Laura said, pulling the door open wider. "Hi, Alice. It's nice to finally meet you." She was nice-looking, with curly brown hair and glasses, and a necklace with a large plastic octopus that covered the top third of her shirt.

"Um, same?" Alice said. It had genuinely never occurred to her that her father might have actual girlfriends, long-term relationships that he didn't tell her about. And thirty-four! Younger than she was! It felt gross even though Alice knew it wasn't.

"Not that you weren't important, Laura," Leonard said. The tops of his cheeks were magenta. "Just that it didn't affect you, Al, and I didn't want to put something else on you. Did I make it too weird?"

"A little," Alice said. "But it's okay. I'm glad you have someone." She wondered how long Leonard had dated this woman, if it had been a brief fling or something serious. Where had she gone? Why wasn't she at the hospital, holding his hand? "Can we talk, Dad?"

Laura gathered her purse and a room key. She was about Leonard's height until she put her shoes on, and then she was a little bit taller. Her face was round and then pointy at the chin, like an exclamation mark. It was a happy face, and kind. She touched Leonard on the elbow and said, "I'll check in a bit later. Alice, very nice to see you in person. I'd like to do it again." She walked through the doorway and down the long hall and then vanished around the corner, toward the elevator.

"I'm sorry," Leonard said. He looked like he might cry. "I wanted to tell you." He clutched his stomach, as if he had a bout of sudden nausea.

"I'm from the future," Alice said. "Honestly, it's both great news and the least of my concerns."

"That is not what I expected you to say." Leonard

held up a finger. "Let me just get my shoes, and then we'll go back to my room." He vanished and re-appeared a moment later with one shoe in each hand. They walked in silence back to Leonard's room, and when they got there, the door was open, and Sam and Tommy were leaning out of it, singing off-key. Alice recognized the song—Boyz II Men's "End of the Road"—but just barely. Sam was clapping, and Tommy had stolen someone's umbrella and was using it as a cane.

"Good lord," Alice said.

"Alice!" Tommy shouted. "We lost you! But now we found you."

"Your dad's friends bought us some drinks," Sam said. "Strong ones."

"Your mother would not be amused by this, Samantha," Leonard said. "Okay, guys, I'm going to take you home."

"Wait," Alice said. She pulled Sam and Tommy into the room. "My friends, meet Leonard's friends. I just need to talk to my dad for one second. Sam, don't barf, okay? I mean, barf if you have to. Howard, can you just talk at them for a little bit?" Howard offered a small bow in acceptance of his task, and Alice pushed her friends farther into the room. She then stepped into the bathroom, flicked on the fluorescent lights, and beckoned for Leonard to join her. Alice pointed for him to shut the door behind him, and he did.

"Dad, I'm actually serious. I know it sounds like

a joke, ha ha, yes, but it's literally true. I came here from the future," Alice said. "I don't know how to say it better than that."

"I heard you the first time." Leonard folded his arms and looked amused.

"Okay, I can see that you find this funny, which I understand, but you may want to sit down." Alice turned and put her hands on the edge of the sink. Her dad's Dopp kit, with his toothbrush and toothpaste and floss and god knew what, was sitting there. Everything was so familiar—all the stupid little objects that she'd seen every day of her childhood, they were all still here. Alice knew that familiarity wasn't the same as meaning, but she couldn't help it—everything she saw felt enormous and loaded and heavy. These were her father's things, the same things that were in the hospital. What would happen to them when Leonard was gone?

Leonard pushed the shower curtain aside and sat down on the edge of the bathtub. He snapped his fingers. "Ready."

"Yesterday was my fortieth birthday. When I woke up this morning, I was sixteen."

Leonard let out a loud laugh. "Boy, are you in the right place!"

"Har, har, har," Alice said, her mouth a flat line. "Dad, I am not joking. I am not a weird dork like you and your friends, no offense. I am **serious.** This is actually happening."

Leonard looked at her and said, **"Wow, wow,**

wow," over and over again. His face made no
sense—Leonard was smiling like Alice had just
told him the best news in the world. It was the
kind of look that Alice assumed parents gave when
you told them you were getting married, or having
a baby—delighted surprise mingled with a note of
their own mortality. Alice didn't know if he actually believed her or thought that she was pranking
him for some reason, but either way, Leonard just
seemed **happy.**

Leonard crossed and uncrossed his legs. "I won't
ask how I'm doing. I'll just assume that you live
with me on Pomander Walk forever, and that we're
both aging beautifully."

Alice swallowed. "You guessed it."

"Okay," Leonard said. "Okay. Let's get your
friends home, and then we can talk." He stood up,
and so did his reflection in the bathroom mirror.
Alice stared at him, trying to understand. Maybe
he needed hearing aids already—those would come
later. Maybe he hadn't heard a word she'd said.
Someone knocked on the door, and Sam pushed it
open before they responded.

"I think I'm going to throw up," she said, and
Leonard quickly moved out of the way. Alice
watched him slip back into the hotel room, and
then lifted the toilet lid and reached for Sam's hair.

35

UNLIKE ALICE'S FRIENDS, WHO KISSED ON the way in and out and sometimes in the middle just for fun, Leonard's friends just waved and moved along, as if they'd all been sitting on a bus.

"Thanks, guys," Alice said. John would get a good part, one where he actually showed his face, and he'd win big awards, and everyone would say he'd been a hidden gem all the while. Leonard would go with him to the Golden Globes and cry when they said his name. Her father had had good friends. But they were also men, and men weren't trained to be in charge of their own friendships. Howard had called the hospital, and Chip, but she hadn't seen or heard from the others in years. People were allowed to out-grow relationships, of course, Alice knew that, but

still—there were times when you were supposed to
show the fuck up.

"The people here are really weird, Leonard," Sam
said. She was still a little bit wobbly, and leaned
against one wall of the hotel while Leonard hailed
a cab.

"The people here are **awesome,**" Tommy said.
He walked up to Alice and kissed her on the cheek.
"I love it."

"Okay, party's over," Leonard said, and shoved
all three of them into the back seat of a taxi, then
opened the passenger door for himself.

The radio was on, blasting WCBS-FM, 101.1, the
oldies station. The taxi turned up Sixth Avenue and
cruised past Radio City Music Hall. Alice closed
her eyes again and just listened. Sam was snor-
ing a little bit on one side of her, and on the other
Tommy was drumming his fingers on her thigh to
the beat of "Bernadette." He lived the closest—the
San Remo was on Central Park West and 74th—
and Leonard directed the taxi there first. All the
lights were yellow for two blocks, then three blocks,
then six blocks in a row, just catching them all.

The cab started to slow down half a block from
Tommy's building, and Alice leaned over. "This is
going to sound crazy," she said. "But marry me.
Not now. Not even close to now. Just eventually.
After college. Promise me. Okay?" Her voice was
low enough and the music loud enough that no one
else in the car could hear her. She didn't even know

if Tommy could hear her. She didn't even know what she was trying to accomplish—more of this, more of sitting together in the back of a taxi, with her healthy dad talking to a cabdriver about how he'd once given Diana Ross a ride. Alice just wanted to push her hands against the walls of her life and see if they would move. She wanted to hit the reset button over and over again until everyone was happy, forever. Tommy looked at her, his brown eyes sleepy, and said, "Okay," like he was agreeing to apple juice instead of orange juice at the diner, and then he got out of the car and waved. Alice watched as his uniformed doorman, gold buttons shining, pushed open the heavy door and then stood to the side to let Tommy walk in.

Sam shoved Alice all the way over in the back seat and then lay down in her lap. "When you go back, I still get to keep you, right? Like, you'll still be here? Will you remember all this?"

"I don't know," Alice said, and put her arm across Sam's body like a seat belt. They were quiet for the rest of the ride up to 121st Street, where Alice helped Sam get into her building and apartment while Leonard kept the driver company down below. Sam's apartment was quiet and dark—Lorraine would have been asleep for hours. The clock in Sam's room said it was 1:30 a.m. Alice pulled back Sam's covers and tucked her in.

"I love being your friend," Alice said. "It's okay that you move to New Jersey."

"Oh my god, stop it, get out of here," Sam said. "I love you."

Alice slipped out the door like a burglar and ran down the wide stone steps to the waiting cab. Her father was still in the front seat, now deep in conversation about something. It took Alice a minute, then she got it—the driver was talking about **Time Brothers.** Leonard smiled at her through the partition and rolled down his window, letting the cool air in as they drove back down to Pomander Walk.

• • •

Leonard unlocked the gate and pushed it open for Alice. The Romans' lights were still on, but the rest of the street was mostly dark, with just one lit window on the second floor here and there—front bedrooms. Alice imagined all their neighbors in their beds, books open or televisions on. She felt like she always had on certain summer nights, like she was already missing the moment that she was still living inside.

"Okay," he said. "Now we can really talk." Leonard jogged quickly toward the door, keys jangling in his hands. "We don't have much time."

"Time for what?" Alice said. She remembered the mess her father was about to see. "Oh, shit. I forgot to tell you. I had a party. It wasn't that big, not as big as it was last time, but—" Leonard opened the door before she could even finish her sentence. The kitchen was a disaster—someone had spilled a beer, and Alice's and Leonard's shoes made sticky thwacking sounds as they crossed the floor—but Leonard didn't even seem to notice. He went straight to his regular seat, pushed aside all the empty bottles in front of him to clear a space, lit two cigarettes in his mouth, and then held one out for Alice.

"Sit," he said.

Alice sat. She took a drag of the cigarette and flicked it nervously between her fingers.

"I believe you."

"Really? At the hotel, before I found you, I was talking to your friends about time travel stuff and, it all made it sound ridiculous. Like, a magic bone? What does that even mean? There is no science that supports this." Alice looked at the yellow spots on her finger, slick little nicotine patches. What if she had exercised, ever? What if she didn't drink forty ounces of beer all in one sitting? What if she had paid attention in math class? What if she had actually enjoyed her father as much as she could, every day? What if Leonard had exercised, or learned to cook, or quit smoking? What if she could fix everything that ever went wrong and he would live until he was ninety-six and then die in his sleep? All she wanted was for everything to change, all the bad stuff.

Leonard raised his eyebrows and took a long drag. He puffed out three perfect smoke rings in a row, and then stuck his finger through them. "Simon's magic bone is ridiculous, of course. Even he knows that. But what you're saying is not ridiculous, and I know it. Because I've done it, too."

"What?" Ursula leaped onto the table, nimbly avoiding all the detritus, and then hopped onto Leonard's shoulders.

"People say things," he went on. "There was gossip on time travel message boards, which are about as unhinged as you'd expect, but I spent a lot of time talking to people and reading crazy theories before I wrote the book. There were a few threads about Pomander, totally unsubstantiated, you know, like people who claim to have a friend who had a friend who had a cousin who had seen Bigfoot, but still. I'd heard of it, and I mean, obviously it was appealing regardless. But people talk about it—time travel—about the real possibilities. The realities, even. And there was a place for sale at the right time, and we moved in, and even after that, it took a while to figure it out." He paused and laughed. "'Figure it out.' There's no figuring it out. I see it sort of like surfing—you just have to go where you go. Not at all like Scott and Jeff, with their clunky station wagon and all the buttons and knobs and thin places. If I'd actually done it before writing the book, gone back, **Time Brothers** would have been different. You can't drive it. You can't choose where you go. Everyone has one destination, one route, that's it. And when you come back, it's always right back to where you started, like a ride at

Disney World. But the exit looks different, depending on what you did. It's like, every time, you make the ride. You decide if it goes fast or slow, if there are big drops or it's just a lazy river, floating along. So you can take it real easy, and come out, and everything looks just like it did when you went in."

"The ride," Alice said.

"Yes," Leonard said. "It's a metaphor."

"Thank you," Alice said. She took a drag. She wanted a piece of paper in front of her—a diagram, a map, something. "Okay. So it's just being here that made it happen? In our house? Like, the whole street? How can that be?"

Leonard shook his head. "Tell me what you did."

"I had dinner with Sam. Then I went to Matryoshka and got too drunk. Then I took a cab back here and I barfed on the street and then I fell asleep outside like a true degenerate, I think, and when I woke up, you were here, like this."

"You fell asleep outside?" Leonard asked.

"In the guardhouse. Your potting shed, or whatever. It was mostly empty, and so I just shoved a few things aside and passed out."

Leonard nodded. "Do you know what time it was?"

"What time I fell asleep? I don't know—maybe three a.m.? Four?" If Alice had her phone, she could check what time the Uber had dropped her off, but her memory was foggy, soaked in too many shots.

"It was between three and four a.m., because that's

the only time it works," Leonard said. He leaned back and ran a hand over his face. "It took me so long to figure it out. Years. I looked and looked. I didn't know for sure that anything was there, but I just **felt** it. And one day, ten years ago, right around the time you started at Belvedere, I was talking to Chip about **Doctor Who,** and it reminded me of our little shed, and I thought, 'That has to be it.' I was out there all night, in and around it, just sure that the Headricks or someone wouldn't be looking out their window at me, but they didn't, at least I didn't think, and I went in and emptied it out—took out everything, all the brooms and the dirt and the shovels and the crap, even the spiderwebs, and I just sat there for what felt like a really long time, and the next thing I knew, I was somewhere else. Not just not in the guardhouse anymore. I was in bed—our bed, me and your mom's—in our old apartment. And it wasn't 1986 anymore—I just knew it.

"At first, I thought it was just, you know, I've got **Time Brothers** brain, or some kind of hallucination, like maybe I was hungover or having some weird DTs, but I walked outside, and to the newsstand, and I picked up the paper, and it was 1980. I had a quarter in my pocket, and so I bought the paper, and then I looked at it again and I realized—it was your birthday."

"My birthday," Alice said. "Today. October twelfth. In 1980."

"Yes," Leonard said. He laughed, and Ursula jumped down from his shoulders onto his lap. "It was the day you were born. Your mom wasn't due for another three weeks. We were still living on Eighty-Sixth then, in that long, skinny apartment, and she was so miserable, she would just pace up and down, up and down, and when I got up and saw her body, like a snake that had swallowed a watermelon, I couldn't believe it. Serena looked so beautiful, even though she was uncomfortable, and huge, and angry—and I knew what she didn't, that you were going to worm your way out that afternoon. Three seventeen p.m." Leonard blinked and blinked, but the tears came anyway. "Do you know how many times I've been in that room? Watched it happen? Watched you come into this world, your perfect little face? I don't know why, but that's my time. That's what I get to see."

Alice could picture the long hallway, and her mother, large and angry. "That sounds bloody and stressful."

"It is. Serena's labor was tough, it was tough. But I know how it ends, and that makes it much easier."

"Did you ever tell her?" Alice asked.

"Who, your mom? No." Leonard shook his head. "I tried a few times, to make it work, you know? Each time I went back I tried to be a better husband, whatever that means, or to be more the way she wanted me to be. I paid attention to every word she said, I rubbed her back, I fed her ice chips. I did most of those things the first time, I think. I hope. I really tried, in that one crazy day, to show Serena that we could be great. Once, when I got back, we were still married, but she was even more miserable than she was before. Angrier. Because I'd been trying to be someone I wasn't, which is a shitty thing to do in a marriage."

"Whoa," Alice said.

"You'll see," Leonard said. He smiled. "The good news is that life is pretty sticky. It's hard to change things too much. What my friends were saying is true, but it's all theoretical." He lowered his voice, as if anyone else could hear. "They're professional amateurs."

"What's happening there now?" Alice had wondered—was her forty-year-old body slumped, motionless, inside the shed, scaring all the Pomander residents going about their day? "Your friends scared me with all their Baby Hitler talk."

"Nothing," Leonard said. "A pause. You go right back. Thirty seconds, maybe? A minute? It can't be more than a minute that goes by. The planets are moving, we're moving, so I'm sure it's not exact, but give or take. You'll find yourself where you are. It's not the exact same forty you're going back to—but it's you, at forty. Doing whatever it is **this day** has gotten you. You see what I mean about it being sticky? It's a day—you wake up in the morning, and between three and four a.m., bingo bango, you're back to when you left. That's all the time you get. Most of the decisions we make as people are pretty stable, and time **likes** stability. I think about it like a car on a track. The car wants to stay on, and so it does, most of the time. I can imagine what Howard and Simon would say—Baby Hitler. What's different? What did you do, what did you set in motion? Sure, that stuff's important. But it's gotta be something big in order to knock you far off the track. Don't worry about it too much." Leonard walked a hand one direction on the table, and then walked it the other.

Alice looked at the clock. It was three. All the lights on Pomander were out except for theirs. "Just give me a minute," she said. She stubbed out the cigarette inside a bottle cap and hurried into her room. Alice looked around, searching for something solid to hold on to. She felt like she was on line for an upside-down roller coaster, a roller coaster she was going to fall out of, and there was nothing she could do to stop it. No change of clothes would help.

Leonard leaned against her doorframe. "Sweetie," he said.

Alice looked at him and knew that she hadn't done it—whatever he was talking about, pushing the car off the track, she hadn't done it. "Dad," she started, but he lifted a palm to stop her.

"It's going to feel a little strange at first," he said. Leonard walked her through it—the fuzziness that would follow. She would remember her life, the life before, but not vividly. Memories were memories, after all, and faded over time, especially without prompts like photographs. Over years, things smoothed out. At least he thought so. Of course, Leonard explained, he couldn't say for sure. He was calm, but Alice was starting to panic.

"But I just got here," Alice said. "It's not fair." She wanted to tell him that it wasn't fair because she hadn't figured out how to make sure that when she got back, or forward, or ahead, whatever the right word was, he would be waiting for her, eyes open.

Leonard nodded. "It's never enough time. I know. But remember—you know how to get here. Do you know how many times I've watched you be born? You can come back."

"And you'll just be here? And we can just do this? So, what do I do?" Alice shook out her hands and feet, a one-girl hokey pokey. "What am I supposed to do?"

"It's late," Leonard said. "I would just go to bed. Or we can sit on the couch."

Alice walked past her dad and down the dark hallway. Ursula rubbed her body against her, and Alice swooped down to pick her up. She lay down on the sofa and Ursula did, too, curling perfectly into her armpit.

Leonard covered her with a blanket and clicked on the television, though Alice knew he was watching her instead. She closed her eyes and tried to breathe normally, but she could only picture shriveled smoker lungs, black like the commercials that were supposed to scare her away but hadn't.

"Will you do one thing for me?" Alice asked.

"Sure, what?" Leonard said.

"Will you quit smoking? Like, for real this time?" Leonard had tried before—he'd tried once a decade since he'd been a teenager himself.

Leonard snorted. "Fine. I'll try, okay? You're catching me in a weak moment here, and so I'll promise to try." He paused. "Al—" Leonard said, half to himself. "Why was it empty in the guardhouse? I'm so careful. How was it just, cleared out? Where was I?"

Alice didn't want to lie to him, but she also couldn't tell him the truth. She hadn't thought much about the hospital, not as much as she usually did. It felt as far away as it was—decades, eons. If they were a hugging family, she would have hugged him, just to make sure she got one in. Why weren't they a hugging family? Was it her? Was it him? Alice couldn't remember. Leonard was close, and talking. That was all that mattered. "I took it out. It was piled up, like normal. Took me forever," she murmured into the arm of the sofa, and then she was gone.

PART THREE

36

ALICE HADN'T FALLEN ASLEEP, OR AT least she didn't think she had, but there was the slightly underwater feeling of awakening from a dream. She stretched her arms over her head, clonking them on something hard. Alice let her hands feel around a little bit—hard, shiny, with bumps, definitely not her father's ancient sofa—before she opened her eyes.

Once her eyes adjusted to the dark room, Alice could see that she was in bed—a huge bed, whatever size came after king. Alice wiggled her toes to make sure that she could, and sure enough, there they were, poking up against the heavy duvet. It looked like an expensive room at a hotel she couldn't afford. A silver lamp with a geometric shade was next to her face, and Alice clicked on the light. The other half of the bed was empty, with the cover thrown back carelessly, as if someone had just climbed out. The walls were cream, the sheets were cream, and the floors were wood, with details laid in a hundred years earlier. Alice knew two things for certain: she'd never been in this room before, and also, at the same time, it was without a doubt her bedroom. It was like Leonard had told her: **You're going to wake up in your bed, wherever your bed is. You're going to be inside your life, just like you're inside your life right now. And there will be a lot of things that you missed. But you'll feel those things, too, eventually.**

•   •   •

She shimmied herself up so that she was propped against the headboard and then leaned over to inspect her drawer. There was her phone, all plugged in, and some earplugs, and a pen, and an eye mask. There was a small stack of books on the floor underneath the table, which calmed Alice down—she was still her, no matter how nice the apartment looked. She remembered what Leonard had said about the tracks, and that calmed her down, too, the idea that even if things looked different, she wasn't, not really. Alice unplugged her phone and held it in front of her face. 5:45 a.m.—she'd slept through the shift. The password was the same—all her passwords were the same, her birthday and

Keanu Reeves's birthday; she'd set it when she was fourteen and had never seen a reason to change it. No wonder it was so easy to steal identities. Only now, instead of the resplendent photograph of Ursula that Alice was used to seeing, there were two smiling, dark-haired children.

They appeared to be a boy and a girl, but Alice couldn't say for sure. Both kids had dark brown eyebrows slashed across their pale foreheads. The smaller one was sitting on the bigger one's lap, like a pair of nesting dolls. The big one had their mouth open wide, and the little one looked nicely chunky. They were, Alice knew, her children. And judging from their coloring and mouths and eyes and how much they both looked like little Raphael Joffey, who had walked into her office that week or never, depending, Alice knew who slept on the other side of the bed.

Alice pulled back the covers and lowered her feet to the floor. The rug under the bed was enormous and probably cost more than three months' rent on Cheever Place. She was in striped pajama bottoms and a Belvedere Fun Run T-shirt that she recognized as being a few years old. Alice pressed it against her body, a soft cotton security blanket. Okay, she thought. Okay. Alice gripped her phone and tiptoed toward the door. She had her hand on the knob when the toilet flushed and a door on the adjoining wall swung open. Alice instinctively curled her body up, as if she were a pangolin or a roly-poly bug, but she remained both human and visible.

"What are you doing?" Tommy was wearing a slim-fitting exercise outfit, with the sweat stains and damp hair to match. He looked much the same as he had in her office, but with a tighter haircut, and an even slimmer face. It had worked—something had worked. Alice thought about Tommy's head on her shoulder in the taxicab, and whispering in his ear. Maybe that was the key—telling people exactly what you wanted, the actual truth, and then getting out of the way.

"Nothing," Alice said. She straightened up. "We live here. You and me."

"That's right. See also: sky is blue, grass is green. Any other shocking revelations?"

"We live here all the time," Alice said.

"Well, not **all the time,**" Tommy said, rolling his eyes. "Can you imagine? How embarrassing!" He was making a joke, but the joke made Alice feel ill. "Is this a weird way of telling me that you want to buy another fucking house? Zillow is not your friend, Alice. Just put the phone down in the middle of the night. One country house is plenty." As Tommy talked, Alice could picture it—a white house behind a hedge, a gravel driveway. Someone else cutting the grass. "Plus my parents'. And they're having the pool redone this year; the kids will love it."

Alice had overheard sentences like these a thousand times. The way she had survived life at Belvedere was by channeling her envy into superiority. Two-thirds of the student body would have described themselves as middle class, a category that Alice did not think usually included access to privately chartered airplanes and houses on Caribbean islands, cottages on Long Island, or full-time help in the home. Leonard had told her, flat out, that he made more money than most of his friends but they had less money than most of her friends, because his money was their only pot, so to speak, and most of the kids at Belvedere were sitting on several generations' worth of booty. New Yorkers were experts at flipping their everyday struggles (carrying heavy bags of groceries, taking the subway instead of driving a car) into value points, and Alice had years of experience making herself feel better because she didn't have a family compound in Greenwich or a horse or a Range Rover. Now that she seemed to have all these things, in addition to a sweaty Tommy Joffey in their shared bedroom, Alice didn't know quite what to do. This was how all the time travel movies she'd ever seen ended—in **13 Going On 30,** Jenna Rink came out of the house in a wedding dress. Bill and Ted passed their history class. Marty McFly got a Jeep. Then the camera slid backward, revealing the whole, perfect scene, and faded to black. In **Time Brothers,** in between rescues, Scott and Jeff went to their favorite

pizzeria. No one was ever standing in their pajamas, trying to remember their life.

The bedroom door swung open, whacking Alice's
right side.

"Mommmmmmy!!!" A small body was attached
to her shins. It felt like being attacked by a friendly
octopus—there couldn't be only two arms. Alice
thought she might fall over, but she didn't, brac-
ing herself against the wall. The child was clamped
on tight. Alice set one hand lightly on the top of
its head. Was this the boy or the girl in the photo?
Alice knelt down to get a better look.

"Hello there," Alice said. It was a boy—not the
boy she had interviewed at Belvedere, but close. His
eyes were the same—Tommy's, on a smaller face—
and the thick, beautiful hair. Alice looked for herself in the child's face but could not find herself
anywhere. It felt like complimenting someone on
their resemblance to their child only to have them
say, **Well, you know, they're adopted.** "What's
your name, again? Firetruck, is it? Xylophone?
Remind me, will you?"

The boy giggled. "Mommy, it's **me,** it's **Leo.**" He
burrowed himself into the tiny shelf of Alice's lap,
knocking her gently to the ground. Despite having
apparently given birth to two humans, Alice's body
felt tight and strong, stronger than it ever had before. She wondered how much money she'd spent
on personal trainers, but decided it was better not
to know.

"Oh, yes, that's right," Alice said. "Leo. And what about your sister? Umbrella? Zimbabwe?" She could feel the name rolling around in her head—Alice could almost see the letters swimming into place, like alphabet soup. These children were hers, no doubt about it. Hers, and Tommy's. Alice was a mom. **Mommy? Mama?** Her own mother had eventually decided that she preferred being called by her first name, because there was only one real mother—Gaia, Mother Earth. Alice felt the skin around her neck go blotchy with panic.

Leo giggled again, his soft, damp hands now pressing against Alice's cheeks. "Poopyface," he said. The boy was so lovely to look at, like a little Italian putto, and Alice liked the way his hands felt on her skin. She put her own hands over his. Alice didn't know if she could talk to Tommy, but she could talk to Leo. This was what she was good at—crouching low, feeling the warm breath of a small person. Leo was probably four. No—he was definitely four. Alice knew. It was the same feeling as waking up in a hotel room and not remembering where exactly you were, or where the bathroom was.

"No, no, it's not Poopyface," Alice said. Leo scrambled off her and ran down the hall, screaming **"Poopyface"** over and over again.

Tommy peeled off his shirt and then balled it up and tossed it into a hamper. The shorts and boxer briefs were next. It was nice to see him in an adult body again, but Alice looked away. It was too intimate, too naked. Standing nude in the lamp-light, inelegantly bending over to pull off one's underpants—there wasn't anything more naked than that. Sex required closeness, and therefore a limited view. Here, from across the room, Alice could see everything. She shut her eyes and pre-tended to have something stuck in her eyelashes.

"Are you still going to go for a run?" Tommy asked. Alice heard him go back into the bathroom, and then the sound of the water in the shower.

"Yes," Alice said. She was desperate to get out of the room, the apartment—she wanted to go back to Pomander. She wanted to call her dad. "Can we, uh, just talk about the plan for the day? I'm feeling a little, I don't know, foggy."

"You know, I thought I could avoid this problem, marrying a younger woman. I didn't think the de-mentia was supposed to start quite this early." His voice bounced off the tiled walls.

"Come on," Alice said. Tommy's birthday was only a week after hers. She would always remember it, so close to her own, hovering there on the calen-dar as if it were written in invisible ink that only she could see. Was this how they talked to each other? Alice felt like she was still in teenager mode, unable to say how she really felt about anything, capable of only sarcasm and feigned irritation. She looked at the date on her phone—it was October 13. The day after her fortieth birthday. The chute had spit her out at the same time she'd gone in, only now, she had managed to knock the car at least partially off the track. Alice wanted to call her dad, but she was afraid. She wanted to call Sam, but she was afraid. Mostly she wanted to do both those things in private, because she wasn't sure how they were going to go, and Alice didn't think she was a good enough actress to play off her reactions. If her father was fine, would she know it? If he was dead, would she know that? Alice didn't know anything for sure, not yet. Tommy emerged from the shower, a towel around his waist.

"Okay, okay. Forty is the new thirty." He put his hands up in defense and leaned away from her. "I've got Leo and Dorothy for now, you'll hang with them after your run, then Sondra is coming at ten. You go visit your dad, then the party is at seven. Whatever else you want to do, up to you!" Tommy kissed her on the cheek. He was being cheerful because it was her birthday week. Somehow this was clearer to Alice than anything else.

"Dorothy," Alice said. "Got it." There was a window on the far side of the room, and Alice walked over to look out of it. Below her, Central Park stretched out like a carpet. The lake, a part of the park Alice had never paid much attention to because it seemed like it had been built for tourists, was right below. To their left, she could see one pointy tower. One tower out of two.

"The fucking San Remo," Alice said. "Where are your parents?" She should have known the answer, of course, but Tommy rolled his eyes, continuing a different conversation.

"Oh, yeah, like they'd be helping with the kids before dawn. Or, you know, ever," Tommy said. He was standing there, completely naked, carrying on a conversation. There were gray chest hairs, tight little coils like the springs that held in batteries. When he turned toward his closet, Alice noticed the slight droopiness of his butt, which felt unkind but also comforting, that she wasn't the only human alive who was aging, that even Tommy Joffey—was her name Joffey now? No, no, she would never have done that—wasn't immune. Tommy got dressed and closed the door behind him, and Alice rummaged through her drawers to find some clothes. Leonard had been right—there was a certain muscle memory in moving around the room. Alice knew which drawers to open, or at least some part of her did. She got dressed quickly and ducked out into the hallway, her phone clutched in her hand like a security blanket.

It wasn't that Alice hadn't wanted children. The timing had never been right. She'd had one abortion, with the first boyfriend she lived with, whom she had very much wanted to marry someday. He hadn't wanted a baby, or at least that's what he said until they'd broken up and he immediately had a baby with someone else. She had a list of names, though, and Dorothy had always been on it. For all of her twenties and thirties, Alice had believed that she would have children someday, until she didn't anymore. It was like balancing a bowling ball in the middle of a seesaw. There were people who were so sure, one direction or the other, and then there were people like her, who had never really decided until one day they stopped paying attention and then got knocked sideways. One of the actors from **The Odd Couple** had had a baby when he was seventy-nine years old. Men never had to decide a thing.

The apartment was enormous. The hall she'd stepped into was long and dark, lined on one side with bookshelves and on the other with framed family photographs. Leo's loud voice echoed from another room, and there was also the sound of a British pig that Alice recognized—it was important, when meeting small children, to keep up to date on their parasocial relationships with cartoon characters. Alice walked slowly, her socked feet silent on the wooden floor. Most of the photos were of the children—Leo as a Ghostbuster and his sister, Dorothy, as the Stay Puft Marshmallow Man; the two kids in the bathtub, surrounded by a mountain of bubbles—but at the center of the wall was a photo from the wedding. From Alice's wedding, to Tommy Joffey. She took a step closer, so that her nose was nearly touching the glass of the frame. In the photograph, Alice was wearing a floor-length lace dress, white, with cap sleeves and a giant bow under the bodice, a human present. Her hair was doing something she'd never seen her hair do, cascading over one shoulder like a swimsuit model's. Alice couldn't quite identify the look on her face—it was slightly more demented than joyful, flush with endorphins or terror, she wasn't sure. There were photos of Alice richly pregnant, clutching the bottom of her massive belly as if the whole thing would fall to the ground if she didn't hold it up. Alice reached down to her midsection, where the skin was soft and squishy, like rising dough.

"Mama!" a high voice called out from the next room. Alice crossed the hall and poked her head into an open doorway. The room—pink, with a canopied bed—was three times bigger than Alice's childhood bedroom on Pomander Walk. A small girl was sitting on the rug, sharing tea with a stuffed bear equal to her size, if not larger. Alice felt her body flood with a feeling that she couldn't quite identify. She wanted to wrap her arms around the little girl, to scoop her up and smoosh their bodies against each other. She wanted to do to Dorothy what Leo had done to her, hug her so hard that they both fell over.

"Hi, Dorothy," Alice said. "Can I join you?"

Dorothy nodded, solemn with the importance of her task, and poured Alice a cup of pretend tea. Alice scooted over so that she was in between the child and the bear. There was a thunderous noise, and Leo leaped into the room, crashing into Alice and hugging her from behind. Tommy followed after.

After her friends had started to get married and

have children, Alice had thought about the by-products of those decisions: an apartment filled with toys, sharing a bed with the same person forever, having someone nearby who potentially understood how to properly file taxes, breastfeeding, what exactly a placenta was and why some people ate it, what happened to love over time, if people found their own children tedious, if people hated their spouses, if she would be good at any of it. At first, it all seemed theoretical, the way teenage girls sometimes planned their future weddings, knowing that everything in their lives would be different when they actually got married but still doing it anyway, but the older Alice got, and the more of her friends actually went through with it, the more it shifted from a fun fantasy into a sad one. Marriage was clearly all about compromise, and parenthood so much about sacrifice, but like everything else that was difficult and unappealing, those conditions were much easier to stomach the sooner they were introduced.

"This tea is delicious, may I have some more?" Alice said. Dorothy nodded and took the cup back with her thick little fingers. "How old are you, you beautiful little person?"

"Poopyface is THREE!" Leo shouted, careening around the room until crashing headfirst into the gigantic stuffed bear. This made little Poopyface explode into tears. She stood up and screamed, her hands clenched into fists.

"Hoo boy," Tommy said. "Come here, baby." He scooped Dorothy up and carried her to a rocking chair in the corner, where he plucked a faded scrap of cotton attached to a pacifier. Dorothy took this object with both her hands and plugged her own mouth with immediate comfort that verged on the ecstatic. She moaned. "Go for your run," Tommy said. "I've got this." He sat in the chair and pulled a book off a nearby shelf. Leo army-crawled across the floor and set his head on top of one of Tommy's feet. Alice didn't know when she'd turned into a person who ran for fun, but she laced up a pair of sneakers by the door and went out into the world.

37

THE DOORMAN SWUNG THE FRONT DOOR
open wide, tucking his body next to a six-foot-tall
potted tree, one of two that flanked the building's
entrance. "Morning, Alice," the man said in greeting. He was small, with a round face and a barrel
chest inside his double-breasted coat. Alice felt terrible that she didn't know his name, because she
could imagine how many people who lived in this
building never bothered to use it until it was time
to write it on an envelope at Christmas.

"Morning!" she said, and hurried into the pre-
dawn air on Central Park West. Unlike Broadway
or Columbus, the busy commercial stretches of the
neighborhood, Central Park West looked exactly
as it always had. The trees leaned over the stone
walls like neighbors sharing sugar, some bending

low to shade benches below. The apartment buildings that faced the park weren't glossy monstrosities
like Alice could see poking into the skyline in midtown. These buildings were limestone and brick,
elegant and sturdy. It could have been any year in
the last five decades. There were flower boxes in front
of the most expensive buildings, and doormen standing sentry by the grand doorways, ready to hail
taxis or help carry groceries. Alice slid her phone
out of her pocket and pressed her father's name.
What had Tommy said? Go visit her dad? Go see
her dad? Had he mentioned a hospital? Alice was
almost positive that he hadn't.

The phone rang and rang and then Leonard's
outgoing voicemail message began to play. Alice
hadn't heard it in so long—in the weeks before her
birthday, she'd had no reason to call—if Leonard
couldn't answer the phone, which was, after all,
just a pocket-sized hunk of metal and plastic, why
would she call? He said to leave a message, and that
he'd call back as soon as possible. Maybe he was
in the shower. Maybe he was having breakfast at
City Diner and had left his phone at home—Alice
had long envied that about her father, that he re-
tained a certain twentieth-century attitude about
telephones, that they mostly stayed at home, and he
could easily go hours without touching his, whereas
Alice could hardly go ten minutes. Alice hung up
instead of leaving a message, then changed her
mind, called back, and after the beep, said, "Hi,

Dad. It's Alice. Just want to hear your voice." She was across the street from the Museum of Natural History, and part of her thought that if she went inside, straight under the whale, she would somehow be able to see herself and her dad lying there. Alice broke into a jog.

A few blocks north, Alice approached the Belvedere corner. She peeked down the street and was relieved to see it empty—no ghosts of Alice past or Alice present. She jogged faster, past ancient couples walking hand in hand, past the hot dog vendors setting up for the day ahead. The steadiness of the city was keeping her upright. New York City could handle any personal crisis—it had always seen worse.

The light changed on the corner of 86th and Central Park West, and Alice leaned over, her hands on her knees, breathing hard. A jogger bobbed up and down next to her, earbuds in. Alice ignored her until the woman waved a hand in front of Alice's nose.

"Morning," Alice said.

"Oh, come on," the woman said. She bobbed faster, like a featherweight boxer, and then began to drum the air. "You say it's your birth-day . . . da da da da! Well it's my birthday, too!" The woman cracked herself up. "I'm kidding, it's not my birthday. Happy fortieth, lady!" Before Alice knew what was happening, the woman's sweaty arms were around her body, squeezing.

"Oh wow, thank you," Alice said. When the woman pulled back, Alice looked at her. It was a Belvedere mom, a real pest. Mary-Elizabeth, maybe? Or Mary-Catherine? There were two little boys, one of whom they'd nearly bounced from the preschool because of a biting problem. Felix and Horace, that was it. Alice could picture their neat haircuts and serial killer manners. "How did you know?"

Mary-Catherine-Elizabeth waved her phone in the air. "Hello, you've been posting on Instagram like crazy. Saw the cake with your kids, so cute. My kids are both off gluten because it makes them—" She drew circles around her ears and crossed her eyes. "Anyway, we got a sitter—finally, a new one— and so Ethan and I will both be there tonight. I'll be ready for some cocktails after a whole day with the kids." She made another rubbery face. "Anyway, gotta get my miles in! Self-care! See you later!" She was off like a shot, zipping across the wide street in a few long strides, and then vanished into the park, heading south.

Alice was having a birthday party. Again. She pulled out her phone to text Sam, but when Alice looked at the thread, it was sparse. Mostly Alice's texts in blue bubbles—**Hi! Just checking in! Free for dinner next week? How's it going? There's a** 90210 **marathon on, FYI**—with Sam's infrequent replies. **Yes to dinner—this week is crazy! Ha!** Alice put the phone back in her pocket. She'd try later.

It took another six minutes to jog to Pomander Walk. Behind the gate, Pomander was quiet, but it wouldn't be for long. Alice unlocked the heavy gate and hurried to her father's door. She didn't want to see any of the neighbors, because she didn't know any answers to the basic questions—even a **how are you** was an existential landmine. Alice shut the door behind her and Ursula was immediately darting in between her legs. Alice leaned down and scooped her up and held the cat against her chest.

"Hi, puss puss puss," she said into Ursula's black fur, whispering in case her father was home and still asleep. All the lights were off, but the sun was starting to rise, and Alice could make her way well enough. She could have made her way with a blindfold. At the end of the hall, she reached for her father's bedroom doorknob, but then hesitated. What did she want to see? Did she want to find him there, asleep? Did she want to see an empty bed? Instead, Alice reached for her own bedroom knob, and thrust the door open into her room.

There was a rug on the floor. It looked old and expensive, Turkish, maybe. It was possible that it had always been there, underneath her piles of belongings, but Alice couldn't remember ever seeing it. There was a desk where her bed should have been, a big handsome wooden one.

"What the fuck," Alice said. Ursula jumped down to the floor and landed with a thump. Alice opened her closet door and found clothes hung neatly, and folded sheets and towels. Nothing that belonged to her. "What the fuck."

Alice backed out of her room and hovered outside her father's door. She knocked once, quietly, and put her ear against the wood. There was no sound, and so she knocked again, and then slowly turned the knob.

Leonard's bed was empty, and neatly made, as always, with four pillows at the top and his familiar patterned quilt pulled taut and even at either side. Alice closed the door again and walked back down the hall. Ursula meowed, clearly asking to be fed as elegantly as she could, and so Alice pulled out a fresh can and emptied it into Ursula's bowl, which was where it always was, on a small tray on the kitchen floor.

Most things in the kitchen looked the same. That was the truth of living in one place for decades, if you were like Leonard—the things you bought once upon a time, on a whim or just because you needed a step stool and so you bought the first one you saw at Laytner's Linen, well, that was just what you had. Leonard had never cared about interior design, or design of any kind whatsoever. But there was something different about the kitchen, and it took Alice a few moments of standing still to figure out what it was.

There were no ashtrays.

Alice looked on the table, and there was none. She

looked on the kitchen counter. The house smelled like lavender and soap. She turned to the fridge and put her hand on the handle, but then stopped—there was a photo of her stuck to the door with a magnet Leonard had had all her life, a circular NASA logo that they'd bought at a museum when she was a little girl.

The photo looked like a holiday card—professionally photographed and printed on thick card stock. **Happy New Year!** it read, in large gold letters. In the photograph, Alice was holding Leo and Dorothy on her lap, the former clutching a toy truck in his fat little hand. Tommy stood behind them, cupping his hands around Alice's shoulders like a bad masseur.

The front door creaked, and Alice jumped. "Dad!" she said, and turned around, her heart beating fast.

"Um, no?" a small voice said. A skinny girl wearing blue jeans and an enormous sweatshirt waved at her from the doorway. "I'm Callie, from next door? I'm taking care of Ursula while Leonard—your dad—is in the hospital."

"Right," Alice said. She swallowed. "Hi, Callie. Thank you. I just fed Ursula, but I'm sure she'd love nothing more than to have you pet her for a while."

"Okay," Callie said, still standing in the doorway.

Alice touched the card on the fridge, covering her own face with the pad of her pointer finger. "Right, thanks," she said, and ducked out the door. Visiting hours started at eleven, so she couldn't go straight uptown. Alice looked at the keys in her hand and started walking back toward the San Remo. She couldn't quite bring herself to think of it as home.

38

THE CHILDREN YELPED WHEN ALICE walked in the apartment's front door. That's nice, Alice thought, a welcoming committee. She had thought a lot about the downsides of parenthood—sleepless nights, diapers, a lifelong commitment of love and support—but she had not spent very much time pondering the benefits.

"I'm hopping in the shower, then I'll be right there!" Alice called out. She'd always lived alone, and it occurred to her now that she'd always been just a little bit lonely, on top of enjoying her quiet and her space and her freedom. In the bathroom, Alice locked the door, not ready for the full-throttle intimacy that Tommy took for granted, and tried calling Sam, but instead of leaving a message when she didn't pick up, Alice sent a text. **Would really love to talk, please give me a call when you can.**

A few things that were different about Alice's body: Her nipples were larger and darker, one more so than the other. Her stomach was soft and domed slightly toward her pelvis, her skin pockmarked with silvery dots and short lines, like a message in Morse code that read **I've had two babies.** It felt like a game, or a puzzle in the back of a magazine—**Spot the Difference!** Her hair was shorter, and Alice could tell it was a more expensive cut than she'd ever had before—the color was what her natural color had been in the summertime when she was a kid, sun-kissed and blond, but it was October, and she hadn't been this blond in two decades. The shampoo choices were expensive, with artistic packaging, and Alice knew for a fact that the giant container of body soap cost fifty dollars. She still didn't know what Tommy did for a living. Part of her knew, of course, but not the part that was currently driving the boat. Alice had so many questions for her father. Had he quit smoking, just because she'd asked? What had happened to her other life, the one she had before? Was that one still happening, without her, or had she pushed the reset button on the whole world? That seemed like too big of a responsibility. He'd been smiling, hadn't he, when he told her how things worked?

When Alice was clean and dry and dressed, she wandered back out into the living room, where she found the children and a strange woman—Sondra?—at the kitchen table, working on something. But of course only Alice was a stranger here, not this woman.

"Look, Mommy! Sondra helped!" Leo said. He whipped something off the table and ran it over to her. It was a folded sheet of construction paper with a pointy crayoned heart on the front and **LEO** in big letters on the inside.

"Thank you," Alice said. "It's perfect." She kissed the boy on the head. There were arranged marriages in so many parts of the world, situations where you walked into a room as strangers and left it as family. People learned how to love each other every day. Alice felt like she'd walked onto the set of a television show, not **Time Brothers** but **Malcolm in the Middle** or **Roseanne,** something that was filmed on a set with a couch at the center and the camera where the television would be in real life. It didn't feel real, but Alice was willing to give it a go. She picked up a crayon and a piece of paper and started to draw.

39

THE HOSPITAL WAS JUST AS ALICE remembered it—a series of large white and glass buildings clinging to the upper tip of Manhattan, with the Hudson River down below. A giant banner proclaiming it the number 11 hospital in the nation was strung across Fort Washington Avenue, which seemed a sorry brag indeed. Doctors and nurses in scrubs stood on line at food trucks outside, professionally impervious to the ambulances and the loading and unloading of sick and dying people. Its familiarity was comforting—again Alice thought about what her dad had said, about life being sticky. Her father wasn't dead. Her father was alive, and here, exactly where she'd left him.

Alice waited inside the hospital to check in. She recognized two of the men at the desk, London and

Chris, who were, as usual, smiling and chatting with visitors as they passed over their IDs. When it was her turn, Alice stepped in front of London's chair and smiled.

"Well, hello, birthday girl!" London flipped some invisible hair over his shoulder. "Look at you!"

The lobby of the hospital was airy and high-ceilinged, with a Starbucks at one end and a gift shop selling cheap stuffed bears and candy bars at the other. It was loud enough that no one else could hear you unless they were straining to listen on purpose.

"How did you know?" Alice asked.

London waved her license at her. "Also, I'm a psychic."

"Right," Alice said, embarrassed. "It was yesterday."

"Go on up," London said. "You remember where? Room is printed on the badge," he said, and handed her license and her pass across the transom.

• • •

The hospital wasn't unlike the San Remo, in certain ways. There were multiple elevator banks, and there were unmarked doors that led to places civilians weren't supposed to go. People made eye contact as little as possible. Alice took an empty elevator to the fifth floor and walked through two sets of double doors, past the sitting area with the good view of the water and the steep gray palisades on the other side, approaching the George

Washington Bridge. The hallways felt sterile, with hand sanitizer pumps every fifteen feet, but also not quite as clean as one would expect, with dust bunnies along the baseboards and people coughing into the shared air. Alice was cold, and pulled her jacket closed. She was close.

It didn't seem fair. It was supposed to be that things were always the same going backward, in the other direction. Alice had assumed—she realized this as she walked down the final hall—that this part would be different, just as her basement apartment had been replaced with a sunny co-op complete with adorable children and a nanny. She had assumed that if things were fixed, things were fixed. Everyone died, of course. Everyone died **in the end,** at some unknown point in the future. People were supposed to die when their loved ones could nod and grieve and say, **It was their time.** What had Alice done, if not undone time? Whatever she had managed to accomplish in between her sixteenth birthday and this moment, it had changed everything else in her life, so why hadn't it changed this? Alice arrived at the curtained-off room that belonged to her father. There was a dry-erase board on the wall just outside with his name and the names of the doctors and nurses on duty and all his meds. The television was on, and Alice could see the closed captions on the screen. It was the weather report. **Warmer than average, highs of 65 today, 70 degrees tomorrow.**

We'll see if it lasts until Halloween. Alice put a hand on the curtain and pulled.

Leonard was in bed. There were no tubes in his nose, no lines in his arm, nothing attached except a port in his forearm that dangled like a limp carrot top. His hospital gown was covered by a flannel bathrobe, flung over his narrow body like a blanket. The room was freezing, like always. Leonard's eyes were closed but his mouth was open, and Alice could hear him breathing out of his chapped lips.

There were often people in and out of hospital rooms—that was one of the things that made the whole experience bearable. An endless parade of doctors and nurses and therapists of various kinds, and staff members who brought clean sheets. One was always dragged back to polite civility and small talk. A new name to learn, a greeting to offer. There was a woman there now, standing by the window. Alice thought that it was nice that she was taking a moment to look out at the Hudson before continuing to deliver fluids or lunch or check vital signs or remove the trash, whatever her job was. Alice took a step closer to her dad. The woman turned and smiled.

"Alice," she said, and held out both her hands, grasping like little pale lobster claws. Alice dutifully reached back and let the woman hold her hands, but the woman wasn't finished, and kept pulling Alice closer until their bodies were pressed flat against each other in a tight embrace. She was small and nicely dense, like a snowman, with a corona of graying curls.

"Hi," Alice said. "I don't think you're a doctor." The woman looked like every Upper West Side therapist she'd ever met, or a middle school principal, a profession that required both warmth and a firm hand. There was something familiar about her face, but Alice couldn't place her. The cheese counter at Zabar's. On line for popcorn at the subterranean Lincoln Plaza Cinemas. She looked like someone's mother. Alice had a momentary panic that this woman was **her** mother, but no, that wasn't possible.

The woman laughed. "Please, can you imagine? You know how well I do with blood." She let go and sat down in the only chair in the room.

"How is he today?" Alice asked.

"He's okay," she said. There was a large tote bag at her feet, and she reached in and pulled out a pile of knitting. "Pretty much the same as yesterday."

Alice turned back toward her dad. He looked yellow and pale under the fluorescent lights, with stubbled cheeks that were now more like a real beard than not. She touched his hand. "Hi, Dad," Alice said quietly.

"How was the rest of your birthday? Kids make you something?" the woman asked.

"Good, yeah," Alice said. She felt a poke in her back and whipped around, saw the woman holding an envelope.

"Your dad wrote you something. A birthday card, I guess." It was a plain white envelope with Alice's name written in Leonard's jumpy, terrible handwriting. Alice took it gently and held it with both hands.

"When did he write this?"

"I'm not sure. But he gave it to me maybe a month ago. To give to you. Today." Her eyes scrunched. "Oh, Alice." The woman's arms were around her waist. "He really wanted to be here for your birthday."

"He is," Alice said. She pulled away, though the woman resisted.

"I'll give you two some time. Want anything from the cafeteria? Soggy lettuce sandwich?" Her eyes were kind. Alice shook her head. The woman dug into her bag for her wallet, took out a twenty-dollar bill, and then put the wallet back. "Be right back."

As soon as she was gone, Alice opened the card from her father—his penmanship was nearly hieroglyphic, but Alice could make out what it said— **Al, welcome back. You'll get used to it. Happy birthday, again. Love, Dad.** It wasn't what she wanted it to say—maybe, **Surprise! I'm awake! Just faking you out!** Or **There's a secret key hidden under the bed; find it and you can turn me back on, like a wind-up toy.** Alice shoved the note in its envelope and slid it into her back pocket. "Come on, Dad, a little help would have been nice," she said to him.

Alice reached into the hugging woman's bag,

grabbed her wallet, and flipped it open. The name on the driver's license was Deborah Fink—the photo was easily a decade old, and Deborah had been slimmer then, with hair that was still brown curling to her shoulders. The address listed was on West 89th Street, just a few blocks south of Pomander. Alice had probably walked past her a thousand times, maybe even sat next to her on the M104 going up or down Broadway.

• • •

A doctor knocked and poked her head in. Alice froze as if she'd been caught shoplifting. The doctor was a tall Black woman with a stethoscope. The stethoscope had a little toy koala clinging to it, which Alice thought made her look like a pediatrician. Everyone would like doctors more if they always looked like pediatricians. Alice wished for a box of stickers and small toys, prizes for having accomplished something scary or difficult.

"Oh, hi," Alice said, stuffing the wallet back into Deborah's bag, poking herself with a knitting needle in the process. "Ouch. I'm fine." She held out her hand and shook the doctor's freshly sanitized hand.

"I'm Dr. Harris, doing rounds today. You're Leonard's daughter?" Dr. Harris pumped more sanitizer out of the dispenser on the wall and rubbed her palms together as she talked.

Alice nodded.

The doctor slid into the room. It was amazing to watch how comfortable people could be with illness, with bodies that were failing to do what they were supposed to do. But of course this was what bodies were supposed to do—fail. It was Alice who had things wrong and was trying to swim against the current. "I spoke to your stepmother yesterday, and will check back in with her today. Your dad is stable, for now. But I do want to send the palliative care doctors in to talk to you two and to give you a sense of what's coming, and how to just make sure he stays comfortable. I think that pretty soon we'll talk about a move to the hospice floor." Dr. Harris paused. "Are you okay?"

Alice was not okay. "Sure," Alice said. "You know."

"I do." Dr. Harris looked at Leonard. "He's been a real fighter, your dad. He's a strong man."

"Thank you," Alice said. Dr. Harris gave a tight smile and left, pausing outside to write a note on the whiteboard.

"I'm sorry I didn't tell you," Alice said. "I liked your version better. Healthy and beautiful and living on Pomander." She lowered her voice. "I got married. I have two children. I don't know if I have a job. How do I find out if I have a job? I don't know how this works, Dad. I should have asked more questions."

Leonard made a noise—discomfort or pain or just an involuntary dream noise, Alice couldn't tell. She leaned over and cupped her hand over his. "Dad, can you hear me? I'm sorry I didn't tell you. But I'm here, I'm back. It's me." Leonard's tongue moved inside his mouth, like a parrot's. "I was there, and now I'm here and everything's different and I don't know what the fuck is going on." This part felt the same—like she was trying to talk to her father from the other side of a giant chasm. No one was going to catch every word, and whatever needed to be said better have been said already. It wasn't like the people who sat beside their estranged loved ones' deathbeds, waiting on a single apology, the code to a safe full of love and tenderness. Alice and her father had always been such good friends. It was luck, she knew, plain luck, that gave some families complementary personalities. So many people spent their lives wishing to be understood. All Alice wanted was more time.

There was a whooshing sound like a shower curtain opening—Deborah was back, carrying potato chips and a Snickers bar and two coffees.

"For you," she said. "Take your pick."

Alice wiped at her eyes, and then plucked the coffee from Deborah's left hand. "Stepmother," she said.

Deborah waved her free hand, which knocked the potato chips to the floor. Both women bent down to pick them up, knocking into each other in the narrow space beside Leonard's bed.

"Oh, please, honey," Deborah said. "You know I'm just your Debbie."

"I always wanted him to find someone," Alice said. "I really did."

"I know that," Deborah said. Debbie. Her stepmother, Debbie, who called her **honey.** "He never would have asked me out if it weren't for you."

"Can I have the Snickers, too?"

"It's still your birthday as far as I'm concerned, love. You can have it all." Debbie trudged forward until the toes of their shoes were touching, then stretched up to kiss Alice on the forehead. She smelled like warm milk and bad coffee and jasmine perfume. Alice thought of all the articles she'd ever read, and the self-help books, every stupid piece of advice about women having it all, and how only counting the things that one was trying to balance in a single life was actually a cosmic lowballing. She'd never even considered all the things she could have, or all the things she couldn't.

"I'll try," Alice said.

40

TOMMY SAID THAT THE PARTY WAS going to be casual, but then he said that the caterers were arriving at four to set up by six, and the bartender was coming at five, but the booze had already been delivered, and when people in crisp white shirts and black vests started arriving, Alice knew that she and Tommy had different definitions of the word **casual.** Alice remembered some things—she remembered wanting the party. She always wanted a party, and then didn't enjoy it.

Her closet was incredible: not quite Cher Horowitz's motorized racks from **Clueless,** but not far off. In addition to all the vintage dresses, many of which she recognized, and the stack of blue jeans, the walk-in closet was overflowing with expensive, well-made designer things that she never could have afforded on her salary at Belvedere. **Okay,** Alice thought. This was more like it—this was the fun part of time travel, this was a scene she knew. Alice pawed through them like a contestant on **Supermarket Sweep.** She kept the closet door open and went back and sat on her bed. She wanted to know who was coming to the party—Alice opened her email and began to scroll. It was mostly junk, as ever. She searched **Belvedere** in her inbox, and about a thousand messages appeared—about vaccination forms, about school fundraisers, about holiday gifts for teachers.

"Fucking hell, I'm a **parent,**" Alice said to herself. Not just a parent, but a Belvedere parent. There was a range of parents, of course, but the range was a puddle, not a river. Leonard had always stuck out like a sore thumb in his T-shirts and clunky sneakers, but he made enough money that people simply excluded him, instead of looking down on him. Alice had had lots of friends at Belvedere who taught and sent their kids—Melinda had; so had most other parents on staff. It was a huge perk, a massively reduced tuition for the children of faculty and staff, though Alice knew from some of her friends that the reduction had gotten less massive over time. Those were the school parents she liked. The other ones—the full-ticket-price parents, as she and Emily would refer to them—were not.

But she knew what they looked like. Alice pulled a few dresses out of her closet—drapey ones, snug ones, ones with elaborate beading and even a few stray feathers—and laid them across the bed. It was like playing dress-up in her own life. At least, this version of her life.

Dorothy toddled in to check on her and immediately ran a jam-covered hand across the bedspread and toward one of the dresses, a beige thing that looked right for a very, very rich nun.

"Hi, Dorothy," Alice said. "You like that one?"

Dorothy licked her palm and then shook her head. "I like the pink one."

The pink one was pretty good, Alice had to admit. It had a high neck with a wide ruffle that reminded her of the prom dress in **Pretty in Pink,** and then stopped short midthigh, where it continued with enough feathers for a dozen ostriches.

"You don't think it's too much?" Alice asked. Dorothy shook her head vigorously.

"It's **like a flamingo.**" Dorothy seemed like a very direct person. Alice was sure that she would love her very much, if she were her mother, if she could remember being Dorothy's mother. Alice could feel something—love, maybe, or devotion—entering the room like an invisible cloud. It wasn't exactly what she imagined motherhood would feel like, but what did Alice know about mothers anyway? Alice could hardly remember being in the same room as her own mother—she had three or four memories, and that was it; everything else was long-distance, and came after Serena had left. People told Alice all the time that it was hard for a mother to lose custody, but it wasn't hard when the mother agreed. Mothering seemed like downhill skiing, or cooking elaborate meals from scratch—sure, anyone could **learn** how to do it, but it was much easier for the people who had seen other people do it first, and well, from a very young age.

Sondra called Dorothy's name and the girl dutifully trotted back to the kitchen, where dinner was being presented for the children. Alice checked her phone again—she tried calling Sam, but there was still no answer. Her mother had left a message, which was just about the only part of her life that felt unchanged. There were half a dozen texts from people whose names she didn't recognize wishing her a happy belated. Alice was popular.

Tommy came in, shutting the door behind him. He was sweaty again, in exercise clothes. A rich-person marriage with small children seemed to involve parents taking turns exercising and then bathing. Alice remembered the sex that she and Tommy had had, and how long ago that night must feel to him.

"Hey," she said. "Remember when we fucked at my sixteenth birthday?"

"Heh," Tommy said. "Did you call the plumber back? There's still a leak in the back of my office; it must be coming from the apartment upstairs."

"Sure," Alice said. She was standing in her under-wear, which was very nice underwear, the kind that came in a box surrounded by tissue paper and that you were supposed to wash by hand. Alice was used to buying her underpants three at a time, and then wearing them until the cotton was too stained or ripped to be ignored, when she would throw them in the trash and buy more. She ran a hand over her lacy bra. "This is nice, don't you think?"

"Yeah, I see the credit card bills." Tommy yanked his shirt off over his head. "How was your dad? Was Debbie there, too?"

"She was. She was really nice. My dad isn't talking, but he made some noises. I think he knew I was there. He definitely knew I was there," Alice said, though she wasn't really sure. What was definite? What was real? She had been standing next to her father—she had touched his hand. None of the grief books she'd bought and hardly read had mentioned this scenario. Or maybe she just hadn't read closely enough. Maybe there were secret chapters written just for people like her, like the handbook in **Beetlejuice.** You didn't need the information before you needed it. Alice sat down on the bed and looked at the books teetering on her bedside table. Brené Brown, Cheryl Strayed, Elizabeth Gilbert. If Oprah had read and loved a book, Alice had bought it, apparently. There weren't any books that she didn't recognize. Tommy walked into the bathroom and she heard the shower turn on and begin to splash the tile walls. There was a small drawer in the table, and Alice slid it open. She put the letter from her father in and shut the drawer again quietly. **Sesame Street** was blasting in the living room. The letter of the day was **L.** Alice's children screamed happily.

• • •

Sondra whisked Leo and Dorothy quickly through the party to say hello and curtsy sweetly at the guests. Alice found herself wanting to follow them into their bedrooms and curl up under the covers, their warm little bodies pressed against hers, but she had put on the flamingo dress, and it was her party, and she was not allowed to leave. Sam hadn't called her back yet, and Alice was starting to panic. Leonard had said it was a chute, a ramp, a slide forward, and this was where she landed. Whatever she'd done, whatever decisions she'd made, they had led her here. Alice was making lists in her head, trying to piece together everything that had happened in between. The marriage, obviously, and the children. But Alice had still gone to art school—there were projects of hers hanging on the walls—and she still loved all the same things. The fridge was full of Fairway avgolemono and Zabar's challah and lox from Murray's, and her favorite books were still on the shelf, in the editions she'd always had. Alice smiled at everyone as they came into the apartment, feeling like a festive amnesiac. As long as no one asked her any direct, meaningful questions, she would be fine. Having been to many parties just like this one at the homes of Belvedere parents, Alice actually thought there was a good chance she could get through it talking about which of the catered snacks were the most delicious and asking people follow-up questions once they mentioned that they were in the middle of a home renovation.

The apartment filled promptly—coats were hung on proper hangers on a long metal rack in the large foyer, and caterers crisscrossed the living room carrying trays of hors d'oeuvres. The living room was full of well-dressed people, and music that Alice loved was playing from hidden speakers she didn't know how to operate. The preppiest parents stayed in a tight knot, only as many as would fit on a sailboat. Same as it ever was.

Tommy was a good host—Alice watched him circulate around the room. He touched women gently on their backs, or on their shoulders, in a way that was neither lecherous nor patronizing. It seemed friendly, if impersonal, like someone running for office. Alice caught his eye from across the room, and he fluttered his eyelashes. Was this what she had wanted? It was something she had thought about, though Alice scarcely wanted to admit it to herself. She had been to these parties and watched the rich hosts swan around the room, full of confidence built on tennis courts and ski slopes, doing everything generously because they had so much to give. She had stared at these marriages, she had gossiped about these marriages, she had made fun of these marriages. But the way Tommy was looking at her wasn't a joke, and the way Alice felt wasn't a joke, either. It almost felt—to jump from time travel to fantasy, which were, after all, kissing cousins—like the part of a fairy tale where a princess finds herself falling under a magic spell and must compel herself to stay awake. Alice could see how easy it would be to sink in.

"This is a very nice party," Alice said to one of the caterers, and plucked a glass of champagne off their tray. "Thank you." The caterer nodded and turned to the next guest.

The jogger made eye contact with Alice from the doorway, and as soon as she'd shaken off her coat, she began to hustle across the room. Alice had chosen a spot near the window with the bookshelves behind her, which meant that she was somewhat difficult to approach, as you had to go around the sofa one way or the other, and if you chose the wrong direction, you would have to squeeze past people's knees between the couch and the coffee table or shimmy around a side table and avoid knocking over a lamp.

Mary-Catherine-Elizabeth had excellent hamstrings and could high-step over anything. She had crossed the room in a minute flat, and picked up a tiny lobster roll on the way. Alice watched as

Mary-Catherine-Elizabeth folded the whole thing into her mouth, stretching her lips wide enough that her fingers wouldn't muss her lipstick.

"Excuse me," Alice said when Mary-Catherine-Elizabeth was in close range. She was still chewing and stuck a finger in the air, telling Alice to wait, but Alice was already ducking around the skinny side of the couch, and snaked her way down the line of legs in front of the couch, the feathers of her skirt tickling everyone's ankles.

There was a short line for the bathroom. Alice smiled at all the women who were smiling at her, which was everyone. The men stood in a solid clump in the foyer—dressed uniformly in button-down shirts, half of them tucked and half of them not. The untucked dads were the wild ones, who didn't work in finance and were instead lawyers, or came from families with enough generational wealth that they didn't **need** to work at all, a group that further divided into a pool of documentarians who made movies about human trafficking and a pool of greedy, power-hungry drug addicts who just wanted to make their daddies proud. Alice got a few nods and one wave. They didn't seem to want to talk to her any more than she wanted to talk to them. Tommy was in a small group of men standing by the bar, his hand clamped on another man's shoulder. Was that how this worked, couples just looked at each other from across the room, and then maybe had sex later, knowing that they'd each probably had a moment's excitement talking to other people? Alice looked at her phone, willing Sam to call her back. Was Sam coming? She felt too embarrassed to ask Tommy.

Alice bumped into one of the cater waiters, nearly sending a whole tray of tiny quiches to the rug. "I'm so sorry," she said. "Emily."

Emily straightened up, blushing. "No, I'm so sorry, I absolutely just walked into you."

"No, I walked into you! What are you doing here?" Alice and Emily flattened themselves against the wall of the hallway to let other waiters get by.

"I'm surprised you remember my name, um, wow, I don't know, you know, the catering is just a side-hustle kind of thing. I'm still at Belvedere." Emily's cheeks were magenta.

"Totally," Alice said. "I didn't mean to make it weird. I'm just happy to see you! How's Melinda?"

Emily drew her chin back. "Mclinda? Finc, I assume? She's been retired for, like, two years, I think? You interviewed with Patricia when you came in with Dorothy, I remember."

"Of course," Alice said. "Must have slipped my mind. And how are you? How's Ray?" Alice felt high—it was obvious that in this life, in this timeline, in this reality, she shouldn't know anything about Emily's private life. She would barely know Emily at all! But Alice was desperate for a real conversation.

It wasn't possible for Emily's face to contort or

purple any more, or she would have burst into flames. "I'm fine. Ray's fine? Did we talk about Ray for some reason? Anyway, I need to get these quiches to all your guests." Emily skidded her back along the wall to get around Alice, who had to move out of the way of the large silver tray. The Talking Heads were playing on the invisible speakers— **This is not my beautiful house, this is not my beautiful wife.** The bathroom door opened, finally, and Sam stepped out.

Alice gasped, so relieved. She threw her arms around Sam's neck and pulled her close for a hug before being stopped by the beach-ball-sized bump in between them. Alice looked down at Sam's belly.

"Oh, wow, sorry," she said.

Sam rolled her eyes. "You don't have to be sorry," she said. "It was a planned pregnancy."

Alice grabbed Sam's hand and pulled her down the hall into her bedroom, leaving stray flamingo feathers in their wake.

41

SAM SAT DOWN ON THE BED WITHOUT waiting to be asked and kicked off her shoes.

"My feet are so swollen, it's like trying to walk on two meatballs." Sam hoisted one of her feet on top of the opposite knee and began to rub.

"How many children do you have?" Alice asked. "Your husband is Josh, right? Who you met in college? At Harvard?"

"Jesus, Alice." Sam let her heavy foot fall back to the floor. "Are you having a stroke?"

"No, I'm fine—" Alice stopped. "I'm not fine. I mean, I might be fine, eventually, but right now I seem to be in a slightly . . . weird place?" She paced back and forth at the foot of her bed, the feathers waving. Alice stopped in front of the window and looked out at the park. Some of the trees were already yellow and orange. It had been almost a whole day. Time was going to keep going, churning away. Alice had to make a decision. "Do you remember my sixteenth birthday?"

Alice watched in the window's reflection as Sam swiveled her body toward her. Sam's belly was the shape of a perfectly taut basketball. Like a three-dimensional clock. This time, Alice knew what it felt like, to have someone swimming around inside your body. She felt a little ghost flicker near her belly button, a reminder.

"I do," Sam said. "Do you?" **Samantha Rothman-Wood,** she wasn't going to give anything up, Alice thought, her gratitude boundless. There was no friend like a teenage girl, even if that teenage girl grew up. She turned around and walked back to the bed, where she and her feathers perched next to Sam. "I have two children, and this is my third. I am married to Josh, and we met at Harvard. What about you, Alice? Where'd you come from? Where'd you go?" Her voice was gentle—Sam was a good mom. She cooked, she played, she let the kids watch television, she loved their dad, she went to therapy. If Alice could have chosen a mother, she would have chosen Sam.

"When you didn't pick up today," Alice said, "I got worried that something had happened, you know? Between us?"

Sam laughed. "Yeah, something happened. Between us, we have four and a half kids. Do you know how hard it is to find a time when no one is saying your name, or touching your body, or needs help going to the bathroom?"

"Have we talked about it ever? I'm sorry. I feel like a really bad friend right now, because not only did I tell you this very big, very weird, crazy thing, but now I have no idea if it's something that we just pretended never happened. Does that even make sense?" Alice put her face in her hands.

Sam put a hand on her belly, and Alice could see it move—whoever was inside was adding something to the conversation. "So, you're like **13 Going On 30,** but it's **40 Going On 16 Going On 40**? Something like that?"

"Exactly," Alice said. She sank down next to Sam and put her head on her shoulder.

"That's trippy," Sam said. "But okay." She paused. "Either I believe you again or I believe that you have ongoing psychosis, which is sort of the same thing, if you think about it. You believe this is happening to you, and I believe that you believe it. And obviously Leonard believed it, too."

"Why do you say that?" Alice asked.

Someone knocked on the door, and then Tommy poked his head in. Both Alice and Sam whipped their heads around to look at him.

"The natives are restless," he said. He made what would pass for a sheepish face, if he'd ever felt sheepish about asking for anything except a blow job. Alice was remembering more. It was like watching someone paint a giant canvas at high speed, all the white getting filled in with details.

"You can't say that anymore," Alice said. "Be right there."

Tommy nodded and withdrew his head from the room.

"Why did I think that marrying Tommy was the answer to anything?" Alice asked. "I mean, it is exactly what I pictured being a grown-up would be like, this whole thing—" She gestured around the room. "And my clothes are fucking amazing. Do you know how many pairs of shoes I have? The kids are beautiful, and funny, and—" Alice thought about her dad. Whatever she'd done, or said, it hadn't been enough. She hadn't told him everything she needed to.

"I get it. I think," Sam said. "You can do it again, can't you? Isn't that how the book goes?"

"How the story goes?" Alice asked. "I don't know."

Sam shook her head. "**Dawn of Time.** You know, the best idea I ever had that I didn't get paid for?"

"I don't know what you're talking about," Alice said.

"Hang on," Sam said. She scooted off the bed and slipped out the door as elegantly as a very pregnant person possibly could, still barefoot. Alice got up and chewed on her beautiful fingernails. A minute later, Sam opened the door again, noise from the party spilling into the room. In one hand, she had a pile of shrimp on a paper napkin, and in the other she had a book. "Here," Sam said, thrusting it at Alice. "Just go—I'll cover for you."

Alice looked at the book in her hand. It was orange, with enormous type, type that took up nearly the whole jacket—**Dawn of Time,** by Leonard Stern. She opened it and read the flap.

An all-new time travel adventure by Leonard Stern, author of the worldwide sensation Time Brothers.

It was exactly what they'd talked about over ice cream—**High school senior Dawn Gale didn't expect her graduation to be momentous, but when she wakes up the next morning as a thirty-year-old, she knows she's got a mystery to solve. Will this smart girl get back to her own life, or will she be stuck forever, going back and forth between these two different points in her life?** The copyright date was 1998, the year that Alice herself had graduated from high school.

"This is real?" Alice said. He'd done it—she knew he could, and he had. She turned the book over and stared at the photograph of Leonard that took up the entire back of the book. His face, in black and white and gray. It was a Marion Ettlinger photograph, Alice could tell—she'd shot every important writer of the decade, and her style, silver and steely, was unmistakable. The picture was **in focus,** every hair on his head. Leonard's eyebrows were raised, as if he weren't expecting someone to take his photograph, as if Marion had just happened upon him in the wild, chin resting on his hand just so. He was wearing a black T-shirt and a black leather jacket and his eyes were fixed straight at the camera, staring it down.

"Okay," Alice said. She clutched the book in her hand. "I love you."

Sam kissed Alice on the cheek. "Until the future." She smiled and opened the door.

42

THE UPPER WEST SIDE WAS BEAUTIFUL during the day, if you had the stomach for the yuppies and the preppies and the bankers and the glossy chains that had eaten up all the idiosyncratic storefronts of Alice's youth, but it was more beautiful at night, when all the shops had closed and the quiet streets glittered under the glow of streetlights. Alice had always loved walking home from Tommy's apartment—her father had given her a rape whistle when she was twelve, just in case, and she kept it in her pocket, next to her sharpest keys, always ready. Despite having to be aware of every man within a block radius and how close they were to her body, the inner radar that every woman naturally possessed, Alice loved to walk alone at night. The later the better. She stepped into the middle of the street, her phone in one hand and **Dawn of Time** in the other, pumping her arms like a mall walker on a mission. She walked up Central Park West until she passed the Museum of Natural History, which was closed, but the rounded towers at either end were still illuminated, little dinosaur-filled light-houses. Alice turned on 81st Street and hurried past the row of uniformed doormen, hands at the ready. She crossed Columbus and walked over the hill to Amsterdam, where the bars were hopping and crowds of revelers were vaping outside, some of them even ignoring their phones for long enough to flirt. So many places from her childhood were gone, like the Raccoon Lodge, where her coolest babysitter had hung out with her biker boyfriend, and the tiny horseback riding stable in a converted garage on 89th Street where she'd begged Leonard to let her take lessons as a kid, but that was New York, watching every place you'd kissed or cried, every place you loved, turn into something else.

Two young women—younger than Alice, college students, maybe—were leaning on each other against the abandoned husk of a phone booth, on the verge of making out or vomiting or both. "I love your dresssss," one of them said, and Alice smiled. Women could say anything to her, and she would smile—if a man had said it, Alice would have scowled and crossed the street. Her phone vibrated in her hand—a text from Tommy. **Where the fuck are you?** She'd missed a few previous missives—**Alice? Alice, where are you? It's time for the toast.** Alice could imagine his face hardening into anger. How angry had she ever seen him? When they were in high school, Tommy had never gotten mad about anything that Alice could remember. Fucking up his SATs by getting two questions wrong? Only getting a two on an AP exam? Not making varsity basketball? Their lives had been in such a thick bubble that real problems would have to have been professional safecrackers to break in. Rich people had problems, of course—Tommy's parents were cold and absent, his grandmother was a famous drunk, whatever else was hidden deeper— but Alice had never seen what happened to Tommy in the face of actual anger, if he turned sad or sour, if his anger went inward or outward. That's what took years to learn, which habits would calcify into immovable traits. Part of Alice was thrilled to be in this part of a relationship—the boring part, the plateau at the top of the mountain. And the kids. Alice sped up, jogging as quickly as her low mules would allow across Amsterdam at 85th Street, the feathers on her dress tickling her now-cold calves.

Two doors in from the corner, in a tiny storefront that had previously housed a Tibetan bead store, was a psychic. A large neon crystal ball filled half the window. Alice could see that the room had been blocked off, so that whoever went in would be sitting in one of two squishy chairs just on the other side of the glass, in full view of passersby. One of the chairs was occupied by a young woman with over-plucked eyebrows. Perpetual surprise seemed an odd choice for a psychic, but Alice stopped anyway.

The woman rose to her feet languidly, as if the future would wait. She tucked her phone into her back pocket and swung open the door. From closer up, the scene looked even dingier, and there was the sound of an episode of **Law & Order** coming from an unseen television on the other side of the flimsy wall.

"Tell the future?"

"How much?" Alice said.

"Twenty for palm, twenty-five for astrology chart, fifty for tarot. Ninety bucks for all three." The woman looked her up and down. "Nice dress."

"Okay," Alice said. "Thank you. Whichever one is fastest." She squeezed past the woman and sat in the chair on the far side of the window, with her book on her lap.

The woman held out her hand, and Alice followed suit. The psychic flicked her ponytail over her shoulder and pulled Alice's palm closer. "When is your birthday?" she asked.

"Yesterday," Alice said, and neglected to make a joke about psychics.

"Yesterday!" the psychic said, looking up. "Happy birthday."

"Thanks. It's a weird one. A weird big one. A big weird one? Both."

The woman examined Alice's hand, both front

and back, holding it between her own hands like the world's most delicate pancake. "Sun in Libra, moon in . . . Scorpio?"

"I have no idea," Alice said. It felt like the nice part of a manicure, when all the prodding and clipping was done and someone else was just holding your hand and paying attention to you for a few minutes.

"Do you know what time you were born? What year? And where?"

"Um, about three p.m.? 1980? Here. Manhattan."

The woman smiled, proud of herself. "Moon in Scorpio. I'm 1980, too. March. What hospital?"

"Roosevelt." Alice could picture her parents in the delivery room, her father on repeat, holding her mother's hand, putting cold washcloths on her forehead, and then watching Alice's slippery red body slide out into the doctor's waiting arms. What did it mean that Leonard went back to that day, and she went back to her stupid party, where she had gotten drunk and thrown up and been a sad girl, just like every other day of her teenage existence? It seemed like a waste, for both of them. Leonard had had such exciting days, more exciting days than Alice had ever had.

"That has nothing to do with it, just curious." In the light of the rosy crystal ball, the woman's face was red. Better lighting would have helped her business, Alice thought, especially in the Upper West Side of today, where everyone wanted their dental

office and their coworking space to look like interior design showrooms. "So here's how this works.
You ask a question, and I answer it. By looking at
your palm, at your sign, and since it's your birthday,
I'll pull a card, too. Now close your eyes, take three
deep breaths, and think about a question. I can't
answer questions about other people, like **is my
man cheating on me,** that kind of thing. Make it a
question about **why** or **how.** You get what I mean?"

Alice did as she was told. She had nothing but
questions. **Do I want to be married to Tommy?
Do I want children? How do I keep my dad
alive? What the fuck am I supposed to do with
my life? Which life, even? Do I have a job? In
some other life, do I have a better one? How do
I know which life to choose?** Each question was
more embarrassing than the last—she couldn't
say any of those out loud, not even to a complete
stranger. Her chest expanded and contracted in
time with the psychic's. Alice took an extra breath
and decided. She opened her eyes. "How do I know
if I'm living the right life?"

The woman let go of Alice's hand and reached
for a deck of tarot cards. She set them on the table
in front of Alice. "Cut the deck," she said. "And
again. Now pick the top card." Alice flipped it over.
A colorfully dressed boy with a bundle on a stick
stood on the edge of a cliff, clearly about to traipse
right off onto the rocks below. **The Fool,** it read, in
large letters along the bottom of the card, closest to

Alice. There was a small white dog nipping at the boy's heels, perhaps in warning, and the boy held a rose in his hand.

"That doesn't seem promising," Alice said.

The woman leaned back in her chair and laughed. "It heard you. The deck. You see? This card, I know, people look at it, and they see the word **fool** and they can get bent out of shape, but that's not what it's saying. If you draw Death, it doesn't mean you're about to die, and if you draw Fool, it doesn't mean that you're dumb.

"Let me tell you about the Fool. He's number zero in the deck, which means that he's always starting from nothing, from innocence, from a blank slate. That's us, all of us—the Fool is always starting fresh. He doesn't know what's coming— none of us do, right? The dog could warn him, he could stop to pick another flower, he could change directions—all he knows is what he sees." She pointed to the different parts of the card. "The blue sky. The clouds. He's at the beginning of his journey. And that can be a brand-new beginning, or a change. All he needs to remember is to be aware of what surrounds him. The journey is what changes him. And it depends what kind of life you mean, right? Some people come and want to know about love—the Fool can mean a new love, a fresh love—some people want to know about their job, their career, their money—the Fool can mean new opportunities in those areas, too."

"What about the dog?" Alice felt dizzy. "Is that, like, some sort of spirit animal?"

"Listen, spirit animals are a whole different thing. The dog is loyal—" The woman whistled once, sharply, and a tiny ball of brown fluff skittered across the floor toward her. She leaned over and picked it up. "This is a dog, but it's also not just a dog. This dog is my protector, my rock." The dog, a dead ringer for Toto, leaned back on its hind legs and stretched its mouth up for a kiss. The psychic let it lick her on the cheek and then gently put it back down on the floor. "That's what the dog is. You have your own dog. A friend, a family member. You might have a few. Someone who wants to protect you, who is always loyal. You gotta listen to your dog."

"Okay," Alice said.

"The Fool is a major card, too. It's not about a promotion, or whether you said the wrong thing one time, that kinda thing. It's the big stuff."

"Couldn't get any bigger," Alice said.

"Basically, this card is saying you never know what's coming, so you gotta be happy when it's there. Whatever it is. I've been listening to this podcast, **The Universe is Your Boss!,** you know that one?"

Alice shook her head. The dog padded over, its nails ticking on the linoleum floor, and sniffed her hand.

"It's good, you should listen. Anyway, the host

ends every episode by saying, 'Joy is coming.' I think it's a quote from a book or something, I don't know. But she says it every week. Joy is coming. That's the Fool. You just gotta keep your eyes open and look for it. Make sure not to fall."

"You say that like it's easy," Alice said. Her phone was dinging, and she took it out of her pocket. The Find My iPhone alarm was going off. Tommy was tracking her. Which she understood. She'd married him young, high school sweethearts. They'd never been apart. Alice thought about having sex with only one person for your entire life—it sounded like a holdover from the days when life expectancy was thirty-five. "I have to go," Alice said. She stood up and hugged the woman, who didn't seem surprised.

"I do Venmo," she said, and pointed to a printed card by the door with a QR code. Alice snapped a picture and hurried out, the dog, little Toto, nipping playfully at her feathers.

43

TOMMY WOULD EITHER CALL OFF THE party and jump in a cab or he'd call the police, Alice didn't know which. Maybe both. She turned off the Find My iPhone button and then turned off her phone altogether. He would probably guess that she'd go to Pomander, and so once she got up to 94th Street, Alice thought about going somewhere else, but there was nowhere else to go. It wasn't a crime to leave your birthday party. It was a dick move, for sure, but it wasn't a crime. She wasn't a missing person. She was just a fool.

It was early yet—only ten o'clock. Alice opened the gate, relieved to hear the familiar creak of heavy iron. There were lights on at the Romans', and at the house directly across from Leonard's, which now belonged to an actor whose face Alice knew but whose name she could never remember. The cat sitter, Callie, lived next door, and Alice could see her parents watching television in their living room. Callie herself was probably in bed. It was such a good street to grow up on, but Alice also remembered how tight it sometimes felt, how short the view was out the window. Maybe that's why Leonard had had trouble writing—he couldn't see anything outside, just a house that looked exactly like his, and a city of fire escapes and windows in the back. But maybe he hadn't had trouble, not this time.

Leonard's lights—the house lights—were off. Alice wondered if Debbie would be there—she hadn't been there that morning. Maybe she and Leonard had the dreamy sort of marriage that Alice herself wanted, or used to think she wanted, where they lived a few blocks apart and could always retreat to their own spaces. Pomander wasn't tiny by New York City standards, but for someone who lived and worked at home, and had bookshelves lining every wall, and who had never learned how to buy or cook real food, it was tight. **Debbie.** The thought of her made Alice happy. She was so clearly kind, the sort of woman who would help you with your homework. Alice could picture Debbie as a loving, supportive teacher so clearly, with her bra line and the waistline of her full pleated skirt one and the same, the word **bosom** personified.

Alice unlocked the door, and Ursula was against her legs. Ursula had ruined Alice for other cats—the aloof layabouts who pretended not to know the humans were there until it was feeding time. "Oh, Ursula," Alice said, and picked her up. The cat scrambled delicately onto Alice's shoulders like a living stole. Some mail was splashed inside the door, where it had fallen through the slot. She moved over to the kitchen table and sat down in the dark. Ursula leaped down onto Alice's lap and batted around some feathers before curling into a tight black ball and closing her eyes. Alice turned on the light.

There was a shelf on top of the fridge that held Leonard's various prizes—an award shaped like a spaceship, another shaped like a comet. Alice had never understood why speculative fiction and outer space were so closely identified—surely the number of science fiction novels that took place on Earth vastly outnumbered the ones that took place on Planet Blork, or in some distant galaxy. Maybe it was because it was easier to imagine a totally different life outside the walls you were used to. Comforting, even, just to spend however many hours in some totally different place. Alice stood on her tiptoes and grabbed one of the silver spaceships. There were two of them, which Alice didn't remember. It was dusty but heavy—a real piece of hardware, not like some flimsy trophy from a souvenir shop. There was a small plaque at the bottom, and Alice rubbed it clean as she read.

Best Novel, 1998
Dawn of Time
Leonard Stern

Alice put the spaceship on the counter next to the book. Ursula leaped up next to her, purring loudly and offering her chin to scratch. Alice turned on the faucet and Ursula began to flick her sandpaper tongue in and out of the water, an inefficient fountain. Alice splashed some water into her mouth, too, and then rested her hand on Ursula's sleek back.

• • •

There were bookshelves everywhere, but Leonard had never put his own books on them, and even if he had, the shelves weren't alphabetized or organized in a way that anyone but him could understand. When Alice was a kid, there were certain areas she knew how to find—the Agatha Christies, the P. G. Wodehouses, the Ursula K. Le Guins. Her eyes scanned the shelves, looking for her father's name, knowing that she wouldn't find it.

Leonard did have a stash, though—Alice could remember him signing copies of **Time Brothers** for various Belvedere fundraisers and things like that, auctions for some cause or another. She flipped on the light in the single, narrow hallway closet, in which Leonard had shoddily built wooden shelves, unfinished and full of splinters. There were several dinged-up cardboard Bankers Boxes. The one Alice could most easily reach was labeled TB FOREIGN EDITIONS. Alice pushed it aside to see the box next to it, labeled DAWN. Alice unfolded the small ladder that was tucked in for changing lightbulbs and heaved the box down with a thud. Dust rained on her pink feathers like fresh snow.

There were hardcovers and paperbacks—the orange paperback that Sam had thrust at her, and a hardcover edition with an understated black-and-white jacket, mostly type but with a small yellow door at the center, like a sunset as seen through a cartoon mousehole. In addition to several copies of those, there were foreign editions—**Alba del Temps, Świt Czasu, Dämmerung der Zeit**—all shoved into the box as if Leonard had been cleaning out his desk in a hurry. There were DVD boxes, which Alice hadn't seen in years. A **Time Brothers** box set had snuck in—six discs, plus bonus material, and right underneath it was a DVD box for **Dawn of Time,** which appeared to have been made into a movie starring Sarah Michelle Gellar.

She put the movie back in the box and shoved it all toward the back of the closet, except for the hardcover copy of **Dawn of Time,** which she tucked under her arm and carried to the couch. Leonard had always been a dedicated napper, and so the couch had a threadbare but still cozy blanket thrown over the top, and a pillow that belonged to Ursula but which she was willing to share. Alice lay down and closed her eyes. It was late, and she was exhausted. Ursula jumped onto the couch and started making biscuits on Alice's chest, poking tiny holes into the bodice of her dress. She opened the book, knowing that she wouldn't stop until she was finished.

If **Time Brothers** was Leonard looking for adventure and for family—he had not had a brother; his parents had been well-meaning but disinterested in his internal life—then **Dawn of Time** was Leonard looking at her—looking at himself looking at her. Alice knew that she wasn't Dawn, that Dawn was a creation, a mix of people, of Leonard himself and what he thought about Alice, and other people, too, and then that strange alchemy of writing, when the character began to do and say things the writer didn't expect. Alice loved her father's book. Books! She wished there were more of them to read, hidden in a box somewhere. It didn't matter if they were published, or if no one else read them. It was better than a diary, because there was nothing that could make her cringe, nothing that felt inappropriate for her to see. People were allowed to have privacy, even parents. But in Leonard's book—his books!— Alice could find little messages. Sometimes it was as simple as a description of a meal that she knew Leonard himself liked to eat—fried eggs left alone in the pan long enough to turn brown and crispy at the edges—or the mention of the Kinks. They were all tiny little parts of him, preserved forever, molecules that had rearranged themselves into words on a page, but Alice could see them for what they were, which was her father.

It wasn't a guardhouse—Dawn, who lived on Patchin Place, in the West Village, with its gas lamp at the end of the lane like something Mr. Tumnus would be leaning against, had crawled through a tiny door in the back of the closet in her bedroom, the kind of door that usually hit fuse boxes or water shut-off knobs, a jerry-rigged space built out of necessity. She was just looking for a small place of her own, but when she made it to the very back of the closet, she emerged into the ramble in Central Park. The story was complicated—portals, a mystery to solve, different years, different realities. But Alice could read it for what it was, which was a love story. Not a romance—there was no sex in the entire book, a few kisses, that was it—the book was about the love between a single parent and their only child. It wasn't funny. It was earnest. It was the kind of thing that Leonard would never have said aloud to Alice, not in a million years. But it was true all the same. Alice wiped at her eyes and looked up at the clock. It was just before three. She sat up and looked out the window at the guardhouse. What had it cost her, traveling back? It had cost her a day. A day when her father was still alive. She couldn't put it off forever, but Leonard had said she could go back. He had, after all. Alice shut the front door quietly behind her and ducked into the guardhouse. This time, she could do it on purpose.

PART FOUR

44

WHEN SHE WOKE UP IN HER BED ON Pomander Walk, Alice knew exactly where she was, and when she was, and where her father was. She stayed in bed for a few moments, stretching. Ethan Hawke and Winona Ryder stared at her from the opposite wall and Alice involuntarily started singing "My Sharona." Ursula was curled up on top of her stomach.

"You really are the best cat," Alice said. Ursula tucked in her paws and rolled onto her back, her eyes still closed. Alice dutifully petted her furry tummy.

It wasn't like **Peggy Sue,** an accidental fainting that caused a dreamlike delusion that wasn't even real. It wasn't like **Back to the Future,** where she could wreck and then unwreck her own life, watching herself from behind. It wasn't even like **Time**

Brothers or **Dawn of Time,** where the heroes were always busy acting out a plot, from point A to point B. Alice wouldn't say that to Leonard, that his characters were always trying to do too much. Why were there so many books about teenagers solving crimes? K-pop fans had raised money, had used the internet to fight evil, but that wasn't solving crimes, exactly. Alice wanted to talk to her father about **Dawn,** but couldn't—he hadn't written it yet.

No—this time, Alice was going to do better. The party didn't matter, the SAT class didn't matter, none of that mattered. He'd quit smoking—that was good, she could do that again. Now she wanted to make sure that he started to exercise, that he went to the doctor when he was sick, that he actually took care of himself. What mattered, too, was making sure that she and Sam said what they said at the ice cream shop. If Sam didn't say it, then Leonard wouldn't write it. And today, Alice knew that she didn't have much time. There was that word again! No wonder there were so many songs about time, and books about time, and movies about time. It was more than hours and minutes, yes, but Alice could see how much each of those mattered, all those tiny moments added together. She felt like a walking needlepoint pillow—**The way you spend your days is the way you spend your life.** She wasn't a teenage detective; she was a scientist. A baker. How much of this did she have to add, and how much of that? Whatever happened, she would see her results in the morning. It had been strange to wake up in the San Remo, but it had also been entertaining, if voyeuristic, like walking through a fun house mirror and getting to see what life was like on the other side. Everything was undoable, give or take. It wasn't like Alice could live anyone's life—she couldn't decide to be a Victoria's Secret model, or a nuclear physicist, but she could start herself and her dad down a path, and if it turned out to be a bad choice, she could always double back.

"Birthday girl? You awake in there?" Leonard called from the hallway. Alice heard him knocking around, getting something out of the closet, then shuffling into the bathroom. The door clunked behind him, and Alice could hear the whir of the fan. Alice had never really loved her birthday—too much pressure to have a good time—but she knew that she would have a good one today. Ursula jumped down to the floor and started playing with a hair elastic, batting it back and forth. Alice kicked back the cover and let her feet touch the familiar mountain ranges of clothing—maybe the Dolomites this time instead of the Andes, but mountains all the same. She was still in her Crazy Eddie T-shirt. Alice gave herself a hug and smiled.

Leonard knocked on her door, nudging it open. "You decent?" he asked.

"Never," Alice said. "Yes. Come in."

The door swung all the way, knocking into the thin wall between their bedrooms.

"So, what's on the docket for the day?" Leonard asked. He had a can of Coca-Cola in his hand.

"Did you just brush your teeth **while** drinking a Coke?" Alice asked. She stood up and took the can out of Leonard's hand. "We're going jogging. Or at least walking. A walk, with a light jog in the middle. And then we're going to have lunch at Gray's Papaya. I'm skipping the SAT class, because, seriously, who cares. Sound good?" She didn't wait for a reply, and walked the can back to the kitchen, where she poured it down the sink.

45

CHEEVER PLACE. ALONE. A BIRTHDAY GIFT
from Serena, a small pouch full of polished crystals and
a lengthy list of instructions about how to use them.

• • •

Melinda packing up her office. Alice threatening to
quit. You had to ask, you had to try. She wouldn't
wait to see how it went, but it was good practice.

• • •

A treadmill in her bedroom at Pomander, vegetables in the refrigerator. No ashtrays. Fridge fully
stocked with Coke Zero.

• • •

Debbie at Leonard's bedside. No change.

46

ALICE ALWAYS MADE SURE THAT SAM
told Leonard her idea, even when the conversation didn't naturally go there. Alice liked his future
full, less lonely, and so she figured out how to
swerve when necessary, to get Sam to say the thing.
Leonard's eyes always opened wide when she said it,
the same lightbulb going on, over and over again.

• • •

Alice and Sam dressed in anime costumes that they
cobbled together from Alice's closet and flirted with
Barry Ford at the convention. They didn't actually
let him touch them, but they threatened to call the
police when they told him how old they were.

• • •

She did have sex with Tommy again, just because she wanted to, in his bedroom in his parents' apartment. It was in between lunch and dinner and his parents were out of town. He had a Nirvana poster on one wall, hung neatly with thumbtacks, and a poster of a Ferrari right next to it, which was the whole problem, really.

47

CHEEVER PLACE.

• • •

Instead of Barry, Andrew McCarthy in the Centrum Silver commercials.

• • •

A workday. Alice went back to Belvedere and found herself alone in Melinda's office, which didn't have Melinda's things in it. She spun in the chair and looked out the window. Tommy Joffey and his wife were on the list again. Alice felt sorry for him, stuck in the San Remo forever, as absurdly fortunate as he'd been every day of his life, but then she remembered the Ferrari poster.

• • •

London at the desk. Debbie at the bedside. Leonard, pale, unconscious.

• • •

She could do better, she could do more.

48

THERE WERE PATTERNS: IF ALICE SLEPT with Tommy and told him something firm, something concrete—**marry me,** or even just **now you are my boyfriend**—she could expect to find herself in the San Remo. Alice didn't like being there any more than she liked being in her studio apartment. The children were always cute, but they never belonged to her. Tommy was always handsome, but he didn't belong to her, either, not like that. It was hard to change a pattern once she'd started it, like her body wanted to do what it had done before, and Alice had to knock herself loose from a clear track. The world didn't care what Alice did, she had no grand illusions about that, but there was clearly some cosmic inertia to overcome. She thought about what

Melinda had told her—that everything mattered, but nothing was fixed. Melinda hadn't been talking about time travel, Melinda had **never** talked about time travel, Alice thought, because Melinda was a sensible, grounded person, but it was good advice. All the tiny pieces added together to make a life, but the pieces could always be rearranged.

• • •

Sometimes things changed a lot, and sometimes things changed a little. Sometimes Alice had rented a different apartment, one that she could almost remember seeing—one that she'd ruled out for having too low a ceiling or a strange step-up toilet, or being up four flights of stairs.

• • •

Alice thought about bringing Sam with her but decided against it just in case there was also a **Freaky Friday** setting, and they ended up in each other's bodies, or exploded.

• • •

Sometimes she just wanted a fresh bagel from H&H, steam rising off the dough, too hot to hold with her bare hands. Sometimes she just needed to walk by and smell it. Childhood was a combination of people and places and smells and bus stop advertisements and local jingles. It wasn't just her father that

Alice was visiting; it was herself, the two of them together. It was the way the Pomander gate clanked, the sound of the Romans sweeping leaves off the bricks.

• • •

Sometimes she didn't tell anyone—not Sam, not Tommy, not her dad. Those were the trips Alice liked best. Just slipping into her own skin and watching everyone around her. It was like going to a zoo, only you could climb behind every fence and get right up close to every lion, every elephant, every giraffe. Nothing could hurt her, because everything was temporary. All she had to do was last the day.

49

ALICE SHAVED HER HEAD WITH LEONARD'S beard trimmer. She'd thought about doing it at various points, but the commitment had always seemed too great. Then she and Sam jumped on the 1 train and took it down to Christopher Street and walked for a few blocks until they hit a cheesy tattoo parlor by the West 4th Street stop and Alice asked for a whale, like the one from the Museum of Natural History, and Sam had gaped happily, her elbows digging into the black vinyl of the tattoo-ist's table as the needle went in and out of Alice's shoulder. She skipped everything except lunch and dinner with her dad and went to sleep happy, blood seeping onto the giant see-through bandage.

50

NEW ZEALAND. WARM ROOM, WITH THE
ocean out the window. Not her house—just temporary. Alice's hair was still short, and bleached
almost white. Her skin was tan, her arms strong.
She carried a camera.

· · ·

Debbie on her voicemail—**Come home. There
isn't much time.** Alice almost wanted to laugh.
**There is always more time, just look at all the
time I have,** she thought, but still, she got on a
plane and flew through an entire day—backward
through a day—arriving before she'd left.

51

ALICE AND LEONARD ATE HER BIRTHDAY dinner at every restaurant she loved: they had dumplings and dim sum at Jing Fong, all the way in Chinatown; they had high tea at the Plaza hotel; they went to Serendipity 3 for giant ice cream sundaes; they had doughy suburban pizza at Uno Pizzeria, which had always secretly been Alice's favorite; they had Gray's Papaya again and again; they had dripping, gooey pizza from V&T; they had lox at Barney Greengrass; they got every kind of cookie from the Hungarian Pastry Shop; they went to City Diner and Leonard made his favorite joke, that he would order the boiled scrod, and then they ate burgers and fries and milkshakes; Leonard let Alice have sips of his margarita at Lucy's, an enormous plate of cheese enchiladas between them.

Bowls of penne alla vodka at Isola. Sometimes it felt like cheating, for it to always be Alice's birthday, and for there always to be a reason for cake and off-key singing, and it was cheating, of course, it was cheating the rest of the year, and tomorrow, but Alice didn't care; she let her dad sing the whole song every time. After one or two birthdays, Alice realized that she was going back mostly for dinner, just to have those hours where she and her dad or she and her dad and Sam sat around a table, talking about nothing in particular but laughing, and happy. Just being together.

• • •

Leonard was always so happy when she told him. Aside from dinner, it became Alice's favorite part. He was surprised every time, and sometimes clapped his hands with delight, pitching his upper body forward. Alice had imagined, over the course of her life, telling Leonard lots of things that made him cackle with joy—true joy, big joy—but there was no going forward, only back. And so she told him this one thing, over and over again, knowing how he would react, a present to them both.

52

IT FELT GOOD, FOR A LITTLE WHILE, TO treat going back and forth like she was just going forward, as if each day were a new day, no matter the year, and it followed the one before it, and like she didn't have to think too far ahead. Alice had never had a problem going from one day to the next. She knew it wasn't true, but sometimes, when she was sitting in the guardhouse, waiting for the past or the future, she felt like she could do it forever, and like no one would ever die, and whatever choices she made, they didn't matter, because she was just going to undo them in the morning.

53

LEONARD'S PALE SKIN, LEONARD'S CLOSED eyes, Leonard's shallow breaths. She could make him better, and so she did, over and over again, a magic trick. Leonard young, Leonard funny, Leonard drinking Coca-Cola and smoking. Leonard immortal, if only for the day.

PART FIVE

54

IT WAS TWO WEEKS AFTER ALICE'S birthday now, each visit pushing forward one day. Now she was used to being forty—truly, what did it matter—but her body did feel creakier than she remembered it, and when she stood up, there were some crinkling noises in her knees, like a freshly milked bowl of Rice Krispies. If Alice had just gone home that night, that first night, her fortieth birthday, if she'd called the fancy car and just given the driver her own address instead of her father's, she would have vomited and passed out and woken up forty plus one day, plus one hangover. She still hadn't fixed one thing in her life. She was no Dawn—she wasn't even a Time Brother. If her life had a tag line, it would be **Go back in time, fix nothing!** Those books had happy endings, or, at the very least, satisfying ones, where there was some definitive resolution. A period at the end of the sentence. Alice's problem was that there was always another sentence.

The Cheever Place apartment was smaller than she remembered, which was always how it felt after a day away. Most garden apartments were floor-throughs, with a door that led to an outdoor space, whether it was grassy or just, like in her building, a large concrete square, but the way Alice's landlady had divided her house, the rental apartment was just one large singular room with a built-in kitchen along one wall and exactly two internal doors: one that opened into a closet, and one that opened into the bathroom. Her desk, which was really just one side of her small kitchen table, was covered with a mountain of paper that was threatening to avalanche at any second. Her shoes, which were supposed to live on their little shoe rack by the door, dribbled out into the middle of the floor as if elves had taken them for joyrides.

Alice flopped over on her bed. The tiny dog who lived next door, with the elderly woman who liked to sit on her front stoop and talk to everyone who walked by, was barking, which meant that the mailman was nearby. The dog was an ancient dachshund and couldn't go up or down the steps by himself, and so plaintively barked every time he wanted to be in a place he wasn't. Alice's bed was a mattress she'd ordered from an internet company that advertised on the subway, on a creaky IKEA bedframe. She wasn't unhappy in her life—she hadn't been **unhappy** in her life. Everything was fine. She was healthy, she had a job, she had friends, she had a decent sex life. She got Sephora points and didn't shop at Amazon. She carried her own bags to the grocery store. Alice didn't know how to drive, but if she did, she would drive an electric car. She voted, all the time, even for city council and state senator. She had a 401(k) and paid down her credit cards every few months. But Alice couldn't look around her apartment and see anything that actually made her happy. There was supposed to be an upside to adulthood, wasn't there? The period of your life that was your own, and not chosen for you by other people?

Alice felt around her bed for her phone, finding it buried under the pillow, her battery nearly dead. It was only 8 a.m., but Sam would be awake.

"Hey," Alice said.

"Hey, sweet cheeks! Happy belated birthday! I'm sorry I've been so hard to pin down, it's been crazy," Sam said. It was always crazy. There were yelps and hollers in the background. Alice thought of Sam's house like a battlefield, where one might be ambushed at any moment.

"Can I come over? I'm sure you're busy, but can I come over? And just hang out?" Alice missed the twisty cord of the telephone in her room on Pomander, watching the pink flesh of her finger bulge through.

"You **want** to come **here** to **New Jersey** to hang out with my **family**?" Sam asked, incredulous. "I cannot stop you, and would be delighted. I personally would vote for alcohol, with grown-ups only, but you do you, baby."

"I'll be there as soon as I can remember how to get there," Alice said, and hung up the phone to map it.

It wasn't complicated: Alice took the F to Jay Street, then the A to 34th, then New Jersey Transit, which felt like the subway but wasn't. Alice liked long train rides. She was feeling too out of sorts to read a book—she'd stared at her bookshelf for almost twenty minutes, unable to decipher if she wanted a happy ending or science fiction or something with death on the first page—and so had turned on the latest episode of her favorite podcast, **Shippers.** The tag line for the podcast was **The Reason the Whole Internet Was Invented,** which was maybe a stretch, but Alice loved it—every week, the two hosts would talk about fictional characters who had not had a canonical romantic relationship, and then gab for upward of forty minutes about why they should have, how they would have, and so forth. Archie and Jughead, Buffy and Cordelia, Stevie Nicks and Christine McVie, Chris Chambers and Gordie Lachance, Tami Taylor and Tim Riggins. The couples weren't always ones that Alice believed

in or would have chosen, but the hosts were entertaining and so she always listened.

"Okay, okay," said Jamie, one of the hosts, after
the theme music played. "I'm excited about this.
It's kind of old-school, but not the most old-school
we've ever done."

"Today we are going to talk about the two books
by cult author Leonard Stern, **Time Brothers** and
Dawn of Time. Now, Jamie, what makes someone
a cult author, and does that mean they're in a cult?"
Rebecca, the cohost, said.

Leonard had always been like that: liable to appear out of nowhere. A question on **Jeopardy!,** an
answer in the crossword puzzle. He was even on
an episode of **The Simpsons,** where he got into a
fight with the guy who owned the comic book store
about some **Time Brothers** memorabilia. Most
people knew his name, and if they didn't, they always knew **Time Brothers,** which had been an easy
cheat for Alice at school when it came to making
friends. She didn't even have to say anything—news
of a famous parent traveled quickly. Alice would be
out of college before she discovered this was a bad
thing and never led to an honest connection.

"Okay, so, before our imaginary call-in line starts
to light up with a thousand of you complaining
that we are about to suggest incest, first of all, no,
and second of all, no," Rebecca said. "In today's
episode, we are going to ship the hell out of the
noncreepy Time Brother, Scott, who was played by

Tony Jakes, and Dawn, who probably had a last name—Dawn Gale!—from **Dawn of Time.**"

A small electronic trumpet noise sounded in the background. "Scott and Dawn! Tony Jakes and Sarah Michelle! I love this pairing." Jamie laughed at her own joke. "Okay, first of all, I want to acknowledge that it's weird, but I can't help it that in my brain, Dawn is Sarah Michelle Gellar, who is a real person in the world, like post–**All My Children** but pre-**Buffy,** and Tony Jakes does not exist, like, I couldn't tell you one thing about him."

"He has a horse farm, according to Wikipedia," Rebecca added, clearly researching in real time.

"Right, a horse farm. Okay, so Tony Jakes has a horse farm, and has not been on-screen in, like, two decades, and according to this super-old profile I read in **People** magazine, he's gay and also renovates houses. So he sounds awesome, and I love him."

"Anyway, here's what I like about Leonard Stern," Rebecca said. "Do you know how old he was when he published his first novel?"

"Twenty-five?" Jaime guessed.

"Incorrect! Leonard Stern was thirty-eight years old! And he didn't publish **Dawn of Time** until he was fifty-two!" Rebecca sounded triumphant.

"I love that," Jamie said. "Snaps for late bloomers."

"Seriously," Rebecca said. "We should start a whole other podcast about people who really tap into their potential after forty. That's a good podcast idea! Tweet at us if you agree!"

Rebecca and Jamie were still talking, but Alice wasn't really listening anymore. She'd never thought about Leonard as a late bloomer. He had bloomed within her lifetime; how could it feel late? But hearing the numbers out loud, from strangers, it did seem notable. These two women were talking about these characters that her father had invented as if they were real, because they were. Sometimes people didn't understand that—Alice wasn't a writer, but she'd spent enough time sitting at dinner tables with novelists to understand that fiction was a myth. Fictional stories, that is. Maybe there were bad ones out there, but the good ones, the **good** ones—those were always true. Not the facts, not the rights and the lefts, not the plots, which could take place in outer space or in hell or anywhere in between, but the feelings. The feelings were the truth.

"Okay," Rebecca went on, "but want to know my actual favorite fact about Leonard Stern, that I learned literally this morning on Wikipedia? He married the woman who played Dawn's mother in the movie!" Rebecca cleared her throat, and Alice sat up, suddenly paying full attention.

"No waaaay," Jamie said. "The woman from that show? About the kids?"

"Yes and yes," Rebecca said. "Dawn's mother

was played by actress Deborah Fox, who was also on the classic eighties television show **Before and After School.**"

It was the image Alice had of her—the bosomy teacher. Alice closed her eyes and could see the whole credit sequence of the TV show—a sitcom about a woman who adopted a houseful of kids and was also their school principal. It had aired on Saturday mornings in the 1980s, and the optics of it were terrible, a multiracial cast of kids and the plump, sweet white lady who saved them. Deborah Fink was Deborah Fox, an actress. And she had married Leonard after costarring in his movie.

"Wow," Alice said out loud. There was always more to learn. How many more surprises did Leonard have that she would discover someday? Alice laughed to herself, thinking of Leonard and Debbie and Sarah Michelle Gellar at Gray's Papaya, the fun house mirror version of her family.

55

THE ROTHMAN-WOODS LIVED NEAR THE Upper Montclair stop, in a big blue house with a porch swing. It was only three blocks from the train station, but Alice came so rarely that she kept having to check that she was walking the right direction. She flipped the phone around in her hand so that it was pointing the way she needed to walk. After only two wrong turns, Alice could see it, the blue floating into view. Montclair's sidewalks were already crunchy with leaves, and the trees seemed to be more full of birds than in Brooklyn. Some houses had already started decorating for Halloween, and headstones dotted the front lawns of Sam's street. Her next-door neighbor had a row of pumpkins leading up to their stoop, and when she got closer, she saw that Sam did, too.

"Hey," Sam said. She was sitting on the porch swing, rocking herself back and forth with her toes.

"Hey!" Alice said. She shoved her phone in her pocket. "It only took me twenty-five years to get here."

"Oh, please," Sam said. Both her hands were spread flat against her belly, which was not flat—it was huge, a perfect half circle. "New Yorkers think they're the center of the world. It takes less time to get here than it does to get to wherever the twenty-five-year-olds live now. Queens?"

"Bushwick, I think."

"Right. It's just New Jersey. Oof." Sam let her sneakers flatten against the wood porch, and the swing slowed to a stop. Sam pushed herself up to standing, her belly in full, triumphant view.

"Wow," Alice said. She hadn't seen Sam very much when she was pregnant before. They had been at dinner at some dark restaurant when Sam whipped out a sonogram photo, the tiny little astronaut profile that would eventually be her eldest, and after that, it was their regular hectic schedule, trying to squeeze in a March dinner that became an April dinner, and so on—Alice had seen photos of Sam and Josh on vacation in Puerto Rico, Sam's belly poking out in between the polka dot slices of her bikini, but even before Sam and Josh had moved to Jersey, even before the kids were born, it wasn't ever like it had been in high school, where they just talked on the phone from the minute they walked in the door until the minute they fell asleep, and where they slept in each other's bed every weekend. It was like watching a plant grow in stop motion. "You look amazing."

Sam rolled her eyes. "I assure you that I do not feel amazing, but thank you. Let's get a drink and then we can sit?"

Alice nodded and followed Sam through the front door. "Where are the kids?"

"The kids? Well, Mavis is in the backyard, and this one's in here." Sam pointed to her belly.

"Right," Alice said. "That's what I meant." She remembered Sam's lists of girl names: Evie, Mavis, Ella. Pregnancies were fragile things—it wasn't shifting the world's balance. Sam had had miscarriages before, and maybe she had again. That was Alice's biggest question, the one Leonard hadn't answered because she hadn't known to ask it—were all those other kids, those other lives, still happening, somewhere? She thought so, but it was impossible to know for sure.

Sam pulled open the fridge and took out two cans of fizzy water. "Pamplemousse okay?"

Alice nodded. The house was so big, like something on a TV show, one of the sitcoms that she and Sam used to watch after school, like Debbie's show. Rooms big enough for siblings and parents and guys hoisting boom mics over all of their heads. Sam led them out the back door. Mavis was on the little wooden play structure they had, dangling upside down by her knees, with Josh standing next to her, his waiting arms ready to catch if she needed to be rescued. Alice waved, and Josh waved back, unable to leave his post. That was fine—they both knew she was there just for Sam.

"Forty's not so bad," Sam said. "You struggling with it? The idea of it?" She popped open her can and took a long sip. "God, being pregnant is like always being hungover. I am always thirsty, and I always have to pee, and I never want to get up to go to the bathroom."

"No, it's fine," Alice said. "That part's fine."

Sam looked at her. "So what's not fine? What's going on? You know I love when you come here, but you never come here."

"I just miss you," Alice said. "And I miss my dad." She let out a noise that was somewhere between a hiccup and a sob. "I'm sorry."

"No, honey, come on! It's okay! You know how much I love Lenny. Did he give me royalties for telling him to write a book that would make him a gazillion dollars? No. But did he thank me in the acknowledgments? Yes. Did he offer to put my kids through college? Also yes. I don't need him to, but you never know. What if Josh gets run over by a bus, and I have to stop working? Your dad is like my personal Oprah." She squeezed Alice's arm. "I'm kidding. Not about him offering to put my kids through college, though—he really did."

"I didn't know that." Alice could imagine it,

though. She could see her dad saying it to Sam, pregnant with her first baby. He had probably wanted more kids—Alice had never considered it, they were always just a team of two, but coming from a tiny family, maybe he had wanted more. Or maybe he'd assumed that Alice would give him a grandkid or two eventually! He would never have pressured her, not in a million years, but Alice wondered if when he had gone back, Leonard had ever tried to find someone else—or if he'd ever gone back after meeting Deborah, to see if he could find her sooner. Have children of their own. Maybe he had. What else had he done that he didn't want to tell Alice about? Probably a thousand things.

"Are you going to go see him today?" Sam asked.

Josh helped Mavis unhook her knees, and the girl disappeared into the top of the structure, which was built to look like a pirate ship.

"I'll go this afternoon." Alice put the cool can to her forehead. "It just sucks, you know?"

"I know." Sam put her arm around Alice's shoulders. "Oof, this kid just will not stop kicking me."

"Can I feel?" Alice had reluctantly touched several pregnant bellies—teachers at school, friends from college, Sam. It always felt invasive on her part, borderline creepy. Alice had never been one of those people obsessed with babies, who would flirt across tables in restaurants and over the backs of airplane seats with any nearby child. Having a baby—carrying a baby—seemed so unfairly public, and compelled strangers to weigh in on your life choices with nary an invitation. But Alice felt like she needed proof that this world was real, that today, whenever today was, was a real day in her real life, and in Sam's, too.

"Of course," Sam said. She reached for Alice's hand and put it low on her belly. "Oh, you know who just moved to Montclair? That kid—man, I guess, he's a man now—but that kid who was a year behind us at Belvedere. Kenji?"

"Kenji Morris," Alice said. She'd seen him a lot recently—he was the very tail of the boy train coming into her sixteenth birthday party on Pomander. A year behind them, but tall for his age, and skinny, Kenji had swayed like a willow tree. His mother was Japanese, and his father was dead. Alice didn't think she knew anything else about him. He'd smoked Parliaments, maybe? No, he hadn't smoked at all. They'd had Spanish together—he was good at languages, and was the only sophomore in the class.

"Right, Kenji Morris," Sam said. "He and his kid live around the corner. He just got divorced. His daughter is Mavis's age, and we met them in the park the other day. He's nice! I never really knew him."

"Let me guess—he's a lawyer."

"No, you fucking snob. Not every single person we went to school with is a lawyer, okay? He's an architect." Sam snorted.

"That's a made-up job for men in romantic comedies."

"That is also not true." Sam put her head on Alice's shoulder. "What do you want for lunch? The menu is grilled cheese or peanut butter and jelly. Or scrambled eggs."

This time—yesterday—Alice hadn't told Sam or her father. It seemed beside the point to tell Sam now, now that Alice knew it wouldn't last and would probably only add to Sam's therapy bills. Even when she hadn't told her, the concept of it was still there, deep in their brains—no one who loved Keanu Reeves could avoid time travel for long.

"Is he bald?" Alice could picture Kenji so clearly, his black hair swooping low over one eye. Haircuts were terrible in the nineties—Caesars, baby bangs, even a few white boys with dreads—but Kenji's hair had always had the freshly brushed quality of a kid on picture day.

"Are you kidding? His hair is as amazing as it ever was. Honestly, better, because there are some grays in there, and I don't know if I'm just getting old, but he is fully hot. Isn't it weird how when you're in high school, a kid who is, like, six months younger than you but a grade behind feels like an actual baby? All the boys in our grade sucked, no offense, but there were some cuties in the grade below us. Why didn't we go out with them?"

Mavis slid down the plastic slide, crunching a pile of leaves with her tiny sneakers. Josh had walked around to the back of the swing set.

"That's a good question," Alice said. She'd always

had crushes on older boys. They were beautiful and adult-seeming and not remotely interested in her, except for sometimes at parties when one of them would stick his tongue halfway down her throat and then walk away when he got bored. "How did you know you wanted to marry Josh?"

Sam laughed. "I mean, did I? I don't know. We were so young. I did, of course I wanted to, here we are, it wasn't against my will or anything. I love him. But I think that I was too young to really know what my choices were going to mean—there's not really any way to find out what you need to find out, you know? Like, if someone is going to be a good parent, or they have some weird, fucked-up patriarchal bullshit that won't surface until they're forty, or if they're terrible with money, or if they refuse to go to therapy. There should be an app for that."

"Um, have you seen all the dating apps? It's literally just penises. No one is talking about the patriarchy. And if someone is, you know it's a front for all the penises that are about to follow." Alice paused. "You and Josh are so good together, though."

"We are. Most of the time. But we're also both humans, you know, with different baggage about different shit. The things that drive me crazy about him might not drive someone else crazy. But it's a choice—still. We've been married for fifteen years. But I still have to choose it. That doesn't stop."

Mavis came down the slide again, and this time, when she crunched into the leaves, she looked up and saw her mother, and took off across the lawn at top speed. Her small body flew into Sam's arms, and Alice watched them giggle and hug. Josh was watching, too. She hadn't thought of it as an ongoing choice, a perennial decision, and the idea of it made her both exhausted and glad. Glad that she wasn't the only one who felt like she was always in the middle of planning her future, and exhausted that there was no way off the ride. It reminded her of when Serena's parents—her grandparents, though she saw them so rarely that they hardly counted as such—had abruptly decided to stop vacationing in Mexico and bought a time-share in Arizona instead, where they could golf and eat Cobb salads and drink ice-cold lemonades all within the boundaries of their gated community. It had something to do with politics, but Serena didn't like to talk about things like that, and so that was all she said, it was politics. **Scottsdale is lovely all winter.** And then, when Serena's father was sick, her mother moved him into a facility with full-time care, and then Alice's grandmother still went back to California. Did she call every day? Send postcards for the nurses to read to him? Who knew what went into people's decisions after fifty years of marriage? Who knew what Serena's parents' relationship had done to their daughter's vision of what her own should look like?

Maybe Alice was alone because Leonard had always been alone.

"Come on," Sam said. She stood up and patted Mavis on the top of the head. Alice winked at Mavis, who blinked back with her whole face. "Time to eat."

56

VISITING HOURS WERE UNTIL 5:00, BUT when Alice passed London her ID at 4:45, he didn't say a word, just slipped her a pass. Alice felt terrible. Not **sick,** not exactly, but slow and heavy, like she was wading through molasses. With a headache. It was disorienting—at least when she was in the guardhouse, Alice knew what to expect. She thought about it like making a mixtape the way she'd done in high school, rewinding until just the right spot and then adding something new. It had always felt so crucial to put things in the right order, to have this song after that one. But you couldn't control how someone else would listen, whether they would care, whether they would play it over and over or whether the tape would get caught and spin out like a ball of Christmas tinsel. She could go back more easily than she could go forward. Going forward was scary, because anything could have happened. Anything could happen. **Anything** had been proven to be within a fairly narrow range, but still—Alice couldn't control it.

The hospital was quieter than usual—the afternoon had turned cloudy and dark, and maybe most of the visitors had gone home early to beat the coming rain. Alice nodded polite greetings to the people she passed in the endless hallways, one leading to the next and the next, until she reached her father's room. She expected the same scene she'd walked into so many times: her father, mostly asleep, eyes closed, and Debbie fussing about in the chair, the noise of television news blasting away in several neighboring rooms. But when Alice pulled aside the curtain, Leonard was alone and awake, his eyes open, with his head propped up on pillows. He looked at her and smiled.

"Finally." Leonard opened his hands, like a magician revealing that something—a coin, a rabbit— had disappeared.

Alice stopped, still clutching the cheap nylon curtain. "Dad."

Leonard smiled. "Were you expecting someone else?" His face was thin, and his stubble was gray. Leonard waved a hand in the direction of the chair. "Come into my tiny kingdom."

"I just didn't know you'd be up." Alice swiftly ducked into the chair and held her arms tight across her lap like they were the safety bar on a roller coaster.

"Debbie just left. She was hoping to catch you, but you can call her later, right?" There were a few bags of fluid hanging behind him, one dripping slowly into his arm. The doctors' and nurses' names were on the whiteboard, and a list of all of Leonard's medications. It was the same as it always was, only he was awake and talking and looking at her. "Good to see you, Al-pal."

"Good to see you, too," Alice said, which was an understatement.

"How was your day?" Leonard said. "You look a little tired."

"I am tired," Alice said, though it was more than that. She felt embarrassed, and anxious, and excited. Alice had already spent so much time grieving in the present that she didn't know quite what to make of having her father in front of her, awake. The idea of Leonard dying, and what it would mean for the rest of her life, was heavy, but it was a familiar weight. Not that Alice thought she had worked her way through it—if anything, she understood that it wasn't actually something one could ever work all the way through, like a jigsaw puzzle or a Rubik's cube; grief was something that moved in and stayed. Maybe it moved from one side of the room to the other, farther away from the window, but it was always there. A part of you that you couldn't wish or pray or drink or exercise away. She was used to him being so close to gone that gone was almost desirable—no one wanted to watch someone they loved suffer. But she was also tired—tired of how tense her body was when the phone rang, tired of how nervous she felt whenever she walked out of his hospital room, tired of how it felt to know that her life was going to change and that she was going to have this enormous hole forever. Soon. Alice thought that it was probably exactly the inverse, the mirror image, of how it felt to be pregnant, and to know that your life would never be the same. A subtraction instead of an addition. So many of the customs were identical—people would send flowers, or cards, or food. Someone would have her name on their to-do list—**Write a note to Alice Stern.** And then it would be done, just her problem again, day in and day out, forever. It had taken a long time for Alice to get wherever she was, and she didn't know if she could do it again.

She couldn't remember exactly what had happened on her last trip—all the days had run together. She hadn't told him, she thought, at the end of the night, as she sometimes did.

"Fine, fine. Yeah, you seem fine," Leonard said, teasing.

"You're better," Alice said. "Better than I've seen you."

Leonard nodded. "You know, they don't know what's wrong with me. They know I'm dying, of course"—here he smiled at the plain truth of it—"but they don't know why. I think when they look at my blood tests, it's like looking at a ninety-six-year-old man." He wiggled his eyebrows. He knew. Of course he knew.

"Dad," Alice said, "I haven't been able to talk to you." She tried to do the math—it had been twenty-four years since her sixteenth birthday, but it had also been a day, a week, two weeks. "Can you just tell me what you know? I mean, I keep going back and trying to help—trying to solve this, like"—she gestured around the room—"this whole thing, but this is the first time you've even been awake! I just don't know what to do. And so I've been going back and forth, because, like, why not?" She tried to laugh but it came out more like a groan. Alice wished that they were at home, and that Ursula was on her lap. Did hospitals have cats? She'd seen segments with dogs on the news, docile and fluffy golden Labradors who would tuck their sweet snouts into the hands of the sick. Leonard wouldn't have wanted some random dog to lick him; he would have wanted the ageless, limitless dignity of Ursula.

"Well, it only works between the hours of three and four a.m., and it has to be empty. Which it usually isn't. I make sure of that. That's that, really. I learned a long time ago, the rules are the rules. It doesn't matter if they don't make sense. It's just how it works. Is that what you mean?" Leonard smiled. "Science fiction only has to make sense within its own walls, even if the walls are your world."

"You explained that part. Once. Who else knows?" Alice asked. "Is it just us?"

Leonard nodded, his face tight. "The Romans know. Cindy used to go back to the seventies and dance all night. That was before we moved in. It gets harder, going back and forth. Harder to come back, really. You feel it in your body. For a long time, I didn't think it actually hurt you, but, well . . ." He gestured around the room. "Cindy used to go to Studio 54 and boogie, the whole bit, and when she came back, she started running into some trouble."

"What kind of trouble?" Alice thought of her own body and how it seemed to be getting slower, the way her head hurt in the mornings, no matter where or when she was.

"It feels like double vision, a little bit wobbly, and the wobbling gets more pronounced the older you get. It's sort of the reverse of what you'd really want, you know—you'd want things to be more and more clear the farther you get away from a certain time, the less you can rely on your own memory, but that's not how it works." Leonard knit his fingers together. His skin looked thin and pale.

"And how do you make sure you get back to where you want to be?" This was what she hadn't figured out. "I mean, how do you know when to stop?"

"Do you know where you want to be?" Leonard raised an eyebrow.

"I don't fucking know. I know things weren't perfect, originally, but then when I got back, things weren't perfect in a totally different direction." She thought about Tommy and the two beautiful kids and the giant apartment and she was so glad not to be there.

Leonard nodded. "Oh, sure. Once, and only once, when I came back, you had moved to California to live with Serena. That was a disaster, so I made sure it never happened again. But you see how it works—you see what changes and what doesn't. Not to sound too Buddhist about it, because I'm not a Buddhist, and I'm sure to get it wrong, but everything outside of you is window dressing, you know?"

Alice shook her head. "Yeah, I'm pretty sure the Dalai Lama has never said anything about window dressing."

"Thank you, miss. But you know what I mean. There's the stuff that changes, and there's the stuff that doesn't. We're all trying to sort out our inner messes—no one has it any better. Even the Buddhists! They're better at trying, maybe, or better at pushing aside all of that. It's not about the time. It's about how you spend it. Where you put your energy—" Leonard closed his mouth in midsentence, and then his eyes, too. Alice could see it now—just because he was awake and talking, it didn't mean that he was better. Whatever she'd done, it hadn't been enough. He'd found love, he'd quit smoking, he'd written another book, he'd taken up jogging, and a thousand more things she hadn't seen, Alice was sure—but none of it mattered. This was still where they were.

"What is wrong with you?" Alice asked. Even as the words came out of her mouth, she realized that she knew the answer. It was this—what she'd been doing, and Leonard had done who knew how many times. It wasn't the Coca-Cola. It wasn't even the smoking. It was this. Of course she couldn't save him.

Leonard lifted his palms toward the sky. "I think any parent would do what I did. Honestly, I wish I could have gotten off at different stops, you know? Alice at three, Alice at six, Alice at twelve, me at thirty, me at forty . . ." He marked the points on his arm, like David Byrne dancing in the music video for "Once in a Lifetime." "No one talks about that—at least not to dads. Maybe moms talk about it more—I bet they do. But no one ever talked to me about it, that's for sure—what it feels like to love someone so much, and then have them change into someone else. You love that new person, but it's different, and it all happens so fast, even the parts that feel like they just last for fucking ever while they're happening."

He was exactly right. Alice felt like it would be hurtful to say so—to tell him how much he had changed, too, though of course he knew it. She loved him now, but not in the same way that she had loved him as a kid, because he wasn't the same and neither was she. That was what she'd been doing, going back and forth—even on the days when she hadn't spent much time with her dad and had gone off and done silly things with

Sam or spent the day in bed with a cute teenage boy. It wasn't that she thought Leonard had been the perfect father—every Father's Day, on the internet, Alice was bombarded with photos of dads hiking, dads cooking, dads throwing underhanded softball pitches, dads building stuff with tools, dads playing dress-up. Leonard had never done any of those things, and sometimes Alice wished he had, but she couldn't fault him for being who he was. He was who he was, and she loved him for it, especially that version of him, the young one who lived like nothing could hurt him. She'd been putting it off, saying goodbye to that version of her dad. Whatever happened on the other end, whether he was conscious or unconscious, he was somewhere else now—slower and stodgier. No one could be young forever. Not even her father, who had time-traveled, who had invented worlds, who had made things that would outlast him. Who had made her.

Leonard let Alice's thoughts fill the room. "It's okay to lose people, Al. Loss is the point. You can't take away the grief, the pain, because then what are you left with? An episode of **Beverly Hills, 90210,** where the tinkling theme song comes in at the end and you know everything's going to be all right?"

"Okay, now I know you have not been paying attention, because those kids were more full of trauma than an emergency room." Alice laughed.

"You know what I mean. That resolution—it doesn't exist." Leonard shook his head. "And you

can't try forever. Or you can, but that's how you
end up like me. That's what's going on. That's what
they don't know. That never happened to Scott and
Jeff—they were always ready to zip off back to the
eighties in their stupid vests. Or Dawn." Leonard
looked over at Alice. "I tried to make Dawn as much
like you as possible. She turned into her own person, like they always do, but when I started, I was
just thinking about you, moving back and forth
like I knew you would. I guess it's the way some
parents feel about their kids getting their driver's
licenses, you know? Like, you're out there, beyond
my reach. And I just had to trust that you were
solid enough. Which you were. Dawn too."

"So what do I do?" Alice asked. It was embarrassing. She wasn't sixteen, she was forty, and she
already knew that he wouldn't tell her, that he
couldn't tell her, even if he wanted to. "Why didn't
you tell me?"

"I didn't know for a long time what it was doing
to my body. And then, when I did—what are you
going to do, be the police? I wasn't going to be the
police. We all do what we have to do, make our
own decisions about how to behave. What we want
to do, what we need to do," Leonard said. "You
wanna watch **Jeopardy!**?"

She did. Alice scooted her chair as close to the
bed as it would go and waited as her dad fished
around in his bed for the giant hospital remote,
which had buttons the size of quarters. He had to

use both hands to press hard enough. Alice laid her head on the plastic handrail of the bed and turned her face toward the screen. Alex Trebek would have the answers.

"I have one more question," Alice said.

"Just one?" Leonard laughed, and then coughed. He pointed at the television. "It's all questions."

"It's always my birthday. When I go back. Why? Nothing happens, I mean, nothing major. For me, I mean." Alice examined her fingernails.

"Not for me to know," Leonard said. He looked so tired. "But I can tell you this—the day that you were born, that was when I became the best version of myself. I know that sounds cheeseball, but it's true. Before you came scampering out, I was pretty happy thinking only about myself, all day long." Leonard smiled. "I've been waiting to talk to you about this."

"About being a selfish cheeseball?" Alice asked. Even now, she couldn't help it—the joking, the teasing.

"About what it feels like to go back. It was just—" Leonard's voice started to waver. He cleared his throat a few times and shook his head. "It was when I felt the most love. In my whole life. You remember when we went to that wedding and the bride told her husband that she was going to love him more than any children they would ever have?"

Alice rolled her eyes. "Yes." She'd been eleven, swigging unlimited Shirley Temples in a velvet party dress.

"Well, I mean, obviously they're still married and I got divorced. But I never felt anything close to the love that I had for you with Serena. Or Debbie." At this, Leonard put a finger to his lips. "And that day, whoosh. There it was, all of it at once. Like when an oil derrick hits, and it all goes shooting into the sky. Maybe that's it. I know I wasn't always the best parent, but I tried. We did okay, right?"

"We did great, Dad. We did great." The hospital made noises—cart wheels on the smooth floor, someone's cough or shout, a nurse's hello, laughter behind the desk—but Alice didn't hear them. She closed her eyes for a moment and thought about everything she'd had on her sixteenth birthday— a father she loved and wanted to spend time with, who also trusted her to be alone. A best friend. A crush. Alice wondered if the day changed over the course of your life. Maybe there was a day in her forties, fifties, sixties that would be so full of love, so full, period, that a ninety-year-old Alice would go there instead. But Leonard wouldn't be there, because no matter what she did, by then, he would be gone. It might not be someone else's best, but it was hers, for now.

"What is **Time Brothers**," said a contestant, hand still on the button, their face flushed with the satisfaction of knowing they were right.

PART SIX

57

THERE WERE BIRDS ON POMANDER—
pigeons, sure, but also noisy swallows and sometimes even some barking seagulls who had
wandered the short block and a half up the hill
from the Hudson. They were congregating on the
fire escape, having their daily meeting about worms
and wind and bread crumbs. Alice listened for a
few minutes, staring at the ceiling. From her bed,
she could see a sliver of gray sky in between the
buildings behind them. She sat up in one fluid motion, her enormous yellow T-shirt riding up her rib
cage as she stretched her arms overhead.

Leonard was in the same spot as usual, eating
breakfast at the table. There was a folded newspaper
beside him, and Ursula sat sentry at the window, as
if she were waiting for Alice to appear.

"Knock, knock," Alice said, clucking her tongue to get her father's attention. He looked bemused to see her up so early. He didn't know how often she was up, she was up, she was up.

"Happy birthday, little vagabond," Leonard said. He ruffled Alice's hair the way he had when she was a kid and came up to his waist. Alice didn't cry, but she did swallow hard, several times in a row.

She had a plan.

58

THE SAT CLASS WAS POINTLESS AND SO Alice skipped it. Leonard didn't even put up a fuss. Alice looked through her drawers for her tape recorder and brought it with them to City Diner, where they had grilled cheeses and two orders of french fries.

"Tell me about your cousins," Alice asked. "Who was your elementary school nemesis? Who was your first kiss? What was Mom like when she was young?"

Leonard laughed into his coffee cup. But then he answered her questions, one at a time. There was a cousin called Eggs who'd ended up as a bookie; there was a girl named Priscilla who had broken his pencils in half; there was Priscilla again, a few years later; there was Serena at twenty-two, blond and effortless. Every now and then Leonard would pause and say, "Are you sure you really want to hear all this?" But Alice would nod vigorously and point to the tape recorder. "Keep going."

59

THEY HAD TO HAVE DINNER AT GRAY'S
Papaya and so they did, even though Alice was
getting tired of hot dogs. She had systematically
worked her way through the juices, and papaya was
the winner. It made Leonard happy when Alice got
more stuff on her dog, and so she loaded it up, the
works. Sam wrinkled her nose, but Alice could tell
she was impressed, too. They had to get the ice
cream and so they did. Alice made sure that Sam
always said the right thing, giving her alley-oops
over and over again until the thought was nudged
out. Sometimes Alice got hot fudge and sometimes
she got butterscotch. That didn't seem to make
a difference.

60

THERE WERE A FINITE NUMBER OF parties in one's life, and so Alice decided to let her dad go to the convention after dinner. There were too few opportunities, as an adult, to be surrounded by friends after midnight. She had decided to let Tommy make his own mistakes—she didn't have to intervene. Alice and Sam wore silky slips and tiaras and dark lipstick like sexy vampires and they were having a great time before anyone else even rang the doorbell. When Helen and Lizzie came over, Helen said, "What is this, **The Craft**?" and that was all Alice and Sam needed to hear. For the rest of the night, they were teen witches, casting spells and making each other levitate by standing behind each other and hoisting up their bodies. When Phoebe came with her brother's drugs, Alice said sure, why not. The boys rang the doorbell and came in like a little parade, like always.

"Did you guys pick each other up, like one at a time? Like a hurricane picking up couches and doors, like in **The Wizard of Oz** or something, only it's just teenage boys?" Alice stood aside, giggling, as the boys all came in, a cloud of Polo Sport carrying them into her living room. Tommy was in the middle of the clump, surrounded by admirers and acolytes, as always, and Alice let him kiss her on the cheek. He was a good guy, even if he wasn't her good guy. The boys collapsed onto the couch and leaned against the counters as if they were all unable to support their own weight. Whatever was in the pill was starting to do its job, and Alice felt the heavy wood of the door against her skin. Kenji Morris was the last one in line and stood on the welcome mat.

"Are you okay?" he asked, tossing his head to the side to swing his bangs out of the way.

"Your hair is really nice," Alice said. "It's like a waterfall."

"Thanks," Kenji said. He looked slightly afraid that she would reach out and touch him, and shimmied sideways through the front door.

Lizzie was on Tommy right away. She had a Ring Pop on and was licking and sucking like she was auditioning for a porn movie. There wasn't a heterosexual teenage boy alive who could have resisted. Sam walked by and turned to Alice, rolling her eyes hard.

"I need more cigarettes," Alice said. A few people threw wads of cash at her and made requests— a pack of Newport Lights, a pack of Marlboro Lights, some papers.

"I'll go with you," Kenji said. He'd been sitting quietly at the end of the table, bobbing his head to the music.

• • •

The closest deli that didn't ask for ID was on Amsterdam. Alice had been so hot inside that she'd forgotten it was fall outside, and as soon as they'd walked out through the iron gates, she was goose-pimpled and freezing.

"Here," Kenji said. He pulled his North Face fleece over his head and handed it to her. Alice quickly shoved her arms through the sleeves. It smelled like laundry detergent and cigarette smoke, though Kenji himself didn't smoke, she didn't think. She'd never paid much attention.

The block between Broadway and Amsterdam was silent. So much of high school was spent roaming around with enormous herds of people— college, too—and Alice had had this feeling before, of suddenly being alone with someone you'd never been alone with, despite having been in the same room with them hundreds of times. She didn't know what to say, but then she thought about it, and she did.

"Hey," Alice said. "I know this is totally out of

the blue, and I'm sorry if it's a weird thing to say
on the way to the bodega, but I'm really sorry about
your dad."

Kenji stopped. "Whoa, okay."

"I'm sorry," Alice said. "I shouldn't have said that,
that was totally weird timing."

"No," Kenji said, "it's cool. It's just, you know, no
one ever mentions it. Or people apologize, like, once,
like they just stepped on your foot, and then it's all
cool, you know?"

Alice thought about how many times she'd done
the same thing. Helen's father had died when they
were in college, after a long illness, and had she
even sent a note? She thought so. The whole thing
had just made her uncomfortable, and she didn't
want to do or say the wrong thing, and so saying
nothing and staying out of the way seemed better.
But it was obviously not better. Alice could already
tell how much she would hate people who did the
wrong thing when Leonard died, and the people
who said nothing at all, even as she would simul-
taneously forgive those who hadn't lost a parent or
a loved one, because they just didn't know.

"I get it. How old were you?"

"Twelve," Kenji said. He shivered in his enormous
white T-shirt.

"Fuck," Alice said. "I am so sorry. It was cancer,
right?"

"Yep," he said. "Lymphoma."

They walked in silence until they got to the

corner. Kenji started to walk toward the door of the deli, but Alice put her hand on his arm. "I'm really sorry that happened. I bet you miss him a lot. My dad is sick, too. And my mom may as well be dead—I know that's not the same thing, but she left us a long time ago, and so it's just me and my dad. And it's scary."

Kenji immediately pulled her in for a hug. "I didn't know that your dad was sick." Alice rested her head against his shoulder. It was bony in the way that so many teenage boys' bodies were—bodies that didn't yet know how big they were supposed to be, where they started and stopped. On her sixteenth birthday, her father wasn't sick at all. Things were getting messy inside her head. It felt like everything was happening at once.

"Were you there? When it happened?" Alice took a step back, and another, until she found herself sitting on a fire hydrant. "I'm sorry if that's too personal."

"No, it's okay," Kenji said. "It's actually nice to talk about it. When no one talks about it, it's kind of like it never happened, even though I know it did. Sometimes I'm like, 'They do know, right?'" He ran his hand through his hair. "I was at school. The nurse came and—I'll never forget it, I was in Mr. Bowman's English class—and said my mom was there to pick me up. I knew what it was, so I got all my stuff so slowly, you know, like in the period of time before she actually said the words, he was still alive. Like, magical realism. Even though I knew it must have happened already."

"Man," Alice said. "I totally understand." It wasn't fair, for that to happen to a kid. It happened all the time, of course, but it shouldn't. There was a girl named Melissa who had gone to Belvedere just for first and second grade, and in second grade, her mom died, and Alice could remember her mom so clearly, and the braids that she gave Melissa every day, these two long, dark brown braids that whipped around when she ran or was on the playground swing. Her father had taken over the braiding, and when she left the school, it was easy to picture her mother still there, wherever they went. It was too much otherwise, too big to even imagine, like learning that the earth could actually explode at any moment. Kenji nudged her toward the door.

"Let's get your stuff before those kids destroy your house."

Alice laughed. They hadn't yet, not once in all her sixteenth birthdays, but there was a first time for everything. By now, Tommy and Lizzie were probably having sex in her bed. Her body was feeling buzzy—whatever Phoebe had given her was kicking in.

"Okay," Alice said. "But I might need just a teensy bit of help standing up."

61

IT WAS NEARLY TWO WHEN PEOPLE started to go home. A lot of kids had 1:30 a.m. curfews, which sounded late at first but then seemed early, until Alice was in her late twenties and it seemed late again. Everything was relative, even time. Maybe especially time. Sam was half-asleep, helping to empty bottles in the sink and then clink them into the recycling. Tommy had gone home— he and Lizzie had stumbled out together, as if they were going to go somewhere, when in reality they'd share a cab and each creep into their parents' apartments, praying no one smelled the beer or smoke or sex on them. So much of being a teenager was pretending that your body hadn't started to do the things that adult bodies did. It was when children had to learn how to be separate humans, a painful process across the board. By 2:30 the house was empty except for Sam, asleep in Alice's bed, and Alice, awake at the front window. She picked up the landline and called the phone number on the fridge.

"Hello?" It wasn't her dad—it was Simon Rush. The room sounded packed and noisy, an aviary full of science fiction writers. Alice could picture him, one thick finger poking into his opposite ear to block out the noise.

"Simon? Hi, it's Alice. Is my dad there?" She would have apologized for calling so late, but there was clearly no need.

"Hey, Alice, sure, hang on." She heard the muffled sound of a hand on the receiver, and then the clink of the hard plastic phone onto the glossy wooden bedside table, she assumed. It took a couple of minutes for Leonard to make his way across the room—Alice could see the whole scene, all his friends strewn about, laughing and talking, drunk and smoking, having a great night. Maybe there were endless opportunities for parties, and for love, if you built a life that made room for them. When Leonard finally got to the phone, he was panting a little bit.

"Al? What's going on? You okay? It's the middle of the night!"

"I'm fine, Dad." She'd wanted him to go to the

hotel because it made what she had to do easier. She had to choose to be an adult, to be that first and his daughter second, instead of the other way around. Alice had always been good at self-parenting as a kid—making curfew, getting good grades—but she'd forgotten to do it as a grown-up, too. "I just wanted to say good night."

Leonard exhaled. "Whew, god, you scared me. You have fun tonight?"

"Sure," Alice said. Her body felt normal again. For the past few hours, she and Sam had mostly been sitting in front of her closet mirror putting on every shade of lipstick she owned and talking about Ethan Hawke and Jordan Catalano and whether the movies they loved were actually good or if the movie stars were so beautiful that it didn't matter. They'd blotted their lips on the inside of Alice's closet door, first in a straight line and then nearly halfway up the whole door, a cloud of kisses, until it looked like wallpaper. "How about you? Are you having fun?"

Leonard laughed. "Well, someone brought a frozen margarita machine from home and is making margaritas, so, yes, we are all having a pretty good time. I'm going to have a headache in the morning, but talking to Barry always gives me a headache anyway."

"Okay," Alice said. "I love you, Dad."

"Sure you're okay, Al-pal? Do you need me to

come home?" His voice sounded louder, like he was cupping the phone with his hand. Alice could picture him turning his back to his friends and facing the wall, maybe shushing them with a finger.

"I'm really okay, I swear."

"Okay. I love you, too, I really do." She could hear him smile. He had been young, and she had been young—they had been young together. Why was it so hard to see that, how close generations were? That children and their parents were companions through life. Maybe that's why she was here now. Maybe this was the moment when they were both at their best, and together. Alice thought about Kenji and his beautiful mother. He'd gone home early—his curfew was only midnight. Alice could understand how hard it probably was for his mom to let him out of her sight at all. Once you had proof of the sudden cruelty of life, how could you ever relax? How could you just let things happen?

"I'll see you tomorrow, Dad," Alice said. She wanted to remind him of all the things he was supposed to do—to write **Dawn,** to find Debbie, to be happy—but she knew that she didn't have to. She would have to trust it this time. Because she wasn't going to come back. Wherever she ended up, that's where she was going to stay. "Will you do one thing for me?" She was going to tell him not to do it anymore, not to travel, that all that love would kill him eventually. But then Alice thought about how good it felt, right now, to hear his healthy, strong voice, to hear him having fun with his friends, and to be so full of it all, and she found that she couldn't.

"Of course, honey, what is it?" Leonard asked. The blender went on in the background. It was so loud, he could probably barely hear her.

"Just take care of yourself," Alice said. "Okay?"

"Until the future," Leonard said, the line from **Time Brothers.** Alice laughed. Leonard must have been drunk, drunk enough to find his own work amusing. He hung up first, and then Alice sat there until the phone started to blare out its complaint. She settled the receiver back in its cradle and looked at the time. The plan was to leave him a note, telling him what she knew, more or less. Telling him not to travel, not to jump, not to visit. Alice started to write it over and over again, but it was never right. Instead she just wrote, **Until the future/my future/your future, what does the future mean, anyway? love, Alice,** threw the rest in the garbage, and went to bed.

62

IT WAS BEFORE DAWN WHEN ALICE OPENED her eyes. She was still on Pomander—in the living room, on the couch, with Ursula purring next to her face. Alice tried to sit up without disturbing the cat. The kitchen light was on, which made it look like a stage set, with Alice the only audience member. Ursula hopped up into the window and flattened one side against the glass. Debbie entered from stage left, dressed in sweatpants and an ancient **Dawn of Time** crew sweatshirt, which made Alice realize that for the first time, she had woken up in the same place she'd fallen asleep, albeit in a different room. She watched Debbie toddle into the kitchen, open a cabinet, and then pour herself a glass of water from the tap. It was still dark outside, and the air was windy, knocking small branches against the window. October was a good month to confront death—this was why Halloween worked. The trees were mostly bare and the air was warm enough that you hadn't yet pulled out a heavy coat. It was a month on the cusp, nature shifting from one mode to another. In transition. Alice sat up.

"Honey!" Debbie said, blinking into the dark. "What on earth are you doing here now? I don't have my contacts in yet." Alice looked around Pomander, as if she would see something that made sense—full daylight, a yellow brick road, anything.

"I guess I was asleep," Alice said. She swallowed, not wanting to ask the question. She had on sweatpants, too—ancient regulation Belvedere gym class attire. They were the Belvedere Knights, as if teenagers on the Upper West Side needed any help thinking of themselves as exceptional and brave.

"Of course. Glad you're here." Debbie pinched the air in front of her until Alice moved into the space and Debbie could wrap her arms around her in a tight hug. Ursula rubbed her body against Alice's ankles. Debbie finally let go, and Alice bent down to pick up the cat.

"I'll just be on the couch. Go back to bed, I didn't want to bug you." Alice kissed Debbie on the cheek and turned around, heading back to the couch.

"I'm sure your dad would want to say hi, Al," Debbie said, her voice now playful. "You don't want to poke your head in?"

Alice turned back around. Ursula climbed up

to her shoulders and bumped her wet nose against Alice's ear. "He's here?"

Debbie cocked her head to the side. "Course he is. The good nurse is in there, too. Mary. He likes her best. Her family's from Trinidad and when she comes she brings these amazing little chickpea sandwich things, doubles, they're called. So delicious."

"Is he awake?" Alice asked. The hallway leading to the bedroom was dark.

"Here and there," Debbie said. She gave a sort of half smile. "Mary thinks we're close. The doctors said so, too, of course, but what do they know. Once he shifted over to hospice, they sort of washed their hands of him. I don't think doctors like to lose. It's not good for their stats." Alice thought of the giant banner stretched across Fort Washington Avenue, proclaiming the hospital one of the best in the country, and imagined if instead it kept a tally of everyone who died, and all the babies born. This many in, this many out.

"Okay," Alice said. She set Ursula back down on the floor. The hall was dark, and when she pushed open the door to her father's bedroom, a nice-looking woman with glasses and a small book with a reading light was sitting in the corner. The regular bed was shoved all the way against the far wall, and Leonard was in an adjustable hospital bed right next to it, which made the small room feel even smaller. There was only a tiny strip of floor to walk on, no more than a foot wide.

"Leonard, you have a visitor," Mary said. She closed her book and put it behind her on the chair. Leonard moved slightly, rolling his head from one side to the other.

"Oh yeah?" he said. Leonard was always better with company—alone, like most writers, he was prone to grumbling, but he turned on the charm when he wanted to, especially with strangers, especially with young people, and women, and bartenders. With most people, really. He was curious and always asked questions—that was why all her friends had always loved him. He wasn't like most dads, who would mansplain about the grill or the Rolling Stones and then vanish after their soliloquy. Leonard was interested.

"It's me, Dad," Alice said. She took a few steps along the wall, until she reached his hands.

"Al-pal, I was hoping you'd come over today," Leonard said. He turned his palm up, and she put her hand in his. "Happy birthday."

"Thanks, Dad," Alice said. It was weeks ago now. "How are you feeling?"

Leonard coughed, and Mary hurried over, squeezing past Alice to adjust his pillows. This was a dance, a duet between Leonard and whatever was on the other side, and the other side was starting to lead. Alice flattened herself against the wall to let Mary by. When she left the room, Alice let herself get closer to Leonard's face. His cheeks were sunken, and so were his eyes. He was smaller than she'd ever seen him before.

"I've been better, Al." Leonard offered a weak smile.

"Should I call an ambulance?" Alice understood what hospice meant, but it just felt wrong not to do everything one could. But of course, they already had.

"No, no," Leonard said. His mouth pulled into a grimace. "No. This is the deal. We all have a time, and this is mine. Whether it's today or tomorrow or next month, this is it."

"I just don't fucking like that, Dad." Alice was surprised to find herself crying.

"I don't like it much, either," Leonard said. He shut his eyes. "But there's no other way. This is how it ends, for all of us. If we're lucky."

"I'm just really going to miss you, you know?" Alice's voice caught in her throat. "I don't know how many people I really, really love, who really, really love me, you know what I mean? I know that sounds pathetic, but it's true."

"It is true," Leonard said. "But that love doesn't vanish. It's still there, inside everything you do. Only this part of me is going somewhere, Al. The rest? You couldn't get rid of it if you tried. And you never know what's going to happen next. I was older than you are now when I met Debbie. Time to go forward into the breach. Until the future, at last."

Alice nodded, willing herself not to cry, not yet.

The talking had clearly knocked the breath out of Leonard, and he closed his eyes, his chest moving in and out in sharp, shallow movements.

Debbie came up quietly behind Alice and put her hands on her back. "You two okay in here? Want some coffee, Al?" It was a kind way of saying **Not too much, not too much, he can't do this all day.** Alice nodded. She leaned down and kissed her father on the cheek and then left the room.

63

THE REST OF THE DAY WAS LIKE FLYING
across an ocean on a slow airplane. Alice and Debbie
and Mary took turns swapping seats—the chair
in the bedroom, the dining room table, the couch.
Debbie took a nap in Alice's old room. She put
out bowls of clementines and grapes and pretzels and
they got eaten. Mary left for a while and then came
back. Alice found that she was anxious when Mary
was gone, even though she knew Mary alone was not
keeping her father alive.

"Should we order Jackson Hole for lunch?" Alice
asked. Debbie looked perplexed.

"Honey, that place closed years ago." New York
City didn't stop, either. That was another banner
that could hang across a city street—the number

of places you loved that were gone and had been replaced by different versions of themselves, places that someone else would love and remember long after you were dead.

"Right," Alice said. She lay down on the couch and pulled the blanket over her legs. Ursula leaped up and curled into place, tucking her head into her body, a perfect circle. Debbie sat by Alice's legs and pushed a few buttons on her phone. No one was going anywhere until it was over.

Leonard was awake and asleep. He didn't say more than a few words—he said so few words, in fact, that Alice thought she might have imagined their earlier conversation.

"Has he been like this for a while?" she asked Mary, who had done this for so many other families, who had seen the end again and again and still got up in the morning.

"It won't be long now," Mary said, answering her actual question.

At seven o'clock, Debbie and Alice had dinner with **Jeopardy!** on the small television, except that it wasn't Alex Trebek, because Alex Trebek had died of cancer. They didn't know any of the questions, even ones in categories they should have, like Broadway Musicals and New York City. Alice was exhausted even though she hadn't left the house all day. The idea of the outside world—noisy, vibrant, **alive**—was too much to handle. After dinner, Debbie forced Alice to join her for a walk around the block, which they did in silence, clutching each other's elbows like sisters in a Jane Austen novel.

Leonard was silent. On her turns in the room, Alice just watched to see that his chest was moving. Debbie and Mary tagged in and out, like Girl Scouts protecting a campfire. At some point, Debbie guided Alice back to the couch and tucked her in. She'd been sleeping sitting up, and fell asleep again once her head hit the pillow, even though she didn't think she would. Alice had a dream that she was in high school again, that she was at her party and Sam was hugging her and Tommy, too, and Kenji Morris was there in the corner, leaning against the wall. But it wasn't Sam, it was Debbie, and she was tapping Alice's arm, gently but insistently pulling her back into consciousness.

Alice blinked and waited for Debbie to speak.

"I think it's happening," Debbie said, her face pale, her mouth open like a bottom-feeding fish. Alice thought that Debbie looked awful, and she recoiled, the way she occasionally had when her mother still lived at home and Alice witnessed some adult thing—Serena plucking a stray hair from her chin with the same tweezers that Leonard used to take out splinters. Whatever was happening on Debbie's face went beyond the mask of everyday life. It was private, and it was real.

"What time is it?" Alice asked. Her eyes were starting to adjust to the dark.

"It's three in the morning," Debbie said. "Gather

yourself, and then come in." She squeezed Alice's shoulder, hard, and then turned back toward the bedroom.

Alice swung her legs onto the floor and sat up. She could see the clock above the kitchen table— it was 3:05 a.m. She could leave now, right now—she could walk out the front door and be sixteen again, and see her father eating breakfast and reading the newspaper. She could watch Ursula curl her body around her father's strong neck. She could make him laugh, and tease him, and she could feel all of his love pointing right at her like the headlights of a car.

• • •

She couldn't save him—Alice knew that. Leonard didn't even like that kind of science fiction, the books with medical advancements that could sustain people for centuries, the books with brains in jars, the books with immortal vampires or power-hungry magicians. He thought that easy resolutions were utterly lacking in verisimilitude, despite the fact that he'd written two books about time-traveling teenagers. He and Serena could have stayed married, he could have gotten a real job, he could have worn things that didn't come from L.L.Bean, but he didn't. Leonard didn't mind doing things his own way. He had always been exactly who he was, better or worse, take it or leave it. And Alice couldn't leave him, not now. She hoped it was true, what he'd said about love, about all of that love still existing in the world.

He wasn't religious, and so neither was she. Fiction, maybe, or art—were those religions? Believing that the stories you told could save you, and could reach everyone you had ever loved?

• • •

Alice pushed herself up to stand and walked into Leonard's bedroom, her own headlights lighting the way.

64

ALICE HARDLY NOTICED THE SUBWAY ride home. It seemed quicker than usual, and she looked up right as the doors were closing at Borough Hall, hurrying off before she missed her stop. The walk from the station was long, fifteen minutes on a good day, but Alice didn't mind. She just put one foot in front of the other until she was standing in front of her building.

• • •

Mary had known what to do. She and Debbie had worked everything out in advance—whom to call and in what order: the funeral parlor, the credit card companies, the friends. There was already an obituary ready to go. Leonard's photo would be in all the newspapers, on Twitter. It'd be in the black-and-white photo montage at the Oscars, with someone singing "Somewhere Over the Rainbow" in a ball gown. Alice made some of the calls to friends—she and Debbie split up the list. No one was surprised. Everyone was kind. Alice cried during the first few, nearly unable to get the words out, but then she got used to the rhythm of the conversation and found that she was able to make it through. That lasted a few minutes and then she was crying again. Alice hugged Mary longer than she'd ever hugged a relative stranger in her life. This was how people felt about their midwives, or platoon mates, or fellow hostages—they had seen things together that no one else would ever fully understand.

• • •

Alice found her apartment key and put it in her lock but couldn't make it fit. Her phone buzzed—Sam—and Alice picked up, even though she found that she couldn't actually speak. "Oh, honey," Sam said, over and over again. "Oh, honey." Sam was a good mom, and a good friend. "I'll come over. Bring some food."

"Okay," Alice said, and hung up. She went back to trying to unlock the door but couldn't open it, and then threw her keys onto the sidewalk. "Fuck!"

Slowly, the door she'd been trying to unlock swung open. "Um, Alice?"

It was Emily.

"Oh, hi. Sorry for the noise. I was having some trouble with my key." Alice felt herself begin to blubber. "Sorry."

"No, no, it's fine," Emily said. "I'm working from home today anyway. Oh, wait, I have a package for you, hang on." She opened the door wide, propping it open with a doorstop. Alice took the two steps down and looked inside, into her apartment. Gone was her bed; gone was her table. Gone was her mess and her clothes and her art on the walls. All of it was replaced with Emily's glittery taste—a pink couch, a rug in the shape of a rainbow, a four-poster bed. Alice could see straight through to the garden, as if the apartment had doubled in size, like it was sitting in front of a mirror. Emily came back with a small box. "Here you go."

Alice took the box and held it against her chest. She wasn't sure where to go.

Emily put her hand on Alice's wrist. "Dude, are you okay? You're upstairs now, boss, remember?" She pointed with her eyebrows, and then a long finger.

"Oh, right," Alice said. "Thanks for this." She looked at the return address—it was from Sam, for her birthday. Late, as always. The tiara, and the photo, Alice could guess. "I'll text you later, okay? Thanks." She didn't mention her father, because she couldn't.

• • •

Her key opened the door at the top of the stoop. It was a duplex—she'd been in it before; her landlady had invited her over for dinner. Original wood-work, a beautiful curving banister. Her things were everywhere, and Leonard's, too—there were posters on the wall that had hung on Pomander. She hadn't noticed they were gone.

• • •

The plan was that Debbie would keep Pomander for now, until they decided what to do. Leonard had owned it outright, and Debbie still owed a mortgage on her co-op, and so the idea was that she would move in, but Debbie had offered it to Alice, too, if she wanted it. Alice had said no quickly—she didn't think she could resist, if she were that close every day. Ursula would stay on Pomander, too, though Alice didn't know if it would be possible to move her even if she wanted to bring her home. It seemed entirely plausible that the cat would vanish into a puff of smoke if one tried. As far as she knew, Ursula had never even been to the vet. It made her laugh to think about all the things that Leonard understood that she would never under-stand, the tiny things and the big ones. Her phone buzzed. She was going to turn it off, completely off, maybe even throw it in the bathtub. It was a text from a number she didn't have in her phone: **Hey Alice, it's Kenji Morris, from Belvedere. Sam gave me your number. She told me about your**

dad. I know we haven't talked in 1000 years, but you know I've been there. Give a call, anytime. Maybe Alice wouldn't throw her phone in the bathtub just yet.

• • •

Any story could be a comedy or a tragedy, depending on where you ended it. That was the magic, how the same story could be told an infinite number of ways.

• • •

Time Brothers, the novel, ended with a scene of Scott and Jeff at the breakfast table, the boys lightheartedly arguing over who had the most maple syrup, after they had successfully saved the world several times. There was no doubt that they would do it all again.

• • •

Dawn of Time ended with Dawn standing at the center of the Sheep Meadow in Central Park. It was daybreak, with a pale sky over a silent city. Leonard spent half a page describing her face, and the way the pink sunlight reflected off the buildings. The year was purposefully ambiguous—Dawn, unlike the brothers, did not want to spend the rest of her life rocketing back and forth through decades and centuries. The reader hoped that Dawn had finally found her way home. Happy endings were too

much for some people, false and cheap, but hope—
hope was honest. Hope was good.

•   •   •

Alice walked over to her front window, which now
was fully aboveground. She could see the brownstones across the street, and the sky overhead. The
traffic on the BQE hummed away. She pressed
her nose and forehead lightly against the glass.
Forward, that was the idea. Until the future, whatever it was going to be.

Acknowledgments

Thank you to everyone who talked to me about the Upper West Side of our youth, about science fiction, about time travel, and about parents: Christine Onorati, Gary Wolfe, Olivia Greer, Julie Barer, Nina Lalli, and Sam Saltz.

Thank you to Gabi Zegarra-Ballon for being a loving friend to the whole family, and whose presence made the writing of this book possible.

Thank you to the staff of Books Are Magic, past and present—I have learned more from you than I could ever hope to teach you, and I am grateful for each of you every single day. Nick Buzanski, Serena Morales, Michael Chin, Colleen Callery, Lindsay Howard, Jacque Izzo, Shulokhana Khan, Natalie Orozco, Aatia Davison, Isabel Parkey, Kristina Rivero, Anthony Piacentini, Abby Rauscher, Eddie

Joyce, and Nika Jonas—thank you, thank you, thank you.

Thank you to my people at Riverhead: Sarah McGrath, Geoff Kloske, Claire McGinnis, Jynne Martin, Delia Taylor, Nora Alice Demick, and Alison Fairbrother. Thank you to Laura Cherkas for copyediting a time travel book without making me cry. Thank you to Jess Leeke and Gaby Young and the team at Michael Joseph. Thank you to my dear, indefatigable agent, Claudia Ballard, and to everyone at WME: Tracy Fisher, Camille Morgan, Anna DeRoy, Laura Bonner, and Matilda Forbes Watson.

Thank you to Justin Goodfellow for always letting me ask questions, and to the entirety of the Penguin sales team for helping my books find their readers.

Thank you to all the bookstores around the world who have chosen to have my books on their shelves. I understand more than ever what it means to have a book in stock, taking up precious real estate, and it is an honor that I do not take for granted.

Thank you to everyone with whom I ever smoked a cigarette, sat on a stoop, ate at a diner, drank too much, and stayed awake all night. I can close my eyes and be there, electric with the excitement of being a teenager.

Thank you to my Mikey, for always making sure there was time (no easy feat this year), for being my tireless cheerleader, and for keeping the bookstore up and running in these uncertain and scary times.

Thank you to my children, my constant companions, for being such wild, amazing creatures.

Thank you to my mom, for still putting small bowls of snacks within reach.

Thank you to Killer, to whom I have granted much deserved immortality in this book.

Thank you to the doctors, nurses, and staff at Columbia Presbyterian Hospital for their vital work, which was made so much harder in 2020, when this book was written.

Most of all, thank you to my dad, for showing me what fiction could do, and for knowing that the real story is both here and not here, that we are both here and not here, and for receiving this book as it was intended, as a gift.

About the Author

EMMA STRAUB is the **New York Times** bestselling author of four other novels, **All Adults Here, Modern Lovers, The Vacationers,** and **Laura Lamont's Life in Pictures,** and the short story collection **Other People We Married.** Her books have been published in twenty countries. She and her husband own Books Are Magic, an independent bookstore in Brooklyn, New York.

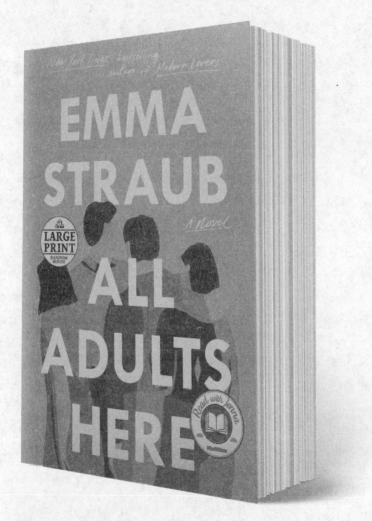